ASH DARK AS NIGHT

BOOKS BY GARY PHILLIPS

NOVELS

The Jook
The Perpetrators
Bangers
Freedom's Fight
The Underbelly
Kings of Vice (as Mal Radcliff)
Warlord of Willow Ridge
Three the Hard Way (collected novellas)
*Beat, Slay, Love: One Chef's Hunger
    for Delicious Revenge* (written
    collectively as Thalia Filbert)
The Killing Joke (co-written with
    Christa Faust)
*Matthew Henson and the Ice Temple
    of Harlem*

SHORT STORY COLLECTIONS

*Monkology: 15 Stories from the World
    of Private Eye Ivan Monk*
Astonishing Heroes: Shades of Justice
*Treacherous: Grifters, Ruffians
    and Killers*

MARTHA CHAINEY NOVELS

High Hand
Shooter's Point

IVAN MONK NOVELS

Violent Spring
Perdition, U.S.A.
Bad Night Is Falling
Only the Wicked

ONE-SHOT HARRY NOVELS

One-Shot Harry
Ash Dark as Night

GRAPHIC NOVELS

Shot Callerz
Midnight Mover
South Central Rhapsody
Cowboys
Danger A-Go-Go
Angeltown: The Nate Hollis Investigations
High Rollers
Big Water
The Rinse
Peepland (co-written with Christa Faust)
Vigilante: Southland
The Be-Bop Barbarians

ANTHOLOGIES AS EDITOR

The Cocaine Chronicles (co-edited
    with Jervey Tervalon)
Orange County Noir
*Politics Noir: Dark Tales from
    the Corridors of Power*
*The Darker Mask: Heroes from the
    Shadows* (co-edited with Christopher
    Chambers)
*Scoundrels: Tales of Greed, Murder and
    Financial Crimes Hollis, P.I.*
Black Pulp (co-edited with Tommy
    Hancock and Morgan Minor)
Day of the Destroyers
Hollis for Hire
*Culprits: The Heist Was Only the
    Beginning* (co-edited with Richard Brewer)
*The Obama Inheritance: Fifteen Stories
    of Conspiracy Noir*
Witnesses for the Dead: Stories (co-edited
    with Gar Anthony Haywood)

ASH
DARK
AS
NIGHT

GARY PHILLIPS

Copyright © 2024 by Gary Phillips

Published by Soho Press, Inc.
227 W 17th Street
New York, NY 10011

Library of Congress Cataloging-in-Publication Data

TK

ISBN 978-1-64129-474-4
eISBN 978-1-64129-475-1

Interior map © Mike Hall

Interior design by Janine Agro, Soho Press, Inc.

Printed in the United States of America

10 9 8 7 6 5 4 3 2 1

To Piere Desir, the Domino King

I feel like the Lonely Ranger . . . I feel
very much like the Lonely Ranger.
                         —Nguyễn Cao Kỳ

Map TK

CHAPTER ONE

Like a runaway virus, fire and destruction was every-where, including this stretch of Vermont Avenue near Watts. Harry Ingram crossed the avenue to click off shots of a burning trophy store. He wasn't worried about being hit by a car as there was little traffic except for fire and police vehicles. Plastic trophies melted on shelves in the display window. He focused on one in particular, the figure of a man on an orb triumphantly holding a bowling ball aloft. Over several clicks of his camera, the figure withered away in streams of plastic yet still the bowling ball remained untouched . . . until it too succumbed to the flames. Ingram felt neither excited nor fearful, remaining stationary as rioters and police tore around him. If he had any sense, he reflected dimly, he should be awash in both emotions.

Most of the other news people out here covering the events were white men from the white press. The *Times* and the *Herald Examiner* didn't have any negro reporters. Now maybe one of these fellas might well get a brick upside their head from a participant, but were less likely to be jacked-up by the law. Ingram realized either side might turn on him. There was another colored freelancer somewhere out here he knew, dashing about for *Jet* magazine. Maybe when they both got a beatdown from the cops, they could compare notes in jail.

Yet here he was, wearing a linen coat and a snap-brim hat like he was on his way to the fifth race at Hollywood Park. He carried a recent model Canon in hand and his battered Korean War era Speed Graphic around his neck, the latter more for good luck than practicality. Unlike the Canon, which used film rolls, the Graphic had to be loaded one 4x5 film plate at a time. Though like the old timers before him, he could deftly remove one plate to load in another rapidly. To top it off, it was Friday the thirteenth. He almost chuckled.

"Get the fuck out of here," a cop yelled at him from his Plymouth Fury prowler as he roared past. "This ain't a god-damn tourist outing."

Ingram resisted yelling back that he wasn't sightseeing but moved along, though he wasn't leaving the area. A man and woman rushed past, taking turns pushing a shopping cart filled with recently acquired goods, including a toaster oven. As one of them pushed, the other held on to the cart to prevent it from tipping over. The thing was filled to overflow.

A ragtop '57 Chevy Bel Air screeched to a stop at the end of the block in front of an appliance store advertising television and stereo sets available on layaway. Ingram watched two soul brothers exit the car. One held a bat and the other a prybar. Both wore gloves. Methodically, they went to work on the store's windows and security gate, busting out the glass. The man with the prybar popped the padlock on the gate. This time, Ingram practiced caution as he took shots.

He crouched down behind the fender of a food delivery truck across the street. Two of the vehicle's tires were flat and the rear double doors hung open at broken angles, the contents long gone. The two regimented looters drove off without entering the establishment.

Ingram flinched at the blast of a shotgun. That wasn't a civilian letting loose with the buckshot. Yet he waited, his Army training kicking in. Without looking at his watch, he had a sense when the four minutes had passed. A pick-up truck and a station wagon appeared in front of the appliance store. Out came several men and a woman. With the collective coordination of worker ants, they quickly transferred those layaway items to their vehicles. Mission accomplished, they too drove away.

Ingram got this all on film. While there was plenty of chaotic, spontaneous stealing around him, there were those who were clearly more organized. He wasn't condoning thievery, but he did appreciate the ingenuity.

It was a hot August and everybody was sweating. He'd worn his coat so as to keep expended film rolls in its pockets along with a few film plates. Ingram supposed one of these days he ought to get himself one of those safari-like photographer's vests. The last two years or so he'd been getting more photography work and doing less process serving—though he'd had a matter that earned him a nice little sum the other week serving divorce papers on an egghead type out in Eagle Rock. An aeronautical engineer who taught part time at CalTech and liked to frequent a certain strip club for gentlemen. Sure enough, he got involved with one of the dancers.

Ingram exchanged a used roll for a fresh one. His hands

were steady, pulse normal. The singed odor of charred wood omnipresent in the air. Yesterday, the first full day of the rioting, he'd gone about like now, on foot. He seemed then to somehow be invisible in the melee unfolding around him. Yet today, Ingram interpreted the shotgun blast and cop yelling at him as warnings he best not ignore. He wasn't turning away but he wasn't going to be foolhardy either. If he was going to get arrested or die, he'd want his pictures to be testament that he'd been doing his job.

A car lurched into view out of the mouth of an alley. It was a Dodge DeSoto, a late '40s model, Ingram estimated. The driver was an older white man who was bleeding from his hairless scalp. The windshield was cracked. A trio of young Black men emerged from the alley and ran after the car as it weaved onto the roadway, losing speed rather than increasing velocity. The young men threw rocks and glass bottles at the car and yelled at the driver. Ingram snapped away. A green 7 Up bottle exploded in emerald shards that sparkled in the sun against the car's trunk.

"Get that old cracker buzzard," one of them said.

"Cheap motherfuckah owes me three weeks' pay," another said. He was running fast and still threw a sizable rock with the force and precision of a Don Drysdale pitch. The projectile busted out the driver's side window, shattering glass and striking the driver. The DeSoto ran up on the sidewalk, nearly plowing through a store. The motor idled, having slipped out of gear. The youngsters descended on the car and yanked the driver out of it, then shoved him back and forth, laughing. Ingram rushed over.

"That's enough, you'll kill him," he warned.

"Fuck you, he has it coming."

Grunting, Ingram inserted himself as best he could between the angry youths and the object of their scorn. "Look, this isn't right, come on. I don't know what he's done, but beating a man to death can't be the answer."

"Who the hell are you, Uncle Tom?"

"Yeah, Rastas," another taunted.

"I'm the one that's gonna put you on Front Street."

"A snitch, huh?"

"No, but you'll be in all the news."

The tough who was holding the older man by his shirt front let go. The man sagged against his car but remained upright, breathing hard. The attacker took ahold of Ingram's camera draped around his neck on a strap.

"What makes you think we won't take your little toy from you?" The youngster was built like a power forward for the Lakers—tall and lean muscled in a crisp athletic-T, crème colored cotton pants, and black canvas Keds.

"You can but you'll have to kick my ass too. I know you can but I'll make it tough and then if you kill me, how righteous does that make you?"

"Makes me the winner, fool."

They stared at each other until the one who'd thrown the rock through the car window tapped this one's arm. "Let's go, we made our point."

"Yeah, we got what we came for." The third one was stocky with rings on his left middle and little fingers. He took several bills from the older man's wallet and tossed it aside. He also held his watch and diamond ring aloft. "When we pawn this, we'll get what's coming to us."

"Goddamn right we will," the taller one said, taking the ring, smiling broadly. "See you around, clown," he said to

Ingram. The three departed, snickering and guffawing, full of their youth and the power of their bodies.

"You just going to let them rob me like that?"

Ingram turned to regard the ingrate, his fear turning into anger. The man's face was lined and his eyes watery. Broken veins were evident along the bridge of his nose. "You're alive, you're welcome."

He glared at Ingram indignantly, alternating between dabbing at his cut cheek and cut head with a bloodied handkerchief. "What kind of Good Samaritan are you?"

"A practical one."

"Oh, I get it, got your hand out like all the rest, that it? Expect me to pay you, is that it?"

"Man, you're lucky they just threw rocks and bottles at you."

"What the hell does that mean?"

Ingram walked away so as not to blow his top. He was pretty sure the indignant bastard was glaring at him. People ran past, some laughing, some seemingly unsure of what they were doing. Sirens and smoke were everywhere. Ingram looked back. The man got in his car, backed it off the sidewalk, and once in the street, righted the DeSoto and left the scene. On Ingram went.

On another block, eerily quiet, Ingram stopped and placed his camera on the hood of a truck and again changed the film roll. He had several exposed rolls in his jacket pockets. Ingram looked around and spotted a wrinkled paper bag on the sidewalk. It had the logo of a chain restaurant printed on it along with their famous slogan, "Don't Cook Tonight, Call Chicken Delight." Luckily, the bag's interior was clean, and he stuck his exposed rolls in there and rolled the top closed. Now where to hide his snaps.

As he tried to figure this out, Ingram continued walking along Vermont. Up ahead, a group of young people were hemmed up in the alcove of a furniture store being routed by several police. Batons jabbed the youngsters in the stomachs or rose and fell on their heads. Additionally, two German shepherds barely restrained on leashes were barking, leaping and snarling at the trapped citizenry.

"Call the fuckin' dogs off, man," one of the assaulted hollered. A gash on his forearm was bleeding profusely.

"Aw, you aren't scared of ole' Bruno are you?" one of the cops holding on to one of the dogs taunted. "He just wants to say howdy."

"Yeah, he just wants to give you a friendly lick," the officer holding Bruno said. They both laughed.

These cops continued terrorizing the young people they'd bunched up. No clear orders were being given and as far as Ingram could tell, the youngsters hadn't stolen anything as there were no items on the sidewalk. He clicked off several shots. One of the cops handling a dog pointed at him.

"Who the hell are you?"

"Press," Ingram answered, making sure to take a couple of close-up photos of the officer and the dog. His hands were steady even though he knew what was coming next.

The helmeted cop broke away from the others and started toward him, his animal baring its teeth. A Channel 5 Ford panel truck was passing by, and the driver applied the brakes. From the rear of the truck a white newsman and a cameraman stepped out. Noting the new presence, the officer flicked the dog's leash and uttered a command. The animal sat on his haunches, still eyeing Ingram.

"What's the problem, officer?" the television newscaster

said. The cameraman was filming the police officer with a Super 8 camera mounted on his shoulder. Ingram had used one at a trade show not long ago. He'd gotten a kick out of making moving pictures.

The cop regarded him blankly. "There's a riot going on, or didn't you notice?"

"Mr. Ingram is rioting?"

"You know this spade?"

"This gentlemen is a newsman, like me."

It took Ingram until then to realize the newscaster was familiar to him not just from seeing him on the TV. He'd met the man briefly when they'd both covered a picket by the Nation of Islam at a White Front department store a couple of years ago. His name was Stan Chambers.

"Then you and him better get a move on."

The cameraman turned his camera to film the other cops.

"What did those folks do?" Chambers asked one of the cops, indicating the youngsters.

"Suspected of starting fires."

"Then why aren't they under arrest?"

"They were resisting arrest."

"No they weren't," Ingram interjected. "The cops were having their fun with them. I've got the pictures to prove it."

The uniformed officer put his blank stare on Ingram. "You a lowlife lawyer in addition to being a nosey picture taker?"

"I know enough," Ingram said.

The cop turned and called out. "Call a wagon and get these negro hooligans booked."

He and his dog walked back to join his fellow officers. Nearby, a fresh plume of black smoke rose behind a row of coming next and watched as a rag was stuffed in the fuel spout. Calmly the smoker sparked a flame on his Zippo lighter. The rag was lit.

Like a pyromaniac waiting for the fire to crackle, Ingram stood transfixed, anticipating what was to come. The fiery rag was consumed, its flame whooshing into the car. For several seconds nothing happened, then there was a muffled blast as the fuel in the gas tank combusted with a loud *woomph*. Everyone reacted, ducking and stepping back. Red and yellow flickered in his lens while Ingram took pictures. Fire consumed other parts of the upended car as unignited gas spread. The windows of the car were up. Lacking oxygen to burn effectively from within, the fire burned quick along the shell, then began to sputter out, leaving blackened remains.

The others having already departed, Ingram marched away too. He felt let down, as if he expected the torching of the car to signal what, a change? A shift in tactics? But this was no organized revolt. The lumpenproletariat, as his girlfriend Anita called them, were frustrated and lashing out, but to what end?

Further along, he spotted a familiar face. G. M. "Gerry" Tackwood was a part-time reporter for the hippie newspaper, the *Free Press*. He was also white, younger than Chambers or Ingram, with a hawkish nose and longer hair, a mod cut it was called. He wore white jeans, a tan short-sleeved shirt and suede boots. His eyes weren't darting around and he wasn't fidgeting. Observing the younger man's apparent calm had Ingram feeling his age, if only momentarily. He supposed to others he appeared that way as well. But his was a practiced state of being while Tackwood's seemed natural.

The Freep's reporter had a portable reel-to-reel tape recorder strapped across his body. He held the attached microphone before an agitated Black woman wearing an apron.

"I'm not endorsing us burning down our own neighborhoods," she was saying. "But you can't have years of unequal treatment just roll off your back all the damn time like water off a duck. Excuse my French."

"I hear you," Tackwood said into the mic. "What do you think will solve this problem of the racial divide in our society?" He shifted the mic back toward her.

"That's too big a question for me to answer, mister. I watched the March on Washington on TV with my grandmother and felt so hopeful, knowing what she had gone through, and her crying when Dr. King spoke." She shook her head. "But here we are two years later and where are we? Maybe it will take something like this to get the Establishment's attention."

Tackwood nodded and concluded his interview after identifying the woman he'd been interviewing. She walked back into a storefront café called the Honey Catch. A plank of plywood was nailed over the display window. Red lettering spray-painted on the wood read: NEGRO OWNED.

Tackwood turned and saw Ingram. "Hey, Harry, good to see a friendly face. Give me some skin, man."

"You tellin' me." They slapped five.

"You've been out since this morning?" Tackwood asked.

"Yeah. You?"

"Got this contact over at 77th Division. When he first got on there, them ofays put a rubber shrunken head in his locker with NAACP written on a ribbon tied around it. Anyway, we're going to meet away from the station house.

The idea was to get his insider's view on what the captains were telling the cops. He didn't show."

"Understandable he'd have cold feet."

Tackwood considered his response, instead checked his watch. "I better hustle back to the office and get my transcriptions down. Art wants a special edition out before nightfall." Art Kunkin, the *Free Press*'s publisher. The office was in the basement of the Fifth Estate, a coffeehouse on the Sunset Strip. Like the others who toiled for the publication, Tackwood was a part-timer, a euphemism for volunteer. They were down for the cause and not about the money. To pay his rent, Tackwood taught journalism parttime at L.A. City College and was a weekend tape editor at the all-news station KNX.

"Trying to beat his capitalist competition?" The *Times* and *Herald Examiner* were putting out extra editions of riot coverage.

"The revolution has many fronts, comrade Ingram."

"Sí, comandante."

The two said their good-byes and Ingram moved further south on Broadway.

"Burn, baby, burn," the driver of a lowered Impala yelled from his speeding car. The driver wore sunglasses, his processed hair agleam. Ingram's picture caught him grinning broadly behind the wheel.

As he walked, he changed his film roll by touch, scanning for cops and rioters. He was still sweating, breathing through his mouth, but wasn't panicked. Air in, air out. This was it, his last roll. He passed by a bank with broken-out windows. A little further down was a shoe store and beyond that, at the end of the block, a small market next to a corner Texaco gas station. Several people were running out of the market, carrying armloads of food. Heads of lettuce flew out of their arms and rolled down the street. Shots boomed as cops ran around the gas station's pumps in pursuit, shooting at those fleeing.

"Stop, you goddamn assholes," a cop hollered.

Instinctively, Ingram ducked, as did those who were running, still clicking away automatically.

"Hey, be cool, boys in blue, ain't nobody has to die for a loaf of bread."

The speaker was a lanky, broad-shouldered Black youth in blue jeans and a matching denim jacket. He stood on the roof of a car, pointing at the police. His mane of unruly black hair was curly, naturally it seemed, not the result of a chemical treatment like the recently departed Impala driver. Three cops stopped running after the looters and circled back to the young man.

"Look, baby, this isn't about greed, this is about need." The man's voice took on a cadence, rising and falling as a small crowd gathered around the car. "We the underclass are fed up with the bullshit the white ruling class has been imposing on us for years. It's time we stood on our own two feet to show we can't be pushed around no more."

The gathered applauded and yelled encouragements.

"Get off that fuckin' car and shut up," a cop commanded.

"Get out of my neighborhood," the young man replied to enthusiastic approval. "Take Parker's occupying army west of La Brea and see how they like it in those neighborhoods. You know what, I'm bettin' them folks won't like it no more than we do. What do you good people say?"

The group cheered. Ingram got closer, counting his snaps

on this last roll. He got a great up-angle shot of the youth on top of the car just as the police pushed through the crowd, jabbing with their batons to clear a path. It was then that Ingram recognized the speaker. He'd seen him at a rally for jobs and justice in Exposition Park about half a year ago, which he'd covered for the *Sentinel*.

"Let Faraday speak," said a woman with curlers in her hair.

"Be quiet, bitch," a beefy officer replied, shoving her aside as he did so.

"Hey, watch yourself, man. We know y'all act like this here is the plantation, but you can't treat our women like that," Faraday said. He backed away from the cops who were reaching for him. The gathered got involved, trying to get in between. There was about to be a riot within the riot, Ingram considered. This young man, Faraday, was giving shape to the chaos. Beyond the fury, he was talking about what could come afterward. He was a man on the rise—he spoke for something, an inspiration.

A police officer climbed on the car's trunk and lunged toward the curly-haired Faraday. The two grappled and both tumbled from the roof, right into the tangled arms of police and civilians.

Now everyone started grabbing and pulling, forms jostling one another with Ingram in the middle of it, snapping away. A baton cracked him on the side of his face but like a veteran pugilist, he shook off the blow and kept taking pictures. He had to keep his cool. This wasn't the first time he'd been hit by a nightstick. Faraday was now being manhandled by all three officers who were attempting to pull him free from the enraged residents. The sleeve of his jacket had torn and a welt was forming under one of his eyes.

"Back, get back," an officer demanded, holding his baton in two hands, and using the end to jab people hard in their stomachs. Another one joined him and they worked in unison.

Ingram followed the cops closely as they marched the young man toward a parked police car. The Canon was now strapped across his torso, the Speed Graphic in hand. Several other officers were forming a semi-circle to keep the crowd back. One of them must have gone off to find a call box, Ingram assumed, to request reinforcements—if such were available, given the altercations happening all over this part of Los Angeles.

"What are you arresting him for?" Ingram demanded.

"Get the hell away from us, shutterbug," an officer barked. "Go find a cat up the tree to take pictures of."

"You know this interfering coon?" another cop said, his southern accent thick like he'd stepped off the set of *Gone with the Wind*.

"He's nobody that matters," the other one answered. He lashed out with the butt of his shotgun, striking Ingram in the middle of his chest. Down he went, the Speed Graphic ejecting from his hand and clattering across the asphalt.

"Now stay down," he said and went off with the others.

Sucking in the taste of smoke, doing his best to keep his head clear, Ingram belly-crawled to his camera and took hold of it. Broken pieces, like the track lock, trailed from the Speed Graphic, but the shutter release was working. Like its owner, the camera had taken worse. Akin to when he'd been in a tight spot in Korea, he partially stood up and ran bent over to a location where he had an unobstructed angle on what was unfolding.

Several of the uniformed officers were now roughing Faraday up. Ingram knew their goal was to beat and subdue the man. Tenderize him, as the cops would say. The other policemen were holding the crowd back, forcing them to bear witness.

"Stop brutalizing him," somebody called out. "You dirty cops."

"You can't get away with this," another said.

Ingram's Canon, strap around his neck, was back in hand, having placed his other camera on the ground next to him. Stay calm, he reminded himself. He hadn't counted how many shots he'd taken but he guessed he had only three or so left on this last roll at best. His third remaining shot captured a knot of cops surrounding Faraday, tugging him this way then that way. The second-to-last framed a baton striking Faraday on his upper shoulder just as he twisted his head away from the blow.

Before his finger pressed the Canon's shutter button again, a flatbed truck with a slat-sided bed carrying National Guardsmen screeched around the corner. A guardsman yelled over the bullhorn mounted on top of the vehicle's cab, "Disperse, disperse."

As if responding to a primal urge deep in his cells, he eschewed using the Canon and was now aiming the Speed Graphic from chest level. Nothing happened, then every-thing happened. A gunshot boomed and a number of Guardsmen pointed their rifles at who knew what. Ingram was sweating, his heart rate thudding. Silence descended until a man in a torn short-sleeved shirt cried out, "You bastards murdered him!"

Ingram gaped. Faraday lay in the street on his stomach.

A gun near him. The officers who'd encircled him stepped back. A Guardsman jumped off the truck.

"He was armed," one of the cops declared.

"That's bullshit," someone from the crowd answered. "Y'all planted that gun."

The Guardsmen re-formed to protect the police. Ingram had to protect his last picture. He was standing in front of the shoe store when the cops returned their attention to him. The one who'd hit him with the shotgun ran toward him, followed by another officer. The latter leveled his handgun at Ingram.

"Give us your cameras, Ingram. Now, goddammit!"

Both weapons were aimed at him now. "You can't have them."

"We can and we will. You got evidence on that film."

"Evidence you killed that kid in cold blood you mean." Voices in agreement went up from the crowd.

"Shut your lying Black mouth," a cop said, eyes on the ones witnessing this.

This time, the barrel of the shotgun swiped upside his head, knocking him back but not down. Preservation overtook him. He lurched forward, cradling his Speed Graphic like a football. He stumbled into the shotgunner cop.

"That's your ass now, colored boy," the struck police officer promised.

Him, the other one and a third joined in beating Ingram to the sidewalk with fists and batons, followed by an assortment of kicks to the ribs. Lying still and moaning, Ingram felt the officers rip open his coat pockets, hearing his last few loose spent rolls scatter across the pavement. "You can't take my film," he yelled. "I'm a reporter, you worthless motherfuckahs."

One of the cops crushed a film roll under his heel.

"I got the one that counts," another officer said triumphantly. He tossed the film roll he'd removed from the Canon up and caught it in his open palm. Smiling broadly, he ripped the film stock from the metal canister, ruining it in the sunlight. He threw the Canon aside. Roughly, he then opened the back end of the Speed Graphic and frowned.

He nudged Ingram with the toe of his shoe. "Where's the film?"

"I . . . dropped the roll off earlier . . . for processing," he managed to say. Ingram was counting on the cop assuming the Speed Graphic used a film roll and not flats.

"Whatever." He let the bigger camera drop then kicked it, sending it skidding across the sidewalk.

Ingram watched him do this, mumbling, barely able to focus as they hauled him off the ground. He coughed blood and his head hurt worse than any hangover he'd ever had.

"He needs an ambulance," someone declared.

They handcuffed and threw him in the back of a patrol car. Fuzzy, Ingram could only distinguish the low murmur from the crowd as two cops got in the front bench seat. The driver started the engine. As the car drove forward, the officer on the passenger side turned halfway around to grin at the beaten photojournalist.

"Man, I ain't wailed on a sambo like that in a month of Sundays. Ooohwee, you gonna be all puffy, some blue on that black." He laughed and his partner did too.

Ingram slurred a reply, but he couldn't understand his words. Then he lost consciousness.

SEVERAL BLOCKS east, the Channel 5 News chopper passed over an industrial section near Alameda and Vernon. Down below were various types of concerns, including a bottling plant and a soap manufacturer. Though the rioting hadn't reached this area, several of the businesses were closed. On the shadowed side of a compact unmarked building, a burglar used a prybar and hammer to break open two heavy duty padlocks securing the hasps on the door. With the police otherwise engaged, and no activity in the near vicinity, he'd picked now to pull off his illegal entry. He'd hit a few concerns in the area and had noticed the double locks on this building, wondering what may lay within.

Wearing gloves, he pushed the door open and, thumbing his flashlight on, stepped inside the gloom. He supposed he'd been hoping to find diamond tipped drills or some such. He was momentarily perplexed by the nature of the equipment he was looking at. What the hell had he found?

CHAPTER TWO

"What is wrong with you?"

Anita Claire stood on the side of Ingram's bed in the prison ward of General Hospital, shaking her head ruefully. She'd already asked him how he was doing before scolding him for fighting with the police.

"I was striking a blow for the working class," he rasped.

"And those cops struck blows for the ruling class. Harry, you know better. This could have ended a lot worse."

"I know, honey. But they were gonna whale on me no matter what."

"It's wrong that you're so right."

"Let alone what they did to Faraday."

The couple got quiet.

Ingram ached all over and it hurt to try to smile. He'd had a grinding headache since he was admitted and the bandage wrapped around his head itched, as did the square of gauze taped to his cheek. His right wrist was cuffed to the bed's railing. The morphine drip stuck out of his arm.

Anita Claire leaned down again, and this time, kissed him. "I'm sure glad you're okay, relatively speaking." She kissed him once more with greater intensity.

"How about a little sugar for me, baby?" another prisoner joked. He was a medium-sized Black man in a bed near the window. His arm was in a cast and suspended at an angle to his prone form. His other wrist was handcuffed to the bed like Ingram's and the three others in the room. There were no chairs or stools in the room and no nightstands either. A policeman sat on guard outside the solid metal door with its reinformed inset window.

Ingram regarded the man, twisting his lips into a sneer.

"Just kidding, soul brother," he winked. "Jealous is all."

One of the other prisoners had been allowed to keep a transistor radio brought to him by a visitor. He was listening to the baseball game happening not far from the hospital. The Dodgers were in a national pennant race and had been playing at Dodger Stadium since Wednesday, the night the riots began. Vin Scully, their announcer, noted that today's crowd was only 29,000 or so, given the "local situation," as he called it, had affected attendance. He also noted that Willie Crawford, who lived in the curfew zone, had spent the night at Johnny Roseboro's house.

When Claire was let in, she'd brought a copy of the morning's *Herald Examiner*, which was now folded over and rested atop the thin blanket at the foot of his bed. Somehow, one of Ingram's shots, from one of the rolls he'd given Stan Chambers the newscaster, had already migrated to its front pages. The picture captured LAPD officers patting down several Black men and women with their hands pressed against a wall. Some had the muzzles of police revolvers pressed to the backs of their heads. The central focus was a male officer roughly searching a female suspect, his hands seemingly lingering inappropriately on her body. Ingram was credited.

Meanwhile, in the Freep, Gerry Tackwood had termed the incidents of the past several days a "civil unrest." As in the Black press, his reporting chronicled the questionable shootings of suspected looters by the police and other actions, like their liberal use of dogs and directing firemen to blow people over with pressurized water.

"I've put in a call to Anton," Claire said.

"Thank you." She was referring to Anton Spurlock, a civil rights lawyer who was a friend of her divorced parents. He was what the authorities called a fellow traveler, both for his ideological bent and his providing legal defense for the likes of striking union members and NAACP leadership for organizing boycotts.

"What about your car?"

"The cops took my keys and wallet. Though I'm pretty sure Jed could get the car going without them."

A Korean War vet like Ingram, Josiah "Jed" Monk was now a mechanic and owner of the Four Aces, a repair shop in South Central. Ingram had done a few photos at his place and a brief interview with Monk the second day of the riots. He and his mechanics had put a NEGRO ESTABLISHMENT sign on their building as well as took turns on guard duty, their pistols within easy reach. They not only kept an eye on their shop but watched a few other businesses on their block, too. Ingram had parked his car at Four Aces before setting off on foot into the riot zone.

"The cops confiscate your camera too?"

"I don't know," he said flatly. "Can't remember."

Claire's face clouded, then cleared. She knew the Speed Graphic meant more to him than just a means to make a living. After a beat, she asked, "Did you see it when it happened?"

Ingram knew what she meant by that shorthand. "Not exactly. But I think it's on the film."

They both kept their voices low, each aware of the possibility one of the prisoners in here was a jailhouse snitch or even a colored cop doing undercover work. Supposedly, they had all been arrested on riot-related charges, but it was not far-fetched to suspect the law had eyes and ears planted to better jam up the soon-to-be-indicted.

"When the Guard showed up, I glanced over at them and when I looked back when the gun went off, Faraday was dead on the spot." He motioned her closer. "I don't know if I got the picture of them killing him, Anita. But I took something 'cause the shutter clicked. It was with my old camera." He started to choke up and she gripped his hand, squeezing hard. They touched foreheads. They both understood the import of what he'd potentially preserved. That this wouldn't be one more time when the police killed an unarmed Black man and there was no counter to that business-as-usual.

"So it's a flat?"

"Yeah. It's inside the black plastic the flats come in. I faked out the cops."

"Like you do, Houdini," she said softly, smiling at him.

He told her where he'd hidden the film.

She straightened up. "I better fetch it. It's small but unlikely to stay hidden for too long. It could get swept up with the other trash."

"Now who's lost their cotton pickin' mind?"

A hand on her hip, Anita regarded him with mock disdain. "Maybe they beat the sense out of you, but I'm a grown woman." Her voice had risen.

"Yes you is," the one near the window agreed.

Realizing arguing was pointless, Ingram beckoned her again. He was worried about the film's safety, too. "I know you know this, but plan this out, okay? And take Strummer with you."

His friend Pete "Strummer" Edwards made his living on both sides of the law and was handy with his fists and a pistol. Ingram's Lenin-quoting girlfriend was no lightweight but still, it was Edwards who hobnobbed with roughnecks on the regular.

"I don't need no one to hold my hand," she said.

"Could you be more stubborn."

She lowered her voice again. "Look, Sergeant Rock, I'm not going off half-cocked. Our people are still in the streets but there are areas where things have cooled down or at least where the Guard has clamped down. Tom has been talking to Dr. King's folks and he's probably going to come back to town." Anita Claire was a field deputy for Tom Bradley, a city councilman. "Once that gets announced, hopefully it'll help cool things down."

Claire continued. "I'm going to do what you soldiers call reconnoitering before I go prancing around. I know how to get my shit together."

"Please do," he emphasized.

She gave him a peck on the unbandaged cheek, then patted his leg and headed toward the door. "Bye, Harry."

"Bye, honey."

When she was gone the man at the window asked, "Say, man, she got a sister?"

Ingram waved him off as the Dodgers got a base hit. If he was a religious man, he ought to pray she'd be all right.

WALKING ALONG the corridor, Claire spotted Josh Nakano approaching from the opposite direction. He was in his formal attire, a dark suit and somber tie, as the funeral director of the Eternal Sands Mortuary should be. She had to shake the sudden chill his appearance gave her. He wasn't here to bury her boyfriend. They greeted each other.

"How's he doing?" he asked.

"For a man beat half to death, not too bad. Crazily he still has his front teeth. Doctor said he was concussed but not as terrible as it could have been." She almost choked up but held her emotions in check.

Nakano looked off. "Motherfuckers." He clenched his fist then relaxed his fingers.

She squeezed his upper arm. "Don't go getting all nuts now, Josh."

"Oh no, of course not, I'll be the good Oriental and smile in the face of adversity. Shit."

"He'll be glad to see you."

"Yeah," Nakano said, a faraway look in his eyes. He adjusted his glasses and, nodding at her, continued on toward Ingram's room.

Outside, tails of gray smoke emanated from the south. Claire got in her '62 Valiant but didn't turn the key. She sat there, staring out the windshield, not focused on the hospital personnel, ambulances and what-have-you passing through her field of vision. Breathing deep, she allowed herself to feel the anxiety she'd tucked away when she'd first walked into Ingram's room earlier. She supposed it worried her how much she cared for him. She knew intellectually how retrograde her mother might say it was for her to entangle herself too much into what happens to her man. *You are*

an individual, women stand on their own two feet, dammit.
Still, Anita couldn't deny that she didn't like imagining her
life without him. At this stage anyway. She turned the key
and, after the engine came to life, left the grounds of General Hospital.

She drove back toward the house she and Ingram rented
on South Cloverdale, on the outskirts of the Crenshaw District. Crossing Western on Exposition, she was stopped at a
checkpoint and had to produce her identification.

"Thank you, ma'am." The fresh-faced young white
Guardsman handed her driver's license back. He touched
the edge of his helmet and she continued on.

Their home was a modest one-story bungalow with a
tended front lawn, a flagstone-bordered porch, a blooming
flower bed and a decent-sized backyard. The couple had done
their share of entertaining since renting the place, including
hosting several dominos games on the patio, some after a
cookout. When Ingram had his bachelor apartment, playing
bones had been the sole providence of his male friends,
Nakano and Monk often among the players. Nowadays, the
women played too. This included Claire, her mother Dorothy
Nielson and one of Claire's closest friends, Judy Berkson. Judy
drank beer and cussed along with the men.

In the driveway, the burnt odor in the air was sharp in
her nostrils. Strummer Edwards would no doubt be willing
to accompany her on her foray to search for Harry's film.
She'd already rolled the idea over a couple of times in her
head on the drive home. She finally dismissed the notion.
She was used to putting it on the line robbing banks—not
that her boyfriend knew that. Here she was, involved with
her oddball lefty divorced parents and their dangerous hobby.

She'd told herself it was to keep them safe. But really, it was exciting. By comparison then, her current task was merely an excursion, right?

Inside, Claire changed out of her skirt and top and put on cuffed khakis, a button-up work shirt and tennis shoes. Ingram kept his service .45 in the house, and she knew where it was and how to use it. What he didn't know was she had a gun, too. It wasn't modesty that kept her from telling him about it. If he knew about the gun, he would naturally ask where'd it come from. If she told him the truth . . . well she wasn't ready to lay that on him just yet.

She went into the fenced-in backyard, past a circular glass patio table and other such lawn furniture to the bar-b-que grill that had come with the house. There was space between the back of the grill and the fence. Shading this area were several leafy branches laden with ripening avocadoes from their neighbor's tree. Claire knelt down on the patch of lawn and removed the brick she'd previously loosened in the back. In the cavity was her gun, a snub-nosed .38 revolver. She put the brick in place again and went back into the house.

In the living room, Claire dropped the pistol into her handbag. Despite revving herself up, she was aware of the risk she was taking. She wasn't too worried about being attacked by one of her fellow denizens, drunk on the hubris of striking back at Mister Charlie, if only temporarily. But if the police should stop and search her, they'd find the gun. More than just her job was at stake for carrying around this unregistered gat, she reflected ruefully. But being out and about at a time like this unprotected seemed foolish as well. Had her extra-curricular activities with her mother and father rubbed off on her?

She sighed. Now was not the time to evaluate her outlaw extra-curricular activities. She decided to dial around on the radio to see if there were any news bulletins on what was happening before leaving the house.

". . . the death in custody of Neal Atkins, arrested during the riots in South Los Angeles, a known sneak thief and house burglar with a long rap sheet, is being looked into by the proper authorities, this broadcast was informed. What is known is he was found hung by a sheet—"

Claire turned the dial and landed on KGFJ, lingering there. Nathaniel "Magnificent" Montague was one of the station's popular disk jockeys. He would often riff on his tagline, "Burn, Baby, Burn," referring to the hot disks he played. But when the riots broke out, his on-air callers started to say his line back to him—but meaning, of course, the actions in the street. Bradley's office, along with other politicians and the police, had received their own calls from irate taxpayers, white and Black, demanding they tell the station, Montague and his listeners to stop repeating it, as the slogan was encouraging law-breaking and whatnot.

Before putting on her sunglasses, she caught sight of a framed photograph above the mantle. The photograph, taken by Harry two years ago, was a clear image of a round white pill being released by female fingers into a glass of beer, suspended just above the liquid's surface. The drink had been intended for Martin Luther King, Jr., who'd come to town to speak. She and Ingram had purposefully spilled the spiked drink. Was the pill meant to kill the civil rights leader, make it seem a heart attack had felled him or inca-pacitate him in some other way? Clearly, they'd concluded, it was intended to derail what he was about to accomplish, to set the movement back. Four months later, Dr. King was able to give his rousing speech at the historic March on Washington. They never found out what was in the pill and the person who'd put it in the drink had disappeared. Claire pushed the glasses firmly in place on her nose, took a last look at the picture, and out the door she went.

Like Harry's, Anita's plan wasn't to drive into the fire zone, but to get close and then travel on foot to where he'd hidden the film. Her destination was near the intersection of 90th Street and Broadway. This was not the Watts section, but the rioting had flooded over various parts of South Central, even as far west and north as Crenshaw, where they lived. If she was stopped at a checkpoint, she'd tell them she was on duty for Councilman Bradley.

As she drove, Claire witnessed people working together sweeping up debris and others already putting in new windows and repairing storefronts. These scenes of rebuilding played out side by side with testaments of the property devastation and the disruption of lives. An S&H Green Stamps redemption store had been looted, its accordion security gate now leaning gently against a wall, as if it was removed with care. Spray painted on that outer wall in vermillion were the words, THANKS FOR THE MEMORIES.

Having reached Figueroa unmolested, she was surprised to see an RTD bus in operation heading further south. At least two of its windows had been broken out. She turned east off Figueroa—smack into a group of women in the process of pulling a cop off his motorcycle, which fell over as she watched, the engine still running. Three of the women were Black and one was Mexican American. Claire stopped her car and didn't back up. She knew she should be on her way—attract as little attention as possible—but this was too good to miss.

"Get this cracker," an attacker yelled. She had a scarf tied around the curlers in her hair. "Teach this bastard he can't ride through here insulting us."

"You broads better get your goddamn hands offa me," the officer said, reaching for his gun.

Though slight of build, the woman in the curlers hit him solidly in the jaw with a punch worthy of boxer Emile Griffith.

"Oh shit," another onlooker said appreciatively. Claire got out of the car.

The jab rocked the man. Another one snatched the gun out of his holster and threw it over her shoulder. A youth ran over and kicked the gun into the gutter then took a bow like a thespian. The officer swung on one of the women, doubling her over as he hit her in the stomach. As this happened, one of the other ladies jumped on his back, wrapped a chain around his neck, and yanked backward. They both fell to the ground. The woman kicked and pummeled the downed officer. As he lay dazed and bloody in the roadway, moaning curses at his assaulters, they ran away to the echo of raucous applause on this residential street.

Back in her car, Claire drove past the symbol of a toppled occupier. Too bad her old man hadn't been around to take a few pictures, she lamented. Nearer to her destination, where Faraday Zinum had been killed, she parked on a residential street. Hands on the steering wheel, Claire took in a slow breath. For about a half a year, she'd been getting more into what readers of newspapers like the *Free Press* called the consciousness movement, including transcendental meditation. She'd been studying and listening to the writings of Aldous Huxley and a man calling himself Baba Ram Dass, born Richard Alpert. He and a fellow Harvard professor had been asked to leave that institution for "turning on" their students via psychoactive drugs. She had yet to make any efforts to find, let alone use, mescalin or LSD—though she had to admit she was curious. She'd also been doing further readings on Buddhism, which she'd initially been interested in as a teenager. The books had been obtained from the library and a few from her mother's bookcase, dusty and unused for years.

Ready, she got out and locked her car. The quiet was soon disrupted as a helicopter flew by overhead, circled, then headed back the way it came. Claire walked down the street, trying to look as relaxed as possible. Then, wouldn't you know it—a police car turned the corner and came toward her.

She consciously didn't change her pace. Fortunately, she wasn't the only civilian daring to be outside, though there was that pistol in her purse.

He pulled up parallel to her and stopped. She stopped too.

"Where you headed?" the officer driving the vehicle demanded. A policewoman sat beside him. Far as Claire knew, the Department didn't assign women officers to the field. Could be this was a day for firsts.

"What's so funny?" the cop said.

"Nothing, officer." The image of the motorcycle cop being wailed on had brought a smile to her face.

Gesturing with his index finger, he motioned her closer.

"I asked you where are you going? And take those damn shades off."

She did as commanded, gazing at the two evenly. "I was

checking in on one of my boss's former office managers for him. She'd been doing poorly lately." She was careful to not have said her boss's "constituent," as this was not Bradley's councilmanic district. The two cops may or may not know the difference, but she wouldn't risk it. She pointed toward Broadway. "I was going to get her some Doan's pills and Ben-Gay at Thrifty's." She had no idea if the drug store was open. The silence seemed to go on far too long.

"Who's your boss?" the female cop finally said.

Claire met her startling gray eyes. That was the response she was hoping for. She tilted her purse toward them as if she had nothing to hide. She concentrated to keep her fingers from shaking. Flipping the clasp back, she opened the purse and removed her wallet, then one of her business cards from that. She handed the card through the open window. The male officer held the card for the woman to see too. They then both shifted their unreadable eyes back on her.

"Go on, but don't be lingering."

"No, sir." She put her sunglasses back on.

The police officer put the car in gear and off they went without giving back her card.

Claire clicked her purse closed and continued in the opposite direction. The slight tremor in the fingers of her right hand ceased. This part of Broadway looked like pictures she'd seen of war-torn Berlin in *Look* magazine. Shops were looted and some of them burned out as well. Pieces of glass, buildings and trash were strewn across the sidewalks. There was a refrigerator lying on its side just ahead of her, the door having been removed and likely carted away. A single loaf of Wonder Bread was inside the hulk.

A National Guardsman had been posted in front of a

Security Pacific savings and loan, his rifle held crossways in front of him. Claire was certain that once it was determined the rioting was spreading from Watts to the north, the tellers had scooped up the money from their tills and secured it in the vault.

The sentry swiveled his head toward her as she neared, but she trained her gaze forward. She felt his eyes on her as she went past.

A skinny woman was using a push broom to sweep up in the roadway and two men in overalls were chiseling out charred sections of wood from a doorframe on the other side of the street. She nodded at these folks before reaching the Kinney Shoes store where Ingram had ditched his film. On the sidewalk were several splotches of dried blood—likely Ingram's blood, she realized. Claire scanned the area. As feared, his camera was gone.

Though the store's display window was missing, there was no glass laying around. She speculated the pane had been removed with precision. The inside of the store had been stripped clean, its aisles of shoe racks unadorned save for an occasional lone sneaker or loafer on the floor. Nearby, several empty shoe boxes had been stacked into a pyramid as if a tribute to the god of shoes for the bounty.

"Soul sister, that white boy with the rifle still out there?" a voice whispered to her from inside the store.

Standing with his back flush to the wall next to the absent window was a young Black man, maybe nineteen or twenty, Claire estimated. He wore slacks and a sweat-stained white T-shirt. He had a do-rag tied around his pomaded hair.

"Yes he is," she replied, also whispering.

"Can you do me a favor?" the young man asked.

"Not sure about that, but I can't just stand here talking to you and not make him suspicious." She'd already turned from the soldier, pretending to be looking in her purse for something. Now she had to deal with this guy and still get inside the store, where the flat was. "I'm gonna come around back," she added, walking away.

Next door, people were straightening up inside a neighborhood market, a large German shepherd in there with them. At first she assumed it was a police dog, that maybe there was an officer present, forcing the people to perform their tasks. But the dog was lazing on the floor, panting. No doubt should she or another stranger step over the threshold, the animal would react. At the end of the block was a closed-up gas station. She cut across the station's cracked concrete apron and was glad to see there was a paved alley that led behind the stores and bank. She followed it, passing stacked wooden crates and tipped-over metal garbage cans. The man in his do-rag had stepped out of the shoe store and now Claire saw the handgun tucked in his waistband. She halted.

"Look, naw, it ain't that," he said, his hands gesturing in front of him, knowing she'd seen the gun. He came closer and she stiffened. There was no way she could get her gun out before his was on her. That didn't mean she wouldn't try.

"I can't have that Guardsman stop me," he said. "Them police put a warrant on me."

"Sneak away." She pointed down the alley.

"My car is parked down the street and I stay in Inglewood. Buses ain't exactly running regular, ya know?"

She also knew where this was going. "He saw me walking up."

"Girl, one spade look the same as another to him."

"Then what makes you think he'll notice you?"

"Sheet," he hissed. "You a female, dig? I mean he might notice you and your brown sugar mixed with cream if'n I was to guess, but you know, like you said, he won't suspect."

"Uh-huh. So you want me to go get your car and drive it around the block for you?"

"Yeah. You know, we gotta stick together."

"Right. Look, I need to get something in the store."

"What, an apple or something?"

"Not the market, here."

"The shoes are gone, baby."

"I'll get your car but I have to do this first."

His eyes narrowed and he smiled. "Oh, you got something hidden in there." He looked past her then back at her. "It must be jewelry, huh? A good-lookin' chick like you. Pearls and whatnot."

"I'm part of a girl snatch and grab gang."

"For real?"

Theatrically, she looked over her shoulder to sell her lie. "Come on, let's get inside." She stepped past him and entered the back door he'd left ajar. This took her down a gloomy passageway. Off to one side was the manager's office, the desk in there overturned. His footfalls were behind her.

"Where'd you hide your loot?" he asked, a slight edge in his voice.

"That's not what I'm looking for."

"I don't get it."

"You'll see."

Claire scanned about. Ingram had told her he'd sailed the wrapped film flat through the busted-out window. It could have fluttered anywhere. Had this young man plucked it off the ground, opened up the packet and exposed the shot, ruining it? He might have figured it had been lost by a photographer for the white press and he could earn a few bucks of a finder's fee, pretending he hadn't exposed the film. What if she told him it was pictures of her and her imaginary girl crew cavorting in lacy lingerie, brandishing guns, kissing each other? That might provide the incentive for him to give it over. Though could she do anything to save the picture?

He grabbed her arm, startling her. "You playin' with me, girl?"

"I'm serious as a heart attack." Hand inside the purse, she pulled her arm free.

"You ain't got no heat on you," he said, taking a step back.

"We can find out." Her palm was sweaty as it held the pistol's grip in her handbag. "Of course gunshots will get that Guardsman's attention." Her mouth was dry and her throat constricted, but her knees weren't wobbly.

"Yeah," he drawled, considering her words. His eyes flicked in the direction of the Guardsman.

Then, peripherally, she saw a lone white heel laying on its side on the floor. It wasn't directly below the window but in the front facing corner of the store. She turned her head slightly to better look at it and damned if the little black rectangle wasn't cocked inside the shoe. If Harry'd tried to make that shot, who knew where the film would have landed?

"What you lookin' at?" He moved sideways to the shoe and frowning, reached down to pull the packet free. "This is what you wanted?"

"That's right."

"What in it?"

"Undeveloped film."

"You some kind of reporter?" There was a loose flap to the packet and he tugged on this.

"Take it easy. Yeah, I'm a reporter," she said, not knowing what else to say. She restrained herself from rushing at him, unless he tried to pull the film flat out, exposing it to the light.

"How much is it worth to you?" he said.

"Thought we're supposed to be sticking together, soul brother."

"Still gotta eat, baby." He shook the packet, grinning crookedly. "I bet you'd pay me not to pull the film out of this, messing it up before it can be developed. Ain't that right?"

"Fifty."

"If you got fifty, you got a hundred." He stepped closer, not intimidated by her in the least. Or if he was, his greed overcame any such concern.

"Not on me."

"Keep fuckin' around and I ruin your shit." He tugged on the flap.

The breath balled in her throat. "Goddammit, wait now, this picture is important." She held her palm up. "Take it all, everything." She dropped the purse, her wallet in her hand, the gun still inside the accessory. Then she tossed the wallet at his head and reflexively, he dropped the packet to catch it. She darted forward, scooping up the purse and bringing it across his face with a loud smack on his flesh.

"Bitch, you done fucked up now," he yelled as he came at her.

Claire side-stepped him and kicked down hard on his ankle. But being young and strong, this didn't faze him, and he grabbed her.

"That's your ass now," he vowed.

"Hey, what's going on in there?" The woman who'd been sweeping up with the push broom stood at the window. She held the broom handle as if at parade rest. "Get your hands off her, you ought to be ashamed of yourself."

"Shut up," he replied.

"Hey, hey," the woman called, waving her hand at the Guardsman not far away.

"Fuck," the youngster blared as he dropped Claire and ran out the back door.

The Guardsman appeared in the window. "What's going on here?"

"A masher, that's all," Claire said.

He glared at her. "What're you doing in there, there's nothing to steal."

Calmly as she could, she again used a business card and told the Guardsman, "Councilman Bradley wanted to get a full picture of the damage. He also wanted us to make sure the authorities were establishing order without undue uses of force."

The Guardsman looked up from the card. "He sent a woman?"

"He sent women and men," she said matter-of-factly.

"But you're okay, right?"

"Thanks to this lady." Claire nodded at the other woman.

"Yeah, well, you be careful."

"I will."

He adjusted his helmet and returned to his post. When

he was out of earshot, the other woman said, "Honey, you and I both know this isn't Mr. Bradley's district."

"What?" Claire said, smiling.

"Okay now," the woman said, shaking her head and walking back across the street.

Claire put a hand to her chest, her heart rate finally returning to normal. Packet in her purse, she left the building and made her way back to her car. If the damning shot of Faraday's death was on the film, the picture couldn't be ignored. What people in the community had been saying about how they are policed differently would be captured in stark black and white.

CHAPTER THREE

The tears were a surprise. Ingram lay on his back in the dark of the hospital prison ward crying softly. Funny how the sadness had dropped on him, out of nowhere—but not really, he knew down deep. Two days locked up and he'd finally been able to sleep. Hoping nothing had happened to Anita and she'd retrieved the flat. The prisoners hadn't been allowed visitors since noon due to some complicated reason their nurse had relayed, but no one, even she, seemed clear on exactly why. Now, early in the morning like a left hook, he dreamed he was back in Chorwa, that village in South Korea.

Being back there wasn't new, but this version was a first. Ingram wasn't dressed in fatigues but in a pin-striped suit and tie, wielding a Thompson submachine gun with a bandolier of bullets draped across his torso like a character out of a comic book. A cigar smoldered in the corner of his mouth. On the upper arm of the coat's sleeve, the three inverted Vs denoting a sergeant's status had been sewn into the fabric. Among the men in his squad was his murdered buddy Ben Kinslow. He didn't have a rifle but his horn which, like Gabriel in the Bible and the walls of Jericho, when he blew a tune aimed at the enemy, they'd fall down dead.

The kid was there, the one Ingram had killed by accident. The child rarely spoke in his dreams, though in his nightmares he did, sometimes in Korean and sometimes in English. Sometimes they talked about baseball and he'd wake up, the youngster fleetingly alive in his mind. This time, the kid ran around a corner trying not to be killed as the aircraft's bomb exploded. He was a flash of movement but Ingram didn't shoot, didn't riddle him with rounds from his machine gun. The kid reached his arms out to the sky and he lifted off the dirt like one of Peter Pan's Lost Boys. Kinslow raised his horn and blew visible notes that swirled around the kid, helping him fly higher. As the two watched him rise, the kid's form disappeared in the glare of the bright sun. They grinned at each other and that was when Ingram felt so bad, he awoke—it was the double loss that hit him, the child and his friend.

At least in Kinslow's case, he'd dealt with the ones who'd killed him. One of them he'd killed in self-defense—Morty, who liked knifes. He had buried one in Ingram's foot. He'd killed Morty's pal Wicks too, gun to his head, pulled the trigger. Murdered him. Justifiable as far as he was concerned. Accepting this cold reality hadn't troubled his sleep since then. Now the man who'd given those two bruisers their orders to take care of Ingram, Winston Hoyt, was rich and white and connected. He remained untouchable. That fact troubled Ingram.

Ingram wiped his wet, unshaven face. He had to use the bathroom. He'd been relying on the bedpan and each time it made him feel worse, like an old man who couldn't even remember how to button his shirt. He was laid up but damn, come on, you can get your sorry ass to the bathroom, can't you?

Before the communication lockdown, Spurlock the lawyer had sent one of his associates, a cat-eye-glasses-on-a-chain-wearing Black woman named Alma Stoner, to visit him. Alma was Ingram's hue and a few years younger than him. She wrote down his account in precise handwriting on a yellow legal pad, at different intervals asking specific questions.

"They cut him down in cold blood, Alma," he'd said. "Not in a dark alley or alongside a building, in plain sight, in front of people. But colored folks, so who's going to believe them?"

"I hope the shot shows that. The police can't just sweep this under the rug like they've done before."

Before leaving, she told him Spurlock's office would be back in touch as they'd be working to arrange bail. Two hours later the police guard had come in and without a word had unlocked the cuff around his wrist, leaving the other end still secured to the bed's railing.

On his third try, Ingram was able to sit up and get his feet onto the cold linoleum floor. He was dressed in a beige cotton gown and nothing else. The man by the window was snoring, as was another man in here. His morphine drip had been removed late last evening. His head still ached but now it was a dull throb, not the lancing pain it had been when he'd first arrived. He got up slowly and instantly sat back down on the bed. He was weak but not dizzy. He rose again and was able to stay on his feet.

Sliding one foot in front of the other, his shuffling gait

took him toward his goal, to pee like a grown man again. Success was his. Returning to bed was an easier walk than getting to the bathroom. In his bed once again, he fell dead asleep with a smile on his face.

CHAPTER FOUR

The printed photograph resounded like a thunderclap across the city. Faraday Zinum was frozen in bold clarity falling backward to the ground. In Ingram's eerily composed photo, the firebrand's body is arching away from the knot of Los Angeles Police officers who'd crowded him on Broadway. It wasn't clear which officer had shot the unarmed man, as more than one had their service revolver out in the image and the muzzle flash hadn't been recorded. But there was absolutely no doubt: Zinum's hands were visible and empty.

"Famous all over town, Harry," Claire said flatly.

"Yep," he said.

Ingram was out of the hospital and back home. Before them, on the front page of the *Sentinel* and the *Herald-Dispatch*, the two Black newspapers in town, was the shot. The image was also on the front page of the *Free Press*, which Ingram had been sent by messenger earlier that morning. The *Herald Examiner*, an establishment newspaper, ran the shot, too, but not on the front page and cropped in such a way as to only show the agony on the dying young man's face.

"Of course your comrades printed the shot," he said, tapping another folded over newspaper, the communist *Daily Worker*. The reds' paper called the riots an insurrection, the police an occupying army. In his accompanying piece in the Freep, Gerry Tackwood likened Ingram's photo to Robert Capa's shot of an Abraham Lincoln brigadista being shot on the battlefield: a photo that singularly summed up courage and injustice, reprinted the world over.

"A bit overblown," Ingram said ruefully.

"You love it."

Ingram was conflicted. He was glad the photo had been printed—but snuffing out this promising youngster's life, that was a goddamn crime. He meant more. His untimely death had to stand for something.

Ingram had learned that Zinum was twenty-three years old but was already experienced in civil rights work. According to one of the articles about him in the *Daily Worker*, he'd been born in Chicago to an Apache father and a Black mother. There seemed to be little known about the father, an ironworker who, when Zinum was five or so, drifted away from the family. His mother, Novina Goodhew, a practical nurse, had thereafter moved him and his sister Dorell out to Los Angeles, where she had relatives. The mother's folks had been involved with Marcus Garvey's Back to Africa movement. Others in her extended family had been organizers with A. Philip Randolph and the Pullman car porters union. *The roots of radicalism*, the article stated, *ran deep in Zinum's family*.

"He was once in Snic," Anita Claire said. The Student Nonviolent Coordinating Committee, SNCC, had been founded in the south when college-aged young people got involved in sit-ins to integrate lunch counters and the like. "Got his head zapped like yours more than once by them crackers," she said, taking a bite of her breakfast. "I read he was a VISTA volunteer but that might just be his legend and not a fact."

"Dedicated cat," Ingram agreed. "Larger in death than life, huh?"

"Yeah, a person of promise cut down so young, we can project on him all manner of what could have been in the years ahead." A mournful look came and went across her face.

Next to his partially eaten plate of eggs, sausage and toast, Ingram had the *Sentinel* open. He tapped the page, pointing at an article by Wesley Crossman, the metro editor, formerly of the *California Eagle* before it closed recently. "Faraday was part of a group that came together last year, according to what Wesley says here. Some of them were involved with CORE and the NAACP. They call themselves the Disciples for Community Defense."

"Like the Deacons for Defense?" Claire asked. The Deacons were initially a group of Black WWII veterans who practiced the art of armed self-defense in the pursuit of equal rights. Currently there were a few other chapters of the group organized in southern cities.

"Sounds like," Ingram agreed. "But I want to dig further, Anita."

"You mean about Faraday?"

"Don't want him reduced to a photo and a slogan."

The rioting had ceased for the most part. Yesterday, Martin Luther King had flown back to L.A. to meet with community leaders and the authorities. Already more militant views than his had been expressed. In some quarters, the desire was to take up where the assassinated Malcolm X had left off.

Claire sipped her coffee. She looked up at the circular electric clock on the wall behind Ingram. "I better get going. Tom's going to be at Dr. King's meeting with the reverends." She rose and adjusted her skirt. The meeting was to plan for a clergy press conference blasting the questionable deaths of colored folks at the hands of the police department and the National Guard's abusive approach to re-establishing order in Watts. Ingram's photo crystalized the various complaints, not just now but for years, aimed at Chief of Police William Parker and his policies concerning the policing of the city's negro citizenry. The official response from the Department stated that Zinum had a gun tucked under his shirt in the middle of his back. That Ingram's photo was misleading because it didn't show the "negro agitator" had been reaching for the weapon.

"Give 'em what for, sweetie." Ingram put his hand just above her knee, rubbing her smooth skin. Earlier this morning he'd enjoyed watching her apply lotion to those legs. How envious would his jail ward buddy be?

She bent and gave him a torrid kiss. When they parted lips and tongues, she said, "You take it easy today, remember you're supposed to be recuperating."

"I know what would help me heal faster."

"Fresh." She pinched his cheek, then started toward the side door off the nook. She paused at the tiled counter, refreshing her lipstick using the reflective door of the bread box as a mirror. "Bye, honey."

"Bye," he said dreamily as he watched her go.

When she was gone, Ingram stretched and yawned. Once more he leafed through the rest of the newspaper as he finished his breakfast. He noted a photo of a National Guardsman on a one-story rooftop manning a machine gun on a tripod. He drained his coffee cup.

The phone rang behind him. Ingram attempted to stand but was wobbly on his legs. Cursing softly as if he were an old timer, he reached for the cane leaning on the wall. The hospital had issued this to him, retrieved from their lost and found. It was made of gnarled driftwood and had a hooked head for grip. Some two years ago he'd also had to use a cane after that Morty had stuck a knife in his foot. He hoped this wasn't an omen and the third time he needed one would mean he'd lost a leg.

Walking slowly, he made it into the living room and plucked the handset free. He was breathing heavier than normal from the effort.

"Hello?" he answered.

"This the commie lovin' blackie who planted that fake photograph in the newspapers to make our police look bad?"

"Why yes it is," he answered cheerily.

"You best understand, boy, that what happened to those thieving darkies during their terror campaign organized by Red China can easily happen to you. Get your head split wide open like a watermelon."

"Let me tell you something, paddy. You come at me you're gonna get a bullet between your teeth for your troubles. Then another one in your gut because you're spittin'."

"You big-lipped nigger, you can't talk to a white man like that."

"I just did."

Calmly, Ingram replaced the receiver and went into the bedroom. Seeking psychological comfort, he took his service .45 from the nightstand and checked to make sure it was loaded and ready. It was.

Satisfied, he put the weapon back in its drawer and sat on the bed. A flash of when he'd last used the gun played in front of his eyes. Two years ago, he'd killed that man in cold blood in a trolley car junk yard. Wicks, Ben Kinslow's killer. Wicks would have done the same to Ingram if the situation was reversed.

Had he let Wicks live and be arrested, given he worked for the rich Winston Hoyt, he would have gotten out of jail. He knew who Anita Claire was and would have hurt her, kidnapped her or worse to get at Ingram. He couldn't allow that. If this call was the start of a hate campaign . . . well, most of that was just assholes spouting what assholes spout. But should one of them get to drinking with a buddy and decide more than a stern talking-to was required to teach this burr head a lesson . . .

Yes, he'd be ready, he resolved. And he'd be practical and get an unlisted number.

Not ready for the gym but wanting to exercise, Ingram left the house for a walk, cane in hand, even though he didn't like to rely on the thing. At least the bandage was off his head. When Spurlock's associate, Alma Stoner, had returned to let him know they'd arranged bail for him, she'd not only insisted on the cane but a neck brace too. The suggestion being these would be necessary implements to utilize when he was arraigned next month. He'd put on the neck brace to appease her before he left the hospital but wasn't about to use it at home.

"Hey, Harry," his neighbor Diane Fitzhugh said. She was outside pruning the shrubbery framing her front window. This part of the Crenshaw area was still mixed, white, Black and Japanese American. Fitzhugh was one of several white folks who hadn't moved away as Black people moved in.

"How are you?" He paused at the edge of her lawn, which was well-maintained, as was the rest of her home. He and Claire had been invited inside more than once.

Fitzhugh stopped what she was doing and straightened up. She was a thin, handsome woman of maybe sixty. Today, she was dressed in khakis and a buttoned-up shirt with a floppy sun hat and frayed cotton work gloves.

"Oh you know, just glad we made it through the troubles." She took a few steps toward Ingram, frowning, and gestured with the clippers toward his cane. "I saw when your friends brought you home, Harry. I'm not a busybody like someone else I could name on our block, but I did happen to be standing near the window at the time. This happened to you because you were out there in the riots?"

"Yeah, got jacked up. Good thing I got a hard head."

She regarded him for several moments then said, "You're young now, Harry, but age has a funny way of catching up on us. You and Norman made it back from war in one piece but that doesn't make you bulletproof."

Norman, her husband, was a World War II vet who passed a few years ago. "Anita gave me an earful too. Believe me, it's not like I go looking for trouble." He wondered if he meant that or if he was like a kid who'd been told not to stick his hand over a lit stove and of course couldn't wait to do the opposite.

"Well," she said, "you sure got a heck of a photo out of it."

"Seems so."

A wan smile crossed her face. "Might do some good, that photo."

He nodded. "Hopefully."

"You be careful, Harry."

"I will. Say hey to Adam when you see him again." That was her grown son.

She nodded, adjusted her hat and returned to her labors. Ingram continued his walk, cane tapping along beside him. The sunshine invigorated him. He passed a Kashu Realty sign planted in a lawn. The owner of the real estate company, Kazuo Inouye, was nisei, a second-generation person of Japanese descent born in America. Inouye's outfit deliberately challenged existing housing covenants, like ones that stated no sale to "Mongolians" or "negroes." He advertised in the *Sentinel* and the *Eagle* when it was in operation, among other newspapers. Ingram didn't know the guy, but his buddy Josh Nakano did. They'd met overseas, both of them serving in the all-Japanese 442nd Regiment, the Go For Brokers.

Inouye was probably always changing his phone number, Ingram considered.

A familiar tinny whistle interrupted Ingram's reverie. The sound announced the arrival of a bright yellow and blue Helms Bakery truck, which was now driving slowly down the street. The boxy custom-built conveyances, which looked akin to a shrunken trolley car on tires, originated at the Helms Bakery plant in Culver City and proceeded into various municipalities across Southern California, selling fresh baked bread, rolls and donuts. Ingram watched several housewives converge on the now-idling vehicle. The starched white uniform of the driver contrasted sharply against his dark skin. The man doffed his cap as he smiled and opened the wooden flat drawers in his truck to fill the ladies' orders.

Ingram went on. At the end of the next block, he turned a corner, heading west toward Crenshaw Boulevard. While he, Claire and their neighbors technically lived outside of the riot area, there had been looting over this way as well. Bunches of tires crowded the doorway of one raided tire shop. Further along there was the Chinese restaurant Lim Fu's Palace of Earthly Delights. The broken-out windows had been boarded over. Yet already one of the sections of plywood had been removed and new glass was being installed. Ingram speculated that, given the restaurant was popular, the goodwill built up among the mostly Black and Japanese customers must have generated favorable karma, since nothing else had happened to the establishment.

He passed other shops that hadn't been touched, then came to the Army recruiting storefront. Spray painted on its window were the words, BRING 'EM BACK ALIVE. Through the open intact glass door, Ingram saw two teenage young men, one Black and one white, sitting at a desk. The American flag and California flag were in a corner at rest on poles. The Army recruiter, a white man who didn't look too much older than these two, was in his uniform, hip hitched on the end of the desk as he worked his charm on the teens. Ingram lingered.

"You can have a career in the service," he was telling the Black kid. "You want to learn electronics, then we'll send you to school for that."

The white kid spoke up. "My second cousin is a marine.

He got sent over there, Vietnam I think it's called. Would we be sent there?"

The recruiter waved a hand dismissively. "A bunch of pajama wearin' rice eatin' dirt farmers ain't nothin' for the US of A to handle, son."

"The French had problems there," the other young man noted.

"Of course the Frogs did. We had to bail their asses out in the Big One and we're going to take care of these Soviet surrogates too. Shoot, by the time you fellas get out of basic, we'll be mopping up there."

The recruiter noticed Ingram and he glared at him. What with his cane and still lumpy face, Ingram figured he symbolized the Ghost of Veterans Past. A reminder that combat took its toll if you lived. The two youngsters saw him as well. Ingram stepped into the office.

"Can I do something for you?" the recruiter said, barely keeping the annoyance out of his voice.

"You might let them know Johnson had deployed more troops into Vietnam lately."

"Yeah, to get the job done," he said, more annoyed now.

"Just sayin', do your homework, fellas. It ain't like it is in the movies."

The two teens exchanged unsure looks.

Though tight-lipped, the recruiter said, "Thank you for stopping by."

Ingram gave the recruiter a half salute and went on. Maybe that recruiter was right, he pondered, but it sure sounded like the re-hashed rah-rah his drill sergeant used to recite. What the hell was that sumabitch's name? Sergeant Hanley, Chip Hanley.

"Jesus," Ingram muttered, shaking his head. "Wonder what he's doing now?"

He walked as far as Nakano's place of business, the Eternal Sands Mortuary a few blocks west of the boulevard on Jefferson. He contemplated dropping in on him but decided against such an intrusion. Though he was morbidly curious if any of the dead from the rioting had wound up here for burial. Nakano hadn't made mention of this during his visit the other day but that didn't mean they weren't here. And it wasn't as if he was going to return to take photos of the corpses—as if his friend would let him. Ingram turned back and by the time he was halfway home, he felt less achy. Less stove up, as his mother would say.

He paused to read a handbill plastered to a telephone pole with his photo on it. The reproduction of the shot was poor quality. Lifted from the newspaper, he concluded. The flyer, produced by the Socialist Workers Party, called for justice for the police murder of Faraday Zinum, the end to the Bantustans of American ghettos, ongoing guerilla warfare— Watts is just the beginning, the SWP warned. Ingram was almost amused. Calling for shit like that could get a lot of Black folks hurt.

When Ingram got back home and had the key in the lock, the phone was ringing. Inside, he picked up the receiver, expecting another complainer. This time he was going to cuss the fool out.

"Is this Harry Ingram?" a pleasant female voice said after he answered. He couldn't help but notice there was a husky quality to it.

"Yes it is," he said.

"Mister Ingram, I work for the Louis Lomax show and

we would like to have you come on and talk about your photograph and your experiences during the recent adversities."

"This on the level?"

"Yes, sir, I can assure you I'm not making this up. If you like, look up the number to the studio and call me back. We're on Channel 11, as you may know. Ask for Phyliss."

"I believe you."

They talked some more, and Ingram wrote down the day and time as well as which gate to enter before ending the call with the sexy-voiced Phyliss Lansdale. He imagined the possibility of doing a photo shoot of her for an issue of *Dapper*, the black men's magazine he occasionally did work for. He also imagined Anita Claire socking him hard on the jaw. He supposed a threesome was out of the question. There, in his living room, the sun shining through the windows, he put his head back and laughed out loud as if he'd lost his cotton pickin' mind.

CHAPTER FIVE

The coroner performed a perfunctory autopsy on Faraday Zinum. The cause of death was listed as a homicide in the technical sense of that word—death at the hands of another. To the surprise of no one, District Attorney Evelle Younger's office announced with a press advisory he wasn't going to bring charges against the officers involved in Zinum's death.

The attorney representing the family, which was to say the mother and sister, was Rita Hansen, a colleague of Anton Spurlock. Hansen wanted an independent autopsy of Zinum's body. Again to the surprise of no one, Chief Parker was applying pressure on the City Council and the DA's office to prevent this. Since the determination had already been made that the city wouldn't be doing any questioning of the Department's version of events, the city had no legal reason to hold the body. The stalemate was getting the attention of the Black and white press.

"You're listening to Cross Currents here on KPFK. I'm your host Tyler McGloughlin. I'm talking with Dorell Zinum, sister to the man we've all seen cut down in vivid

cold-blooded detail by the Los Angeles Police Department
. . ." Cross Currents on KPFK, the FM Pacifica station
where programs about meditation, Buddhism and left of
center points of view could be found, was what they called
listener supported. They too had fielded volunteer reporters
during the conflagration.

"Dorell in her own right has been active in the struggle
for civil rights as he was," McGloughlin continued. "And I
don't think I'm speaking out of turn saying that she and the
station give thanks to that intrepid photographer who dared
to be out in the streets to chronicle the truth of what happened to her brother."

"That's right," Zinum said.

"Don't get too swelled a head, Intrepid," Claire said.

She and Ingram lay in bed in their matching pajamas,
snuggling and listening to the broadcast. The radio blared
from a shelf of the bedroom's wall bookcase. Not far down
the shelf was a small stone statue of the Buddha. Figuratively
and literally, it had been a hot summer and the evening was
warm. The sash of one of the windows was partially raised.
There was at best a listless breeze.

"I'll try not to." Ingram sampled more whiskey from
the tumbler on his nightstand, then set it back down next
to a plastic bottle of prescribed pain pills. He'd stopped
taking them two days ago and was no longer using the
cane.

"Of course they're going to great measures to cover up
this murder by the police," Zinum's sister said. "And really
it's not just the death of my brother that should be remembered and investigated. Leon Posey, Emmerson Walls, I
could go on and on about those shot down by Parker's police

during, well, I won't go so far as to call it an insurrection, but it was more than a damn riot." After a pause she added, "It was an uprising, that's what it was."

"Yes, it was inevitable what happened in South Central," her interviewer replied. "Years of state sponsored abuse and neglect can only be tolerated so long."

"There's going to be a memorial for Zinum soon," Claire said. "At the Watts Towers."

"Before there's a second autopsy?"

She reached across him for his drink. "The feeling is to keep the momentum going. It would be a mistake to wait weeks to get the body and get the examination done." She sipped and put the glass in place on her nightstand, next to a book entitled *Early Buddhism* by Thomas William Rhys Davids. "Already Brown is talking about putting together some sort of commission to yet again study the 'Negro Problem.'"

"Us negroes got a lot of problems, baby."

"Ain't that the truth." She bared her teeth and said, "I'm about to give you all the problems you can handle."

"Good thing I'm on the mend."

He was reaching to kiss her but she held up a finger and got out of bed. She turned the radio dial to KBCA, the jazz station. Claire slid back in bed and reached her hand inside the slit of Ingram's pajamas, taking hold of him.

"Oh, my," he said.

A heated gust blew in and encircled their entwined forms. Jazz organist Jimmy Smith's melodic rendering of "Prayer Meetin'" was their soundtrack as a shudder worked its way along Ingram's spine and he held Claire tight in excitement and foreboding of what was to come.

ARRANGEMENTS WERE made and Faraday Zinum's body was transported to Eternal Sands. His body would be held there in preparation for the independent autopsy to be conducted. The autopsy went forward due to community pressure and the intervention of Black councilmembers Tom Bradley and Billy Mills. Bradley in particular had cited Ingram's photo as troubling.

"We must get to the truth," Bradley had said over the radio. "In some quarters faith in our institutions are being frayed. I believe that faith can be restored only if all avenues are explored."

Eternal Sands was chosen because the dead man's sister knew Kazuo Inouye, the owner of Kashu Realty. He'd helped a friend of hers buy a small tract home in the Hyde Park section a few years ago. The friend knew about Josh Nakano and that he in turn was a friend of Ingram's. Ingram was drafted to be the official photographer of the memorial.

"Okay, I'll see you later," Ingram said to his friend.

"Hope it goes well today," Nakano replied.

The two were standing on the side of the mortuary near an opal black Cadillac hearse. While the body remained at the funeral home, the hearse would depart from here and be driven to Watts. A stylized wreath made of black and red crepe paper was secured to the roof. In the center of the arrangement was a blown-up photo of a smiling Faraday Zinum. Several people were in the lot including members of the Chosen Few, a predominantly Black motorcycle club begun in South Central a few years ago. Aside from Ingram, the only other newsperson present was Mike Piedmont, a white reporter with the *Herald Examiner*. He was talking to Dorell Zinum.

"Even Parker knows to reign in his cops now and then."

Nakano cocked his head, lifting his hands palms upward. "Hope he does."

"Time to go," the driver of the hearse said. He was one of the Disciples. He held the door open for Zinum's mother and sister. Both women were slender of build, their features favoring one another. They shared grim but determined expressions as they got into the vehicle.

The Cadillac maneuvered around the other departing vehicles and paused in the driveway on the Jefferson Boulevard side of the building. Several motorcycles lined up on either side of the hearse. Ingram clapped Nakano on the shoulder and headed toward his transportation, a sidecar attached to one of the motorcycles.

As the hearse passed through various neighborhoods, people exited houses, laundromats or what have you to gather on the sidewalk to clap or, for some, raise fist in salute. The Chosen Few on their motorcycles and a number of lowriders in Impalas, '57 Chevys and other types of cars formed the procession for the empty coffin. More than one LAPD patrol car kept pace at numerous intervals but they didn't interfere. A police helicopter circled overhead. Ingram took his pictures, at times standing up, managing to keep his balance as he took his shots with his Nikon. The club member handling his motorcycle was Thiggs, a friend of Strummer Edwards. He was easily six-three and had a wide chest over which he wore a blue striped shirt.

"'Preciate the ride, man," Ingram told Thiggs over the roar of the engine. Both wore goggles to protect their eyes from wind.

"My pleasure," he said back.

When the assembled reached Central Avenue, they went right, heading farther south past burned out businesses and the occasional torched hulk of a car or pick-up. About three blocks from its destination, the hearse and its entourage pulled up to a roughhewn wooden funeral bier on wooden wheels that looked to have been erected in the latter part of the previous century. Across the street stood a row of the members of the Nation of Islam, a wall of dark blue suits and matching bowties. Darker blue was also evident in the crowd—the police presence.

The rear of the hearse was opened, the dark wood and iron plate casket extracted. The Zinums had eschewed extravagance for humility as befitting her dead brother's status as one of the common folk. Ingram snapped away as members of the Chosen Few and Thiggs, who wore a leather newsboy cap, lifted the casket onto the bier.

Ingram hung his camera around his neck and helped roll the wagon and its cargo to Watts Towers, where the memorial was taking place. The Towers' three main spiraling structures, made from plumbing pipe and found material joined by other minor spirals and arches, rose from a triangular piece of land. The tallest spire was nearly a hundred feet high. The whole of it, with its seventeen towers of various heights, had been erected over decades by a headstrong man named Sam Rodia. Born Sabato Rodia near Naples, Italy, Rodia scavenged materials such as tiles, the bottoms of glass bottles, wire mesh and rough concrete to create his signature work. While there had been fires and looting nearby, the Towers hadn't been vandalized. Rodia had passed about a month earlier in Martinez, in the northern part of the state. Ingram covered the memorial, held here at the

Towers, for a piece he'd been commissioned to do for *Jet* magazine. His earlier interview of Rodia was set to be reprinted along with several articles in an upcoming issue of the *Nation* magazine analyzing the recent unrest. Ingram's connection to the left-leaning organ came through a free-lance writer named Eddie Burrows, whom Ingram had met while covering King's previous visit to L.A.

A stage with black bunting had been set up on one side of the towers. Together with the Chosen Few and Thiggs, Ingram rolled the bier in front of the stage and secured it in place. On the stage was a wooden podium with a micro-phone. In place of a photo of the deceased, the podium bore a graphic in a circle, a stylized rendering of a stalking California cougar—the symbol of the Disciples. It had been showing up spray painted on buildings in various parts of South Central in the week after Zinum's demise. Even Chief Parker couldn't be tone deaf to the meaning, Ingram thought. The Disciples were watching the police and what they do.

Reporters for print and radio were present to cover the memorial, but it was only Ingram who'd traveled with the hearse. He'd figured correctly to capture the reactions of regular people to the procession. He was not only taking his usual black and white shots, but was using color film today too, which he was starting to utilize more. Several of his steady customers like the editors at *Dapper* magazine had requested he adapt to modern times. He'd been reluctant at first but as he got used to working in color, he came to see the medium could expand his visual vocabulary.

The crowd was mostly Black folks but there were many whites present as well as other races and ethnicities. People still milled about as more arrived, including a contingent of

American Indians. Ingram spotted his lady love and walked over to her. On the way, he passed a loose-limbed, bearded white clergyman shaking hands with one of the Black Muslims in greeting. Mimeographed programs were available. A line drawing, traced from a photograph, depicted a smiling Faraday Zinum on the cover.

"Looks like the governor is going to have this guy McCone head his causes of the riots commission," Claire said after he gave her a peck on the cheek.

"Wasn't he the head of the CIA?"

"Um-hmm," she said.

"Damn, what're we supposed to make of that?"

"It's a signal to conservatives this won't be no bones thrown to the mau-maus and rabble rousers. The CIA don't play."

"Like what they did in the Congo." She'd told him about the Agency's involvement in helping to overthrow the left-leaning prime minister Patrice Lumumba of the then newly formed Democratic Republic of the Congo, once a Belgian colony. Emerging from the coup forces was the pro-West Joseph-Désiré Mobutu, who was more than glad to take advantage once Lumumba was arrested and killed.

"Tom says McCone likes to boast about knowing Watts," she added.

"What're you talking about?"

"McCone says he used to play ball down here when he was a kid, forty some years ago."

"Sheet," Ingram said, grinning. "Nigger go fetch. He might as well have said he milked cows when with Bojangles when Compton was dairy land."

A man in a tan windbreaker signaled to Claire. She told Ingram, "That's my cue. See you in a bit, honey pie."

Claire puckered her lips at him while walking away. After letting his gaze linger on her, Ingram moved about, taking several shots of the police whose patrol cars were parked haphazardly in the roadway where 107th ended at Graham. Now he was using a Canon single-lens reflex camera strapped around his neck. He'd taken a night class at L.A. City College to better understand the Canon's capabilities and how to push the limits of using color film. Ingram also hefted a camera bag containing another camera loaded with black and white film. Given the number of people who were present, including other members of the press, he hedged the cops would hesitate before they took his stuff this time.

He nodded to friends and familiar faces, including Frank Wilkerson, who'd once worked for the housing authority in town, jazz saxman Red Holloway, who was currently gigging at the Crystal Tea Room, and Edwards, who was lighting a cigarette as he got nearer to him.

"Surprised to see you at this, Strummer."

"Ain't I Black too, Harry? Brother don't always think with his fists. Sheeit."

"Don't tell me you gonna start a Marcus Garvey block club."

His friend regarded him seriously. "Soul brothers and sisters getting out there wasn't just a passing fad, man. It's a new day."

Ingram swapped out one lens for another on his camera. "On the level, you plan to take a few pages from the Book of Malcolm?"

"You damn well know I like chitlins and smothered pork chops too much." They shared a laugh. A few members of the NOI walked by, causing them to snicker more. Then

Edwards said, "Can't say I'm about to reform my wicked ways, but it is about time to stop singing and start swinging, ain't it? I mean, come on, Harry, I've been doing shit like that since I don't know when anyway."

"Old dogs and new tricks, Strummer?"

"You the one that's been doing the reading."

"Seems you been too."

Edwards blew a stream of smoke into the air. "Yeah, well, can't always just read the Sports section." He looked over at Ingram. "Not that I've given up betting."

At their periodic domino games, particularly when it was only the men, invariably the conversating included sports, women and current events. It wasn't just Ingram who might make mention of something they'd read in an essay by James Baldwin or a heated discussion on a news show they'd watched. Indeed Jed Monk, who hadn't completed high school, was up on the latest debates about such matters as the US's growing involvement in Vietnam. Ingram too was aware his perspective about life had broadened since he and Anita Claire had started going around together.

The speakers began to gather on the stage, including Dorell Zinum. Her mother took a seat in the first row of the folding chairs behind the podium. She was dressed in black, a wide-brimmed matching hat with veil on her head. Her daughter too wore black, but a fashion chic version of bell-bottom slacks, a midriff tan colored shirt and a long black polka-dot vest over that.

"Well, well," Edwards muttered, eyeing her.

"Careful, you're drooling. And by the way, she's young enough to be your daughter."

"You know what Redd says."

"About beauty being skin deep?"

"I was thinking of something a little dirtier." The cigarette bobbed in the corner of Strummer's grinning mouth. He tapped his friend on the side of his arm. "I'll let you get back to work."

"Later, man."

Zinum's sister took her seat with the other speakers on stage. Standing umbrellas shielded them from the sun. Ingram recognized the older white woman she was speaking to, Dorothy Healey—the Red Queen of L.A., as she'd been called in some quarters, for her radical activities. He'd met Healey on more than one occasion over the years, including a poetry and jazz event Johnny Otis held at the 5-4 Ballroom on Broadway, located a little more than four miles north of where Zinum had died.

Someone tapped the microphone to get the crowd's attention. Ingram was mildly surprised that the first person to speak at the podium wasn't one of the Black clergymen he'd spotted but the youngish, blond-haired and blue-eyed white clergyman he had seen earlier.

"My friends, let us begin the proceedings with a modest invocation, shall we?" he said. Heads and bodies turned toward him. "My name is Mark Schmeling and I'm the pastor at Ascension Grace Lutheran and quite pleased to see a few of my parishioners here today. For we are gathered here today to mourn, but to also not forget what Faraday Zinum stood for. We come to ask the All Mighty to look upon this troubled city. While we seek a healing of the soul, we also seek a healing of the intransigence that plagues us in the form of the so-called authorities."

Applause and cheers erupted from the gathered. Ingram

angled to the side of the stage to get shots of the pastor. His words were a mixture of the designs of the otherworldly and the need to apply those aspirations practically. Not unlike what he'd seen King do, Ingram wrote on his notepad.

"Hello, Mr. Ingram."

He turned to see a woman he didn't immediately place. Then he felt his expression brightened. "Sister O'Shay." She'd worked at a neighborhood clinic sponsored by her order and had sewn up his bleeding foot after the knife attack two years ago. They shook hands.

"After all we've been through, you can call me Violet." She was dark haired and dark eyed and regarded him steadily.

"Then I guess you should call me Harry."

"May I?"

"Can't you get in trouble for being here?"

"I don't think Cardinal McIntyre knows about me or what I do."

"I'm getting the impression that's more than managing the clinic."

"Maybe we'll have coffee one day and figure it out."

"Well, sure, yeah," he stammered, as if she could discern the impure notions about her going through his head. He nodded in the direction of the stage. "You know this Pastor Schmeling?"

She nodded. "We sit on an interfaith council that advises the city's Human Relations Commission on the matters of poverty. He's a good guy who got sent out here by his synod from French Lick, if you can believe that. A little wet behind the ears, but earnest."

"He sounds it." Ingram put a long-range lens on his

camera and began adjusting the focus, then took a few more shots as the pastor wound up his talk.

O'Shay asked, "How's it feel to be famous?"

"If you mean the photo, that wasn't what I was after." He lowered the camera to regard her. "I knew though what it could mean once it got published. When I first got back home, I used to chase those kind of shots like a junkyard dog after a raw steak. A dude lying in his own blood, a switchblade sticking out of his forehead, his old lady who did him in standing there, looking down on his cooling body, maybe some thigh showing through from the robe she's wearing. Quiet as it's kept, I sold them pics to mags like *Bronze Thrills, Jive*, you name it."

"Would it surprise you to know I'm familiar with that kind of material?" Sister O'Shay said.

"Telling on yourself, huh?"

"People are complicated."

"Ain't they?"

"And these days you wonder about the folks in your pictures. What got them to the point when you showed up?"

"That's why you joined the church? About seeing to them once the ghouls like me were gone?"

"You too, Harry," she said, touching his arm. "Let's skip the coffee. Why don't you drop by the clinic after hours soon and we can bat around what makes you and me tick. I keep a bottle of rye in a bottom drawer."

The pastor finished speaking.

"That also doesn't surprise me," Ingram replied. The last time they'd met they'd rolled dice to see if she would patch him up or not. She'd said if he lost, he would have to wait for the doctor to be in. He'd figured she'd been jiving him—she'd have tended to him either way. The back of his neck was warm, and he was unsure if she meant more than what she was saying or not. Her enigmatic smile perplexed him.

They both then looked to the stage as people clapped for the next speaker, Charlotta Bass. She'd once been editor-in-chief of the *California Eagle* and was active on various issues, including fair housing. She was a stout woman with an alert face. She began talking.

"Like in the days of the infamous Sleepy Lagoon case, where Mexican American lads were railroaded on a murder charge, we know that the people of Montgomery and Philadelphia, Mississippi and Los Angeles are at the mercy of forces that seek to terrorize and cow us. To deny us the rights granted to us by the Constitution. We can see it on our televisions each night."

In addition to his shots of Bass and the speakers following her, Ingram captured images of known figures in the crowd as the number of attendees grew. By the time Dorell Zinum came to the podium as the last speaker, there were more than two thousand people here, he estimated. While the number of police remained the same, a contingent of National Guardsmen had arrived and parked their trucks along Santa Ana Boulevard. Guardsmen assembled in front of their flatbeds. Notably, their rifles were shouldered but certainly within easy reach.

Eventually, Dorrell Zinum concluded her remarks, all eyes on her. "Crying time is over," she said. "Faraday is not a victim where flowers are left on his grave on the anniversary of his death and we go on about our business as if things were the usual. No, he wouldn't want sentimentality and empty gestures any damn way. What he'd want is for us to carry the torch forward."

Ingram took a picture of the young woman leaning into the microphone, an arm raised.

"For sure as night becomes the day, the time for the usual is over. We don't need yet another blue ribbon commission to study the problem. We know what the problem is and there they stand in their white helmets and batons at the ready." She pointed at the police.

The chant of "Burn, baby, burn," rose among the gathered. Collectively the cops visibly tensed.

"All right now, y'all be cool," Zinum said, her hands raised. "We have to honor Faraday by not tearing down but building up!"

Whoops of approval travelled through the crowd.

Two of the television news people rushed toward Zinum as she stepped off the stage. One had a cameraman in tow, who aimed a 16mm film camera on his shoulder at the firebrand. After the interview, Claire spoke to her. They soon separated and Claire walked over to Ingram along with her mother and another white woman.

"Hello, Dorothy," Ingram said.

"Hello yourself." She kissed him on the cheek and he affectionately squeezed her shoulders.

He stepped back and took a snap of her. "Maybe I'll do a piece about the two Red Dorothys plotting the overthrow of the ruling class." He was aware she knew Healey.

"Not even the *Daily Worker* would go for that," Nielson quipped.

Her daughter crossed her arms, clearly bemused by their exchange.

"At any rate, I want to introduce you to a friend of mine. This is Betty Payton."

He stuck out his hand. "Good to meet you."

The tanned white woman was medium height with styled reddish-brown hair cut short to frame her angular face. Payton was dressed in a form-fitting linen skirt and matching belted jacket. She carried one of the programs. She seemed at ease, her eyes steady on Ingram.

"I know your name," he said. "You're part of that group who saved the Towers."

"I am," she said. "How'd you know that?"

Ingram recognized it from the articles he'd done on Rodia and told her so. Betty was part of the group who protected the Towers from being torn down for being structurally unsafe, according to the city. They'd gotten an aerospace engineer to conduct a stress test. Turned out Rodia, who was not trained as a builder or an architect, had known what he was doing. The seemingly haphazardly constructed Towers passed the test.

"Betty and her board have already been talking about opening an arts center here," Nielson interjected. "Maybe you could teach a photography class, Harry."

"Never taught before, but I'd give it a try."

"Sorry, didn't mean to get us off track. Go ahead, Betty."

She began. "I've heard about you too from Dot. I was also very impressed with that photo you took, Mr. Ingram."

"Call me Harry."

"Of course." She paused, glancing toward Nielson, a slight frown creasing her brow.

"Let me buy you all lunch," her friend said, breaking the silence. "And Betty can fill you in on what's on her mind."

Claire interlaced her fingers with his. "I'd like to join you but I have to get back to the office. Tom wants to debrief me before he meets with Dr. King later today. Miss Zinum and the Disciples are on a lot of people's radar." To her mother she added, "I'll call you this evening."

"You better." They kissed.

"Bye again," she said to Ingram, pulling him close by his waist and squeezing.

"You're strong for a girl."

"Don't you forget it."

She went in one direction and the three another.

Ingram said, "There's a Mexican café on Willowbrook a few blocks over."

"Lead the way," Dorothy said.

THEY WALKED southward. Their path took them past LAPD and Guardsmen, who stood around talking and smoking. The trio earned stares, at this ruggedly proportioned Black man escorting two white women of a certain age through the ghetto. Yet no snide remarks were made—at least not loud enough to reach Ingram's ears. Several attendees of the memorial service were inside the café, but they were able to get a table. A window had been broken out, plywood tacked in place to cover the opening.

"Do you have lemonade?" Payton asked the waitress when she came over with menus.

"Yes, we do," she answered.

"Beer for me and this gentleman," Nielson said in Spanish.

"Pacifico okay?" the waitress asked, also in Spanish.

"Sure," Ingram said.

The waitress walked away. "You speak Spanish, Harry?" Payton said.

"I know how to say beer and how to ask for the restroom." He scanned the menu. He then looked at the two of them sitting opposite. "So, what's up?"

"Can't a potential mother-in-law enjoy her daughter's manly man's company? And I'm not even asking yet again when is that grandchild coming so I can dote on her or him while I'm not yet infirmed."

She and Ingram shared a soft laugh. Payton looked ill at ease and Nielson patted her arm. "Betty has a favor to ask, Harry."

Ingram smiled at Claire's mother. "Is that right?"

"You make it sound ominous."

"Just trying to see all the angles."

"She intends to compensate you for your time."

Payton added, "Absolutely."

"All right then."

The waitress brought the drinks and once she took their orders, left again.

"I'm worried about a friend of mine," Payton began. "He disappeared sometime during the riot . . . the uprising," she corrected herself.

Images of the sour white man being chased by the young Black men materialized in his head. "You think he got caught up out there?"

Betty frowned, then sipped her lemonade. "I don't believe it's that. Mose has been in South Central since after the war—World War II, I mean. I know from Dot you served in Korea." She glanced at her friend then back at Ingram. "He's well-liked by his employees, he hires locally and sponsors a bowling team. His business was untouched during the recent events."

It occurred to Ingram he should be taking notes, if only to show Dorothy he took this seriously because she did. He got his steno pad out of his camera bag and, leafing to a blank page, clicked his pen. "What's his name and where's the business?"

"His name is Moses Tolbert and he owns Restoration Building Supply on Slauson near Figueroa." She recited the exact address.

He recalled seeing the truck during the riots. "They sell lumber, doors, that sort of thing?"

"Yes," she said. "Over the years he's developed quite a customer base, including people who build sets for movies and TV. He's done business with the housing authority."

"Is he married?"

"At one time he was. He has no children."

Ingram noticed Nielson giving Payton a sideways look but he kept his face neutral. "Do you know when he went missing?"

"It was that Friday. From what I understand he, Chet and several of the others had returned to the business after ferrying other employees away. They were keeping watch, making sure they and their neighbors weren't burned."

Ingram nodded. "Do you know if he had words with anyone in particular that day?" He almost chuckled. He sounded like he was starring in one of those private eye shows he watched.

"I don't believe so, no. At least Chet didn't mention it and I think he would have."

"And who's Chet?"

"He started as a driver for the company and has worked his way up to being the manager. See that's what I mean about Mose. He's a good and fair man."

Ingram finished sipping his beer. "Chet's a colored man."

She grinned. "Yes."

"And a red. Mose, I mean." Those two he'd seen in the building supply truck during the riots, had that been them?

"It's certainly true that Mose was involved in several campaigns, particularly when we were active in the Civil Rights Congress."

Ingram was familiar with the Congress and its work in Southern California around equal rights in employment and its ties to unions and the Communist Party. From Nielson and Claire, he'd heard the inside stories, including how the L.A. branch had been subverted by the FBI like other locals had across the country. The local Party's executive secretary had turned informant, naming names and providing internal files.

The waitress returned with their food on a tray and distributed the plates. "Thank you," Nielson said.

"My pleasure. Hope you enjoy the food." Off she went.

Betty said, "I suppose you might as well know Mose and I used to be an item but that was during those times. We have, though, remained good friends since then."

Ingram figured she was admitting things that Nielson knew and would tell him if she didn't. The question he was interested in asking, he did. "Are you an investor in the company?"

"I am."

"Me too, Harry," Nielson acknowledged. She held up her thumb and forefinger a small distance apart. "A little bit."

Taking a bite of his enchilada, he wrote additional notes. "Just trying to be thorough. Okay, back to that Friday."

"From what I understand, once evening came and what with the Guard in town to impose the curfew, Mose said his good-bye and presumably was heading home."

"Where does he live?"

"In View Park."

"But he didn't get there?"

"Maybe he did but it's unclear. Restoration is normally open half a day on Saturdays and closed on Sundays. Come Saturday, Chet and a couple of the others were in, but not Mose, though he'd been expected. Chet called his house and got no answer. He has no wife or children. No one thought much of it. They went about doing inventory and what have you. Surprisingly, they even got a few orders."

"But he doesn't show up on Monday," Nielson added.

"Now they get a little worried, so Chet drives over to his house and Mose's car isn't there." She paused, gesturing. "In the past Mose would sometimes go off on a bender, drinking and gambling. But he'd calmed his wild ways. He hadn't gotten carried away like that for a few years I'd say."

Ingram said, "Something was different this time."

She nodded solemnly. "The police found his car parked not too far from the airport."

Ingram worked that over in his mind. "Could have been abandoned there, or maybe he took a plane to beat it out of town? Is there money missing from the till?"

"No, the books are intact, and as far as anyone can tell, the money's in the bank."

"Only Tolbert can write a company check?"

For the first time, Payton smiled. "No, there's a longtime

bookkeeper and she hasn't gone anywhere." She looked over at Nielson. "She's what our folks would have called a spinster. Just her and her cats in the little cottage she lives in by the ocean."

"It's the quiet ones you have to watch out for," Ingram said.

"Could be," Payton allowed. "She's an interesting person."

"How do you mean?"

"Well," she began, searching for the words. "I know from Mose she's something of a spiritual seeker. For someone who deals in adding and subtraction, she's into self-discovery, it's called."

Anita Claire had recently been reading about eastern philosophies, and Ingram also recalled articles he'd read in the Freep. "Like meditation, you mean."

"Exactly. You get it."

Ingram asked, "When was Tolbert's car found?"

"Tuesday past. According to the police there was no blood on the seat or any other signs of violence apparently."

"The car was locked?"

"Yes, and no keys were inside. It was towed to an impound yard."

"Can you pay the fees if I can get it towed?" Ingram asked.

"Yes," she said, "but to where?"

"Got a friend who fixes cars. I'll talk to him to see if he'll keep it there rent free for a week or so."

"Jed?" Nielson said. They'd met at one of his and Anita's cookouts.

"Yep." Ingram swallowed more of his food and said, "Couldn't he have just run off with a lady friend?"

"A big, bosomed gal, Harry?" Nielson said.

"I know better than to answer that."

"Correct."

"That doesn't seem like Mose," Payton said.

He recalled an article in *Dapper* about men trying to realize their fantasies when they reached a certain age. Some took up wood working or even more vigorous pastimes. Gesturing, he said, "Man gets to a point in life where looking forward is shorter than looking back . . ."

"That's why I'm willing to pay you to find out."

"You must really like this Mose," he mentioned.

"Could be it's the capitalist in me. Protecting my investment." She smiled crookedly.

"Could be. Or there's something you're not telling me. The car left by the airport, you know he didn't run off. Was he grabbed?"

Nielson regarded him, then her friend.

Payton said, "You're right. I'm worried Mose has run afoul of his other investor, Gavin Rickler. That is, he may be on the run from him."

"Rickler's a gambler," Ingram guessed.

"Yes, he owns the Emerald Room, a card club in Gardena."

"Mose is into him large?"

Betty hunched her shoulders. "I really don't know. It's not as if he's talked to me about this. That is, I know he and Rickler do business. The sort probably no one reports to the IRS."

"That's why you didn't want to go to the police." Ingram was quiet for a moment. "You think Rickler could come for you?"

Dorothy turned to her friend. "Betty?"

Betty met Dorothy's concerned look. "I should have been up front with you, Dorothy. I guess I hoped to engage Mr. Ingram, and that alone would give Gavin pause. I don't think he's capable of outright murder but, honestly, I don't know what to think." She turned her head back to Ingram. "He might not be involved at all."

"Me and Betty go back. Hell, she used to babysit Anita and her sister. I told her what you and Anita had done around King's visit to town in '63," Nielson admitted. "Bragging on my child and her old man." She shook her head. "You would think I should know better.

"It was that and you knowing the lay of the land," Nielson added. "I'm sorry I wasted your time."

"I haven't said no." Since the time Dorothy Nielson referred to, Ingram hadn't had that kind of engagement to command his attention. Putting the pieces together, that was the thing. Process serving involved a degree of tracking but the results were usually finding someone who was trying to avoid getting their car repossessed or being taken to court over back child support. This had the potential to be different, the outcome could matter.

Nielson put a hand on his arm. "Don't do this for me, Harry. Anita would kill me if anything happened to you. Not to mention, I've grown fond of you."

He put his on hers. "My reasons are more mercenary."

"I'm not looking to bring trouble to your doorstep," Payton said.

"As long as you're up front with me, we're solid."

They talked more and continued eating. Payton provided a home phone number for Chet Horne and gave him the address and phone for Tolbert's home too. She didn't have a home phone number for the bookkeeper, Arlene Domergue, but she knew she lived in the beach area of Venice.

"Yeah?" Ingram had said at that information. Venice was sometimes affectionately referred to as the "Slum by the Sea," with its dilapidated housing, surfers and what had been beatnik coffee houses turned hippie hangouts. Ingram'd once served papers on a muscle-bound individual who worked out in Muscle Beach in Venice. The individual's girlfriend, also a weight-lifter, hit hard too.

His fee plus expenses were also agreed upon, including a check—a $500 advance. He hadn't made that much in the three weeks prior. Ingram walked with the women to their cars. Down the street at the Towers, the crowd had dispersed and workers were dismantling the stage. The police had departed as well, though a trio of Guardsmen remained. They seemed to have no particular orders. One of them stood outside the main entrance to the Towers, which was closed, and two others walked back and forth along the residential street, rifles slung over their shoulders.

The three stopped next to Payton's aqua-blue Thunderbird convertible. "I should tell you, Mose has a gun and carried it with him from time to time, particularly if he found himself transporting a lot of cash for the shop."

"Is that missing too, the gun?"

"I don't know, and according to Chet, Mose hadn't had to take money anywhere for a few weeks. Just figured you should know."

"Chet and Mose good buddies?" he asked.

"Sure, they pal around. You think Chet knows what happened?"

"I'm going to see what I can find out." He considered if

Tolbert were up to his wild ways again, what would that mean for him?

They shook hands again and he and Nielson watched her drive away.

"Betty is a rarity," Nielson said when she finished waving at her departing friend. "She's a native Angeleno. Her grandfather and his brother made their money in California's first oil boom back in horse and buggy days. By all accounts they were greedy, rapacious sonsabitches with her granddad winding up bankrupting his own brother."

"Damn."

"Mind you, this was a few years after the brother that would be bankrupted had shot the other brother in the butt after he'd kicked his dog."

"I'll just say it again, damn." Ingram reflected on the information Betty shared. "You know anything about this Rickler?"

"No. That surprised me too."

"She called him Gavin. Sounds like they're chummy."

"I'll ask around. Quiet like."

They got to Dorothy's car, which was parked a few blocks from the Towers. As he'd left his vehicle at Eternal Sands, she'd offered to give him a ride instead of him having to take a bus. He gladly accepted. As Nielson piloted, she continued her narrative. "At some point Betty's father inherited the business, then sold it off to Pinnacle Oil for cash and stock. It's the stock that allows her to do what she does."

"You saying she's a dilettante and a Red? Ain't that a contradiction?"

"There's degrees of class traitors, Harry," she joked. "Betty doesn't mind certain trappings what with her split-level in

Tujunga Canyon. But she don't let it go to her head. She's definitely one of those who understands money is a means of exchange. She put up the bail several times when the hammer came down on us in the '50s. Mose was sometimes her courier."

"She could be quite used to certain trappings these days, Dorothy."

Nielson regarded him.

"Why do you think she wants Mose found? Just being a good friend, or worried about her investment?"

Nielson said, "Honestly, Harry, I'm not sure. Could be she's more worried about this Rickler than she lets on. To your point, she could be wondering about getting muscled out of her percentage if Mose isn't around."

Now he kept quiet.

Ingram stared out the window at destroyed businesses and those left intact. "The hammer hasn't exactly let up."

"Yeah," she said. "Betty and I agree that there was probably at least one paid informant if not more at the memorial today. A police agent or two as well." She made a face as if tasting something bitter. "I'm worried about our young people, Harry. The history of times like this, the authorities can't let the hoi polloi get too rambunctious. Knowing Parker as I do, he'll send in their infiltrators to cause disruption and disunity. The FBI too."

This was not a new observation from his girlfriend's mother. She'd lived through those times when comrades turned on one another for real and imagined reasons. The results weren't simply hurt feelings. People had lost their jobs, their families, and in some cases gone to prison due to the poisoned fallout from the red crackdown, as she'd called

it. There was a toughness in Dorothy that Ingram had recognized in Anita Claire, who was like those career soldiers
he'd encountered on occasion in the Army. They didn't growl
or sit at the end of the bar telling whoever was in earshot yet
again about how gloriously they killed and in what magnificent battle. To them there was a distant kind of hardness
borne of seeing too many casualties on both sides of the line.
Not a war of bombs and machine guns, but a psychological
assault inciting paranoia and fear. This too wrecked body
and mind.

They arrived at his parked car. Nielson put hers in neutral
and engaged the parking brake, letting the engine idle.
Ingram's car was a late model Falcon Squire station wagon
with the fake "woodie-style" trim on its flanks and rear drop
gate. Having plenty of room in the cargo area of this car,
he'd reconfigured his mobile dark room which once occupied
the trunk area of his departed Plymouth Belvedere. The car
had been intentionally torched when he was looking into the
death of his Army buddy Ben Kinslow two years ago. The
new setup included black curtains on rods installed over the
two rear-side windows and the center back one.

"Thanks for the ride, Dorothy." He damn sure wasn't
going to call her "Dot."

"Of course. I'll have you two over for dinner soon. Oh,
and good luck on the Louis Lomax show. Anita told me
you'd been invited to appear."

"Thanks." He leaned over and gave her a smack on the
cheek and, as he slid back toward the passenger door, noticed
something peeking out from underneath the bench seat. It
was a torn paper currency strap like what banks used to band
together specific amounts of money. He picked it up and

held it toward her. "Been counting your stacks at the Savings and Loan."

She stared at the strap. Smiling, she said, "Had to take out a little for an emergency." She took it and crumpled the paper up in her fist and put it in her purse. "Bye, Harry," she said, putting the car back in gear and waving at him as she drove off. He returned the wave.

He stood there for a few moments after lowering his hand. The denomination and amount in the strap was handwritten on the paper as was customary. Two thousand dollars in hundreds. Heck of an emergency, he reflected as he got in his car.

He keyed the ignition and drove off as well, heading for Tolbert's house in View Park. He didn't expect to discover a clue checking out a missing guy's pad from the outside. But as his girlfriend had told him, nothing wrong with a little reconnoitering.

CHAPTER SIX

"Weren't you at the memorial?" Ingram asked.

Chet Horne was a stocky, solid-looking individual. He'd come up front when Ingram arrived and they'd introduced themselves one to another. This area of Restoration Building Supply was occupied by three chairs, a small table with several issues of *Popular Mechanics* and *Sports Illustrated* on it, and a wilting potted rubber fig in the corner. It was the following day. Ingram had made this appointment yesterday after returning from checking out Tolbert's house.

"That's right. I saw you there taking your pictures, too," Chet said. "But Miss Betty says she's asked you to see about what happened to Mose. That is if something did happen to him."

"I'm gonna see what I can do."

Horne was in his early forties with close cropped hair with some gray in it, weightlifter's arms and a pleasant face like that of a county clergyman. "Jack of all trades, huh?"

"Looks like," Ingram amicably agreed.

"Well, come on back," he said. "Thanks, Hillary," he said to a white woman standing nearby.

"Sure, Chet."

The woman in jeans, a flannel shirt and work boots had greeted Ingram when he first came in. She'd made it clear that she was not the receptionist but one of the order pullers.

He followed Horne through a metal door past stacks of lumber organized by size—two by fours, four by fours and so on. They side-stepped a forklift backing up with a load of planks.

"Coffee?" Horne asked over his shoulder.

"Sure. Can never have enough."

Horne stopped at a rickety wooden table with a two burner electric hot plate and a carafe of coffee on it. He poured measures of coffee into two ceramic mugs. He handed one to Ingram and pointed to the sugar and Coffee Mate.

"Help yourself."

"Thanks."

Horne gestured with his coffee cup. "We can talk over there."

Horne opened an unmarked green door and entered the compact wood-paneled room. The plaster had been patched and sanded smooth in several spots awaiting a new coat of paint for the entire surface. Ingram followed, stirring in a spoonful of the coffee creamer while he sat. The sounds of the workers going about their business filtered through the walls. A mini fridge hummed in the corner. On top of that was a toaster oven. A clipboard with bills of lading hung on the wall next to a pin-up type calendar. This display for August depicted a bikini-clad blonde caressing a giant floating spark plug as if the object was the love of her life. The second hand on the clock on the wall audibly ticked off the time as it rotated the dial. There was a phone on a corner of the desk, and an aqua blue Admiral clock radio rested on a rickety narrow stand. The time on the radio was five minutes different from that of the wall clock.

"Let me ask, 'cause I was out that day taking shots, but I think I saw you and Mose driving around in one of the company trucks the afternoon he was last seen." Ingram wasn't trying to trap him in a lie but was curious as to his answer. He'd figured to be straightforward with him.

"Yeah," Horne said. "We were taking people home or elsewhere, figuring the Restoration name had goodwill."

"Y'all stayed open?"

"Big order to fill and we're far enough north, but naturally we guessed wrong and once we knew the riots were spreading, we decided to get folks to safety."

"Look man, you think Mose ran off with a flashy chick he met in a bar?"

"Can't say Mose was that kind of dude," Chet Horne said. "He likes the ladies like we all do—but lose his mind over some young thing who flashed him some thigh, hardly." He hunched a shoulder. "Leastways I ain't seen no filly prancing around about, and me and him shared a beer now and then. Hell, right in here for that matter." He wagged a finger. "Pretty sure he would have made mention."

"Right," Ingram said. He had his notepad open and circled where he'd printed "girlfriend" and finished his notation with a question mark bifurcating the circle. "And no one you recall coming around asking about money he owed or something like that? Like this guy Rickler?"

Horne shook his head. "Don't know no Rickler. And let me tell you not a nickel gets spent around here that Miss

Arlene don't know what it's for and when it's gonna get allocated, dig?"

Ingram wondered if Horne was lying about Rickler but nodded in understanding. "By the way, where's her office?" There was only the one desk in here. There was no safe, but Ingram assumed there was one elsewhere in the building, given Tolbert occasionally took amounts of cash to the bank.

Horne hooked a thumb over his shoulder. "She has her own office out back near the loading dock." He smiled, revealing a silver front tooth. "Even got a couple of neighborhood strays that like to hang around 'cause she feeds 'em."

"I heard about her cat fancy."

"Guess that's one way of putting it," he agreed. Horne paused, folding his arms, his mood shifting. "You think somebody did Mose harm? That what Miss Betty say?"

"Like I said, she's worried, him up and vanishing like he did."

Horne paused. Ingram took this to mean the other man was weighing holding back or not.

"Sure, I see that," he finally said. Then his mood seemed to lighten as he clapped his hands together and rubbed them, rising from his seat. "Look, I better get back to it. I was told by Miss Arlene it was okay for you to look through his papers and whatnot, help yourself."

Ingram stood too. "For the time being, are you the one has to take money to the bank if it's necessary?"

"Hasn't come up yet, but yeah, I guess I would be. And brother, you can believe I'll keep a rod on me. Parker's goddamn police or not. I ain't about to get knocked upside my big head."

"Yes, sir."

Horne added, "Miss Arlene already looked through Mose's desk but didn't find nothin', just so you know. But I guess you'll be talking to her too?"

"I will. Thanks for your time, Chet."

"Hope you can find out what happened and he's okay." He took hold of the clipboard on the wall.

"Me too." They shook hands and the manager left.

Alone in the room, Ingram approached the desk, extending his hand. He stopped, his hand motionless, the only sound that of the clock marking time. He momentarily felt unmoored. Here he was playing at detective, realizing to be effective he was going to have to intrude deeper into Mose Tolbert's life. He'd plunged in because he estimated Payton's money would buy him freedom to work on not just an article about Faraday Zinum but maybe a book, one with his photos and reflections on Black life before and after the fires.

This gig was different than looking for a deadbeat dad or a hit and run driver who dented a fender to serve them court papers. He usually had a last known address, the license plate number of their car, and a list of known associates and the like to go on. In that respect he had similar information for Tolbert. Yet once he'd served the papers on someone, he was done. How matters turned out for them dealing with the legal system, maybe going to jail or prison, he didn't know and if he was being honest, didn't care. Sure, sometimes a square head would cuss him out or come at him with a tire iron. But he'd handled those situations accordingly, bruises and all. It was all part of the job.

This though might turn out to be more like when he jumped in to unravel the death of his friend Ben Kinslow. What he saw and learned from his questioning might mean nothing at first but could be useful to know as he dug deeper. And like with his buddy, would there be roughnecks coming at him? Would he be ready for that? Too if he found Tolbert, he wouldn't just be cashing Betty Payton's check and moving on. She was friends with his damn near mother-in-law and the love of his life. For whatever reason Moses Tolbert went missing, he and the others, people he cared about, would have to live with the consequences.

Ingram got unstuck and went to work. Taking possession of the situation he was in, rather than standing at the desk and looking through the papers and items as if wishing to not impose, he sat behind the desk—defying Tolbert to burst in catch him. The drawers of the desk were unlocked. Ingram wondered if they had been left that way by Tolbert. Or had that been done by Miss Arlene, as Horne called her? She probably had keys to the whole place. Did Horne?

In the middle drawer were handwritten notes about orders to be filled and scraps of paper with a name and phone number on it. That was expected. There were also some paper coasters with beer brands on them and several books of matches bearing Restoration's name. In the other drawers were letter-sized envelopes, onionskin and carbon paper for the typewriter, "Paid" and "Overdue" rubber stamps, mailing stamps, index cards with names of specific kinds of lumber and on and on. In the left bottom drawer was a can of gun oil wrapped in a soft cloth and a few loose .45 bullets.

As Payton had told him, the missing man had a gun though it was reportedly absent from his abandoned vehicle. Could be Tolbert had the gun with him. It could also be the gun was at his house. Ingram wondered if he would have to break into the man's home to get some answers. He also came across a worn deck of cards. Did he and Horne while away the time some nights playing Blackjack as they sipped on libations stronger than beer? Looking through the paperwork on the desk was also a bust insofar as a clue to where Tolbert had skirted off to, willingly or otherwise.

Ingram got up from behind the desk, stretched and drained his now tepid coffee and left the office. He walked across the shop floor, keeping out of the way of another forklift as an employee drove by with a load. He and the operator nodded at each other as he rolled past. The building was located less than fifty yards to the north of the Southern Pacific Railroad tracks which paralleled this part of Slauson Avenue between Olive and Broadway. The entrance to the Harbor Freeway, the 110, was accessible on the north side of Slauson at Flower. A few miles west, the tracks curved to the south. A narrow dirt track that served as an access road lay between the gravel lining the railroad tracks and Restoration. The loading dock was on the west side of the building.

Ingram took this all in, then wound back to Arlene Domergue's office. It was, as Horne said, along the way to the loading dock. The hallway leading to her door was situated between two tall racks containing sacks of cement, scores of rebar and a stack of drywall which was being used more and more these days as opposed to plaster and lath. Domergue's door was dark stained pine and solid, no wording on it. He knocked lightly, announcing himself.

"Miss Domergue, it's Harry Ingram."

"Come in," she said.

He opened the door and stepped through as Arlene rose from her desk. She didn't look as he'd imagined a spinster with cats might appear. His notion derived from late night movies like *Arsenic and Old Lace* and episodes of *Maverick*. She was his height in low heels and wore up-to-date attire, a gray conservative skirt and buttoned up white shirt, the sleeves at half-mast. Her coiffed black hair was streaked with white, like that of an aging fashion model. While the lines of her face suggested a woman of a certain age, she was handsome with observant eyes. She put out her hand in greeting, a sparkly bracelet on her wrist.

The accessory triggered a memory in Ingram, but he didn't hesitate and shook her hand.

"Pleased to meet you, Mr. Ingram. Have a seat why don't you?"

"Thanks," he said, sitting. What did live up to his expectations was the papers and manilla file folders on her desk in orderly stacks. There was a row of three metal file cabinets in a corner. Her credenza was wood, part of her desk set, and had an adding machine on it.

Domergue left the door slightly ajar and she took her seat back behind her desk. "You talked to Chet?"

"I did. There doesn't happen to be a spare key to Tolbert's house around here, is there?"

"What are you suggesting, Mr. Ingram?" she said flatly.

"Didn't mean it the way the way it sounded, Miss Domergue. Wanted to see in case of an emergency that maybe there was one."

"There isn't."

"Understood. Anything you can share about Tolbert's habits? He go to the prize fights at the Olympic, chase the ponies at the track, that sort of thing?"

"Why would I know about those manly pursuits? Did you

ask Chet these questions?" Her tone wasn't accusatory, but connoted mild curiosity. She sat forward, her forearms crossed atop the desk.

Ingram said, "Tolbert and Chet are drinking buddies. It occurred to me he might not be inclined to level with a stranger about certain things concerning his pal."

"But a woman would? A white woman at that?"

"Betty says you seek enlightenment." He'd borrowed that term from a program on KPFK, when Anita Claire was listening to a reading of Aldous Huxley's *Doors of Perception*.

"That doesn't make me somebody who tells tales out of school."

"I know from her he'd go off the rails now and then, and you're the one that's been here the longest, Arlene."

She interlaced her fingers. Ingram noticed several gaudy rings on each hand. "You want to know if he liked to gamble?"

"Does he?"

"You got that from Betty?"

"I did."

She looked past Ingram, then back at him. "Mose appreciates a game of poker now and then. In fact, so do I. Nothing fancy, no outlandish stakes, I can assure you . . . Harry."

"Any strongarm types ever come around collecting on a bet?"

"Not for years. Back in '57 he got carried away and brought a danger to the business. But we cleared that up."

"You and him?"

"Chet too," she admitted.

The goddamn Three Musketeers, Ingram noted. His face blank he said, "Who was the debt to?"

"I don't recall."

He didn't believe her. He wondered if it was Rickler, or he was involved somehow and she knew that. Like with Horne, it would be counter-productive to call her on it now, he judged. She was direct only to a point. Ingram hedged he was going to have to circle back to her at some point and didn't want her to freeze him out. "I appreciate you telling me this." He rose.

"Let me know if there's anything else I can help you with," she said, but notably, she remained in her seat instead of seeing him out.

He thanked her and walked back outside. Ingram watched one of the Restoration panel trucks drive away from the business, then plucked a crooked hand-rolled cheroot out of his coat's inner pocket. He lit the crooked cigar and blowing a thin plume of smoke, took a stroll around the neighborhood rather than return to his car. Partly this was due to Claire complaining about the stale odor that would be trapped inside the Falcon. But this was also a way for him to consider his next steps. He walked west along Slauson toward Figueroa. It was clear to Ingram he was going to have to take a run at Rickler. He'd told himself he would walk away if it got to be too much. But who was he jivin'? Was he so shell-shocked he liked this kind of challenge?

His cheroot almost spent, Ingram stood in front of a deactivated Water and Power pump station. The grounds the structure sat upon was a rectangular half acre of city-owned land that started at Slauson and continued north to

58th Street. Ingram had once been inside on an assignment. He took a last puff.

Just as the cheroot left his fingers, a police car rolled past. The two cops in it eyed him but kept going, heading south along Figueroa. Three weeks ago he supposed they would have stopped and harassed him for littering. He watched the patrol car recede. The cop car reminding him of the riots, he drove to Whitehead's Market to check on his friend Arthur Yarbrough, who he last saw then. And while he wasn't articulating this to himself, in the past he and Yarbrough had shared their ruminations on surviving combat. There was comfort in talking to his friend.

"COLORED FOLKS had to get it out of their system," Yarbrough opined.

"Until the next time," Ingram said.

"Yep," Yarbrough agreed. The two stood in the front of his store, Whitehead's. He held a push broom. He knew the layout of his store well and, as if guided by biological radar, often swept up.

During the riots, Yarbrough, who'd been blinded by an exploding land mine in the Korean War, had nonetheless stood guard with two of his employees inside. The business occupied the ground floor of an old-fashioned apartment building Ingram had once lived in before taking up house with Claire. Across the street and a few doors down, an upholstery store had been torched. Flying embers had ignited the wood trim around Whitehead's display window, threatening to burn the entire establishment. Fortunately, there was a threaded spigot inside the store and a hose was attached to deal with the emergency. The front wall had been discolored and smelled of charred wood from within. Repairs would have to be done but that was as far as the flames had gotten. Ingram had been to the store the first full day of the unrest but hadn't been back until now.

"You should have seen Arthur being all fire chief," Eric Coley said. The young man of twenty-two, who was also taking plumbing courses at Trade Technical College, had guarded the store by Yarbrough's side. He'd also been the one to call Ingram to tell him the store had survived. "He was directing us how to put out the fire."

Ingram smiled. "Figures."

"The heat had me light-headed," Yarbrough cracked.

"I hear you, man. Mind if I make a call? Want to see if Strummer's around."

"Be my guest."

Edwards would hopefully have a better sense of who Rickler was. Was the gambler volatile? Reasonable? In the back office, Ingram first dialed his blind pig joint, the Stockyard, but there was no answer. He then tried the office Edwards maintained on the second floor of a two-story cinder block building on Western Avenue near Adams. Pest Be Gone extermination services occupied the first floor. The name on Edwards's door in Art Deco relief lettering read: RENARD ENTERPRISES. Edwards's enterprises were varied. Some were above the line—he and Ingram were among the investors in Whitehead's—but there were underworld dealings as well. He imagined one day, the life Edwards led would catch up to him, possibly sucking him and Yarbrough down, too. Ingram reached the man's answering service.

"I'm not sure where I'll be," he told the pleasant-voiced woman on the line. "Just let him know I called and will try him later." He could hear someone typing in the background on her end.

"Very well, Mr. Ingram."

"Thank you." He hung up.

After saying good-bye to Yarbrough and Coley, Ingram got back in his car and headed to the Ascot branch of the library. He was putting his search for Mose Tolbert on pause until he talked with Edwards. At any rate Ingram needed to get his notes together before his appearance on the Louis Lomax show on Thursday. True, he had a desk with a typewriter in the detached garage where he'd set up a darkroom. Claire also had a desk in there. But he was used to using the library and liked the idea that if he needed to look something up, such was instantly accessible. Walking into the quiet space, carrying his note pad and a yellow legal pad, he was pleased to find an unoccupied desk at a window, the blinds drawn against the bright sun. Ingram sat and got to work.

About an hour later, he was finishing up and preparing to leave. He'd been checking particular dates and had taken a book off the shelf, *From Slavery to Freedom* by the historian John Hope Franklin. He picked up the book and went toward the section where it belonged to reshelve it. Heading down the aisle, he saw a familiar face.

"Doing your homework, Sister?"

Violet O'Shay smiled at him. She was holding a book and had been scanning for another one on the shelf. "Something like that," she said. "I've been asked to do an article on the recent troubles." She pointed at the book he was returning. "And in fact I was looking for that."

He handed the book across. "Is the article for that Catholic magazine, *Tidings* it's called?"

"A bit more this way," she said, veering her hand to the left. "It's a tabloid called the *Catholic Worker*."

Grinning, he said, "Of course it would be called that, like the commie's newspaper."

"Wait till you read my article."

"You mean it's not going to have the headline, 'Get Whitey?'" That had been part of a headline on the front page of the *L.A. Times* the first day of the riots.

They chuckled. She said, "Believe me, that's not the approach I'm taking. Really, I might need to call on you, Harry, for a quote or two. Part of what I want to get at is about the police department and how they treat us in this part of town."

He cocked his head at that. Playfully, she tapped the back of her hand on his chest. "You know what I mean, smart ass."

"You haven't gone native have you, Violet?"

"I'll let you know when I do." She allowed her words to linger for a moment, her gaze steady on him.

His cheeks warm, he said, "I'll let you get back to it."

"Okay. I know where to find you when I need you, Harry."

"Yes, ma'am."

She waved at him as she returned to her research.

Walking to his car, he warned himself—what kind of foolishness was he trying to do? Flirting with a Sister and him practically a married man. He loved Anita and he damn sure better not mess that up. Maybe, he reasoned getting into his car, he'd been unduly influenced by one of those articles in *Dapper* about the playboy lifestyle, a different girl for each day of the week. And what did it say about Violet, who surely knew what she was saying to him. She had vows and whatever, right? Wouldn't they both go straight to hell if they had an affair?

Slipping into traffic, he considered that at least Anita wasn't going to be on that one-way ride to demons and pitchforks. Her folks were atheists, but they'd brought her and her sister up to learn for themselves what it meant to be spiritual. Tomes such as the Bible, the Talmud and the Quran had been in their household and what these various religions meant was often discussed around their dinner table. It was religion as viewed through the lens of her parents' politics. That was certainly different than how he'd been raised, typical of any number of Black households with roots in the south. He clearly remembered a framed print of a painting of a bearded, beatifical Jesus aglow in his purple robes, arms outspread as he ascended to heaven. The reproduction hung in his mother's bedroom before his father had left them. He'd been a trolley conductor here in town and when he'd abandoned him and his mother, he went to Texas and took up with another woman.

To his mother's credit, religion didn't become a crutch for her after he left. When it was the three of them, they went to church probably once a month. After he was gone, the two of them attended only on certain occasions like Easter and Christmas. If anything, his mother became more driven after his father departed, going from a secretary at the Black insurance company Golden State Mutual to one of the few women selling policies. It was initially limited to types of businesses associated with women, such as beauty shops and bakeries, but she diversified and could count enterprises like an auto parts store and a furniture shop as clients.

In the house he shared with Claire were her books about

Buddhism and memoirs written by people searching for enlightenment or just wandering like John Steinbeck's *Travels with Charley* and Zora Neale Hurston's *Tell My Horse.* Books that wouldn't have been in Ingram's purview until he'd met her. They did discuss their ideas about the afterlife and both were unsure. Or as Claire had said, flexible on the subject of what, if anything, waited for them once the last breath left their body.

He stopped at a red light. Never mind a fantasy about fooling around with Sister O'Shay on the side and all the implications of that . . . if doom was to be his, surely it would be for killing the hood, Wicks. It was only at this moment that Ingram noted the strange coincidence of his shooting Wicks in a junkyard of trolley cars and what his father's job here in Los Angeles had been. He'd replayed that night among the junked trolleys several times since then but hadn't made the connection until this moment. Having heard Claire and her mother talk about Freudianisms several times, had part of his willingness to squeeze the trigger been a desire to kill his father? But he didn't think about his father that much and wasn't of the mind to reach out to him—wherever he might be these days. Neither the dead Wicks nor the fate of his absent father gave him bouts of sleeplessness. The light changed and on he went.

CHAPTER SEVEN

After his workout at the 28th Street Y, Ingram called Strummer Edwards again, hoping to get information on Rickler, but he was still unavailable. Feeling the need to justify the money Betty Payton was paying him, he made a call over to the Four Aces auto repair. Jed Monk the owner was out on a parts run but Howell Exum, one of the mechanics, answered.

"You must be like that cat, Criswell," Exum said after they'd greeted each other and Ingram said why he was calling.

"That's right, man, I see all and knows all. Like chicken ain't nothin' but a bird."

"Ain't that the truth? Anyway, that car you wanted towed is here. We got it this morning."

"I'm on my way."

By the time he got to the Four Aces, Jed Monk had returned. He took Ingram to Mose's car, a 1962 Chevy Bel Air. Not too fancy but not too plain either. The car had been placed behind the enclosed service bay area on an open rectangular concrete pad bordered by a chain-link fence.

"Far as I can tell, this ride's in pretty decent shape," Monk said in his bass voice. "I checked the dipstick and the oil's not too dirty, so he must have kept up the maintenance."

He wiped at an upper portion of the car with a clean shop rag. "It's the Sport coupe, low milage, 409 V8, nice." He nodded appreciatively. "They call this the Bubbletop 'cause of how the roof is shaped."

"I'm not angling to buy this short, you know." Ingram stood looking at the car with his hands in his pockets.

Monk smiled. "Okay, Boston Blackie, I'll leave you to it."

"The car's unlocked?"

"Yeah, they'd jimmied the door open when it was first towed."

"Thanks, man."

"Sure."

Monk returned to his office. Ingram opened the driver's door and leaned in, a knee on the bench seat. There wasn't anything of interest in the glovebox. Ingram discounted a used roll of Life Saver candy as a clue. He felt under the seat and produced a few old receipts. One of them was from the bar at Hollywood Park racetrack. The date was from several months ago. He pocketed this. In the backseat he slipped his hand between the crevices and except for a few coins, came away with nothing else. He pulled the seat back away to gaze inside the trunk, spotting several items in there. Rather than wrestle removing the seat back out of the car, Ingram decided he'd instead pop the trunk.

Borrowing a screwdriver and a hammer, Ingram tapped the blade end of the tool into the trunk's lock. He twisted the screwdriver's handle, turning the lock and opening the trunk. Inside there was a medium-sized carboard box, its top interlocked by the flaps. There were several loose 45 records in their colorful paper sleeves, a picnic basket and a roadside kit containing a flare, jumper cables and the like. There was nothing in the picnic basket and he noted the 45s were doo-wop numbers like "Earth Angel" and "Yakety Yak."

The man had a social life, Ingram mused. Tolbert likely brought his records to house parties or to barbeque out at the pool. Sifting through the contents inside the carboard box, he noted a jumble of parts—rollaway casters for a couch, a small block and tackle pulley with a hook, and a mechanical fuel pump for a car. He took the box and the other objects out of the trunk and lifted the flooring to peer into the cavity where the spare tire and jack were. He took the tire out and set it aside but there was nothing underneath where it resided in its circular hollow. He put it back. Ingram also put the flooring back in place and returned the other stuff he'd taken out. He was about to close the trunk when he paused.

"Damn Sergeant Saunders," he mumbled. *Search thoroughly, soldier,* he heard him warn. *The NKs boobytrap the corpses of our dead, don't forget.*

He got the carboard box back out and emptied the contents onto the ground. This time he took each part in hand to better examine it. He shook the fuel pump. Something rattled inside of the device. It could merely be a loose part, but it didn't sound metallic. Curious, he took the pump into the shop and borrowed the correct-sized crescent wrench to remove the lower section from the upper body. In the lower portion was an envelope held together by a rubber band.

He put the pieces of the fuel pump aside and undid the rubber band over the letter, which wasn't sealed. Oddly, there were several garments' cloth tags in it. Each were marked "Exclusively, Sabine of Beverly Hills." He took out the receipt he had in his pocket and inserted that in the envelope, then folded it over again and tucked the envelope in his back pocket. He went to Monk's office, wiping his hands on a shop rag he took off a work bench. Monk was just hanging up the phone.

"You got a Yellow Pages?" Ingram asked, setting the rag on Monk's crowded desk. There was a glass ashtray shaped like an amoeba on one corner of the desk with several crushed cigarettes in it.

"Here you go." His friend opened a bottom drawer in his industrial metal desk. He plopped the thick directory on his desk. "Find something?"

"Not sure," Ingram said, taking hold of the book. Sitting before the desk with the directory balanced on his knees, he leafed through the listings and display ads. He got to the one for Sabine of Beverly Hills. "Damn," he muttered.

"What?"

Ingram put the opened directory on the desk facing Monk. The display ad, which featured a lush rendering of a Grace Kelly-like woman with dark stylish short hair, took up half the page. Turned partly away from the viewer, the illustrated woman wore a form-fitting skirt and heels with a mink stole wrapped around her shoulders. The copy read: "For the Finest for the Woman in Your life, Only Sabine for Exclusive Furs That Will Endear Her Evermore to You." There was an address, store hours and a phone number listed.

"Don't you be showing that to Nona and I won't show Anita," Monk said. Nona was his nurse wife.

"How do I know you want to rip this ad out and mail it to Anita? A not-so-subliminal message."

Monk jabbed a blunt finger onto the ad. "Now that I think about it, I'm sure there's a sign over the door that says, 'Negro, this is as far as you go, this is mink, not rabbit 'round here.'" They both had a good laugh. Monk added, "What's this got to do with your missing man?"

Ingram told him what he'd found. "Could be he had hisself a couple of chicks he was squiring and keeping track of what he bought them. But there's too many tags."

"So what's it mean?" Monk said.

"Hell if I know." Ingram rose.

"You'll figure it out."

"I better. Let's get a game together soon."

"For sure."

That evening at home he and Claire had a humble meal of pork n' beans from the can and hot dogs Ingram had charred, frying in a skillet rather than boiling. She'd made a cucumber, tomato and avocado salad—the avocadoes liberated from Diane Fitzhugh's drooping tree. He had a beer to go with his dinner and she drank iced water. As was their habit, once they sat down to eat, they began discussing how their respective days had gone.

"We got a call from Chief Parker's office," she said.

"Let me guess."

"Apparently he was not pleased with what Tom had to say about his asinine remarks." Parker had been on television and radio pontificating as to the cause of the riots. Not surprisingly, he'd deflected the assertions that the heavy-handed way his Department policed the city's colored citizenry had anything to do with the anger that had boiled over into the recent destruction. Rather, he'd claimed in the interview more than once that the people who had made something of themselves had moved out of places like Watts, leaving the flotsam and jetsam behind.

Ingram wiped his mouth on a paper napkin. "Parker figured if us poor darkies heard what he'd said, it would go over our heads anyway."

"Imagine his surprise." She reached over and took a pull of his beer.

Ingram observed, "So the Chief is keeping up with the Black news?" Tom Bradley had been quoted in a *Sentinel* article stating Parker's comments demonstrated how out of touch he was with modern notions. Suggesting that it might be time to step aside to allow for more forward thinking to take place among the leadership of the LAPD.

She smiled. "Probably has a bleary-eyed negro sitting in an office reading Black newspapers all day long and listening to the calls into rhythm and blues radio stations."

"Or gets weekly reports from guys like Shoals."

She fixed him with a look. "You haven't talked to him since then, have you?"

"Nope, and don't plan to."

James "Shoals" Pettigrew and Ingram had been friends since kids in grade school. The events involving Winston Hoyt had revealed Pettigrew had ties to a group of power brokers Hoyt was a part of, the Providers.

"I know what you're feeling, Harry. My folks had friends who for one reason or another turned on them and the ideals they'd shared. Sometimes naming names to a particular government agency or actively becoming informants or worse, agent provocateurs, trying to set them up."

"Yeah . . ."

When the meal was done, they washed and dried the dishes and went into the living room. Ingram put on the jazz station while Claire mixed them vodka tonic cocktails at their rollaway bar. They both took off their shoes and sat close on the corner sectional couch.

"Here's how, baby," Ingram said.

"Salud," she said in Spanish and they clinked glasses.

Drinking and relaxing, Ingram filled her on what he'd found in Tolbert's car. He pointedly didn't mention the cash band he'd seen in her mother's car. Whatever that was about, Dorothy's business was hers to handle.

"Do the tags indicate what sort of coat they came off of?" Claire asked.

"Hadn't considered that," he said. He took the envelope out of his back pocket and shook the tags out. On the back of each were different numbers.

"Inventory numbers I'd say," Claire mentioned. "And why take them off to begin with? He'd want to impress whichever lady friend the coat was for, wouldn't he?"

"An insurance scam?"

"What do you mean?"

"Putting these labels on fake furs and selling them as if they were legit?"

She pursed her lips. "Why go to all that bother to hide them?"

"Cause it's illegal. He wouldn't want to keep the labels in his office or his home, and who would figure they'd be inside a junked fuel pump?"

"You did," she said.

"Could be I'm good at this."

"Could be."

"You don't sound too convinced."

"Should I swoon next time I say it?"

"That might help."

"Don't hold your breath, honey."

"Sadly I won't." He drank in silence. "Think I should ask Betty Payton does she know anything about Sabine of Beverly Hills?"

"She could have gotten a coat there, but so what?"

"Isn't the Buddha about asking the right questions?"

"Look at you."

"She knows more than she's telling me. Tolbert, her and Rickler could be in bed together on this or that shady deal. Or maybe this is her way to edge Tolbert out."

She halted the martini glass at her lips. "Yeah?"

"Just trying to dope it out."

"Sure you're not confusing your feelings for Shoals with her?"

"No, I got it separate in my head. Maybe it's your mom I should be asking."

"She wears plain peasant cloth coats, I'll have you know."

"Uh-huh, what Nixon said about his wife's coat.'

"That was a respectable Republican coat," she said with mock indignity. "My mom's was made by the workers for the workers." She tapped her chest, smiling. "Anyway, she knows where Betty's money comes from."

"Does that mean she's also connected to the Association of Merchants and Manufacturers?"

"Betty has her hand in above ground and underground enterprises?"

"Like Strummer. And while they all aren't part of the

Providers, you know the big wheels of the Association's hands aren't clean either."

"Maybe," Claire considered. "Deep dark secrets . . ."

He put a hand on her stomach and leaned close to her face. "We all got 'em, right?"

"Do you want to know mine?"

"Little by little . . ." He gave her a kiss and leaning back on the couch, let his body slump more into the cushions. His hands now rested in his lap.

Claire regarded his profile while saxophonist Sonny Rollins blew stratospheric cool. She put her hand on top of his and they both got lost in the notes, there on the couch, eyes locked on the faraway as if in a spaceship traveling to a place where strife and injustice were alien concepts.

LESS THAN six miles from where Ingram and Claire drifted on a sonic cloud, a figure in dark clothing was using a ten-inch prybar and screwdriver to try and get inside the Eternal Sands funeral home. The man had already cut the wires to the burglar alarm. The double doors on the side of the building leading to the parking lot where the caskets were loaded into hearses was too visible, even at this time of night. He'd chosen a sash window toward the rear.

Having successfully inserted the prybar at the base of the sash, he forced it up, breaking the bevel lock.

"The fuck you doing?"

A light snapped on. The surprised white man turned to see a substantial figure semi-outlined behind the flashlight.

"Shit," the would-be intruder exclaimed. Concurrently, he brought up a can of gas he'd set down, knocking the flashlight out of the taller man's hands. He'd let go of the prybar, which was sticking out from between the window sash and frame. But as he turned to retrieve it, the guard grabbed him and spun him from behind the tree, bending him forward.

Before the man could get his balance, the guard drove a fist between his shoulder blades. The blow caused the man to stumble, and he skidded onto the asphalt, skinning his chin badly. The guard lunged for him but the other man was quick and scrambled away. He was now back on his feet. The two moved in and out of light and gloom, their altercation partly illuminated by the beam from the fallen flashlight. The intruder threw the can of gas at the guard.

"That ain't gonna stop me, chump," the guard said as he batted the can away. Some fuel spilled from the flexible metal nozzle, splashing on his arm and upper body.

"Who you tellin'." He squared up and took a swing at the bigger man as the guard came at him.

Now it was the larger man's turn to be taken aback because when the punch landed, he was surprised by the force behind it. Clearly his opponent had fisticuffs experience. Still, he wasn't shook and he countered with a blow that doubled the intruder over. He swung again but the other man eluded the hit. Changing tactics, the guard feinted and this time, when the burglar ducked, he was ready and sent his knee up and into the already bloody chin. He stunned him this time and got behind him, wrapping a muscular arm around the intruder's windpipe.

"You about to tell me who the hell you are and who sent you, white boy. 'Cause I know you trying to break in here is no coincidence." He increased the pressure.

The trapped man had both hands on the bigger man's

forearm but couldn't force the arm loose. "Okay," he wheezed, "I'll tell you, but I can't breathe." Sweat bubbled on his brow and ran down the sides of his face.

"Too fuckin' bad."

"Come on," he said, tapping the corded arm, "If I pass out I can't talk."

"You can when you come to, asshole." He tightened his arm even more and held it that way for several seconds. "You'll remember real good."

The intruder sagged. The ad hoc Eternal Sands guard pushed him hard, intending to send him to the ground again. The other man crumpled to a knee. The larger one smiled and reached for the switchblade tucked in the shank of his worn boot. Distracted only for a moment, he came out with the knife and, pressing the release, the blade flicked into place.

"Now I'm gonna ask you seriously." He advanced, the knife unwavering in his mitt of a hand.

"Suck on this, John Henry."

The intruder had palmed a paper matchbook. He'd bent one of the matches out of the pack and, swiping the head between his thumb and striker, lit the matches and threw them at the larger one.

"Motherfucker," he yelled, holding up his arm to block the lit matches. The spilled gas on his sleeve sparked instantly. He was determined to not break off his attack, but part of his shirt was now on fire.

He hadn't been what you'd call an attentive student in school, but he remembered moving too fast would only increase his predicament. He beat at the flames as the other man ran off into the nighttime. Worried but not panicking, he recalled a cartoon film strip he'd seen once about dropping and rolling if you were on fire. It had been in Sunday School of all places. He did the maneuver, extinguishing the fire. Just as quickly, he rose from the asphalt, pawing at his body with his big hands. His burns seemed superficial—or at least flesh wasn't hanging off him, he noted satisfactorily.

Unfazed, he plucked the flashlight off the ground and swept its light around. The only evidence of the intruder was the gas can and the prybar. He took them and went back inside the funeral parlor, past where he'd been stationed in a corner of the show room with its array of caskets. In a back office he hitched a leg on the desk and dialed a number on the phone. The call was answered after three rings.

"Hey, this is Thiggs," the Chosen Few motorcycle club member said after Josh Nakano said hello. "You were right. Somebody tried to break in but not just steal the body. They weren't playin'. These bastards meant to torch this place to burn Zinum up."

In a measured tone, Nakano replied, "I'll be right over."

CHAPTER EIGHT

A bullet clipped the marble pillar.

"Oh, shit," the masked robber yelped, instinctively ducking behind the pillar he'd been running past. Some of the bank employees sitting on the floor gasped. An older man covered his head and began uttering a prayer quietly.

The Morning Bandit lost his footing on the slick, recently polished tile floor, landing in such a way that he was now facing the security guard who had taken the shot. The guard shot at him again and the bandit returned fire as the bullet whizzed past his shoulder. His round struck the security guard in the upper thigh causing him to topple over, but he still held on to his gun.

"Shit, goddamn motherfuckah," the Bandit said.

"Let's go, let's go, let's go," yelled his female accomplice nearer the entrance as she levelled her sawed-off at the guard. She wasn't a thick-set woman, but she handled her sawed-off shotgun with ease. "Slide the piece to me," she demanded.

The aging security guard balked, looking as if he might try his hand at taking her down.

"Go ahead," she warned, the twin barrels of the shotgun steady on him.

The guard slid his gun across the floor toward her and she picked it up. It was a backup piece he'd had on his ankle. That's how he'd caught them robbers by surprise, as they'd already taken the revolver on his hip. This was their second surprise in the bank, despite the robbers' precautions. The front door had been relocked and the shades pulled down. The blinds facing the street had been closed too. To allay the suspicion of a potential customer, a professionally painted cardboard sign was taped on the outside of the front door stating the bank was closed today due to minor renovation.

The woman motioned with the shotgun for the guard to join the huddled others on the floor and this time, he didn't hesitate. Back on his feet and carrying the swag, the Morning Bandit limped, skidded and hopped as fast as he could to the door and his compatriot. The shotgun woman got an arm around his upper body to support him.

"Twisted my ankle," he breathed in her ear.

"We'll make it," she assured him.

Together, they exited the bank into the crisp morning air in Maywood, a small municipality located not so far east of South Central. While there had once been a Ford assembly plant here, Black workers in the facility knew to be out of town before nightfall or at least across the dividing line into the City of Commerce.

The two hustled down the steps just as a battered-looking Buick roared from around the building, smoking the tires as it screeched to a halt. Scrawled next to the bank's doors were the initials A.M.—the gang's reference to Black Cuban freedom fighter Antonio Maceo. Though the time of the day interpretation had led to the Morning Bandit designation. The shotgunner handed her weapon to the Bandit and tossed the duffle bag with their score into the back of the car. Several onlookers glared, including two painters in their splattered overalls who were painting a nearby storefront. One was up a ladder and he called down to the second one.

"There's a reward for that Bandit guy. Five thousand simoleons."

"Yeah," his buddy agreed. He let the paint can he was holding drop to the ground. It tipped over upon landing, a light beige hue called Desert Sunrise eddied across the sidewalk. The two started toward the Buick as the injured Morning Bandit and his fellow robber got inside. The one who'd been on the ladder was carrying a small crowbar he'd been using to loosen a rotten section of wood.

Out from behind the driver's wheel of the Buick, the third member of the gang appeared above the top of the car, a revolver in her gloved hand. She deliberately shot over the heads of the two would-be bounty hunting painters.

"Drop the crowbar," the masked Anita Claire said.

His better sense overcoming visions of a sweet payday, the painter did as ordered.

"Now, both of you get down on the goddamn sidewalk or my next bullets are through your skulls."

Again there was quick compliance.

"Jesus," she muttered. She got behind the wheel of the idling car and drove away from the bank. Like her mother and father, Claire was dressed in dark attire, capri pants, black tennis shoes as well as a bulky dark windbreaker. Her mask, also like that of her folks, was a variation on a Kabuki demon mask, half white and half red, split horizontally down the middle. She removed the mask and turned off the main throughfares to head down residential streets. Not too fast so as not to attract undue attention. A siren sounded in the air.

"I think this is a sign, Solly," Dorothy Nielson told her ex-husband and partner in crime. "I hope that poor man you shot is going to be all right."

"Yeah on both counts," he said.

This wasn't the first time gunplay had factored in one of their robberies. Due to the increased notoriety about the Morning Bandit gang and other matters in each of their lives, five months had lapsed since their last caper.

"I won't argue the point," Solomon Claire said, also removing his mask from his sweating face. "Anyway, it doesn't seem that I hit a major artery, given how feisty he was."

"By pure luck," his daughter said.

Her folks remained quiet. She pulled to a stop where another car, a plain-looking Chevy Nova, was parked. An old oak offered a leafy canopy of green and shadow. They had crossed into the industrial city of Vernon, where there were many types of warehouses. The steady hum and diesel aroma of big freight trucks was ever present.

The three got out of the car and quickly transferred their loot and guns to the trunk of the Nova. They'd taken off their windbreakers to reveal colorful tops. The idea was to blend in not only driving a different car than the one the tellers at the bank would have described to the police, but being seen in the car not wearing dark clothes. A key reason the thieves chose the smaller municipalities of the Southland was such entities had smaller police forces, though some were patrolled by the Sheriff's Department.

"I saw a curtain move," Neilson said, nodding toward a modest house.

"We stick to our protocol, Dorothy," Solly Claire said.

Their mixed race daughter cracked, "It's not like we don't already stand out."

As they'd done before, they left their jackets in the get-away car, which had stolen license plates on it. The car of course could be traced via its vehicle identification. But the cars had been purchased at distant used car lots where a cash sale over the asking price coupled with presenting a false driver's license resulted in less scrutiny.

"You okay to drive?" Nielson asked her ex.

"Yes'um," he said, affecting a Stepin Fetchit accent.

"Keep being funny."

"Oh, I will."

They continued on, with the two women in the rear seat. Leaving Vernon by way of Vernon Avenue, they were soon back in South Central. The remnants of the recent rioting were evident the more they headed west. Now it wasn't vigilantes they were worried about. During the riots there'd been a picture in the *Times* showing several big rigs block-ading the avenue at the Vernon city limits, the white truckers armed with rifles and pistols.

"There's a motorcycle cop behind us," Solly Claire said calmly, eyes on the rearview mirror. "He rolled out from behind another car. Good thing the plates on this heap go with it."

After another block, the motorcycle officer put on his siren and lights. Nielson put on over-sized sunglasses, pat-ting her daughter's hand.

"Here we go," the father said. He pulled to the curb and shut off the engine. His driver's side window was already partly open but he made no move to roll it down further.

The officer came up, looking inside the car. His gaze rested on the two women, a frown forming. "Where you folks heading today?"

"I'm taking Miz Dorothy to her business appointment," Solly Claire said.

"That right, ma'am?"

"It is, officer." She removed her sunglasses. "I own some rental property in this part of town and have to see to my investments. Not the least of which is what damages might have happened to them during the recent . . . well, you know." She nodded toward the back of her ex-husband's head. Continuing she added, "Smitty here is not just my driver but a handyman too." She put the sunglasses back in place.

"And who are you?" the cop asked her daughter.

Making sure to look right at him, she answered, "I'm her assistant. I take care of Miss Dorothy's bookkeeping, tallying and what have you. I also collect the rent in this part of town."

The cop kept staring at her. Given the sunglasses and that the daughter to many was simply another colored gal, the three hedged the odds were in their favor a stranger might not notice the familial resemblance. This was not the first time they had been stopped. They'd rehearsed their roles for a situation like this.

"Let me see your license and registration."

"Of course." Solly Claire got his license out of his wallet and removed the registration from where it was wrapped around the steering column. He handed them across and the officer read them carefully.

Without a word the cop walked back to his motorcycle

to radio in for any wants or warrants on the car or for the man. A few minutes later he returned and handed the paper-work back. Leaning down some and looking into the back he said flatly, "How come you two look alike?"

Without hesitation, Nielson responded. "People have told us that." She took the sunglasses off again. "Me, I don't see it."

Whatever notions the policeman might be harboring about miscegenation, he kept them to himself. "You can be on your way."

Breath still in their throats, they waited until the officer roared away before they too continued toward their destina-tion, Solly Claire's granny flat over a friend's garage.

"Too bad it's too early to have a drink," Nielson said, plopping down in a chair. The humble apartment was appointed with a shower and bath in its own room and an all-electric kitchenette.

Solly Claire limped some as he walked over and dumped the contents of the duffle bag onto his only table. Claire closed the blinds. This was the first time they'd taken items from safety deposit boxes in addition to cash. The trio had used a hammer and screwdriver to force the locked panels on several open, the tools taken from a toolbox inside the bank's janitor's closet. It was Nielson who'd suggested they look for them. As if it were an everyday family gathering, the three sat around the table. After taking off the paper bands around the money, mother and father began counting. Anita Claire examined the goods taken from the vault, including a clutch of pearls and a set of silver dollars from the 1800s in a drawstring cloth bag.

"I've got a little over fifty thousand," Solly Claire

announced when he'd finished his count. Imitating a high rolling gambler going all in, he shoved his stack into the middle of the table.

"Seventy thousand, six hundred for me," his ex-wife announced, smiling.

"For the love of the people," he declared.

"You pulled off the big dream this time, Solly."

"The three of us did."

As with their other robberies, the bulk of the proceeds would be used to support civil rights activities in the States and funneled overseas to the likes of Spear of the Nation, the armed wing of the African National Congress seeking to end apartheid in South Africa. Nielson leaned over and gave him a kiss. In the months the three had been pulling off heists, the two exes had renewed affection for one another. The shared cause of stealing money from the capitalists. The Bonnie and Clyde of the Atomic Age.

"Ain't you two cute," Claire said. She tossed a squarish memo book onto the table. It was black leather bound and the pages were lined. Inscribed throughout in pen were numbers and letters in an obvious pattern. "What do you make of that?"

Her mother picked it up and opened it to no particular page, then another. "Some sort of code, I'd venture." She handed it to her ex.

The father also studied a few pages in the notebook. "I remember this, it was by itself in one of the boxes." During the robbery he'd randomly busted open several of the safety deposit boxes and emptied them while Nielson kept watch on the tellers and manager they'd made sit on the floor. When they were heading out of the vault toward the exit, their backs momentarily turned on their temporary hostages, the guard chanced to use his backup gun.

Solly Claire held the notebook aloft, shaking it. "Could this belong to a bookie or somebody like that?"

Mother and daughter exchanged a doubtful look. Anita Claire said, "Maybe . . ."

"We should find out," her mother declared. "Clearly the book has value."

"Or leave it alone. I think you're right, Dorothy. This is a sign we should retire our extra-curricular method of fund-raising before one of us catches a bullet."

"Who you trying to kid, Solly?" she said.

"Gangsters use this kind of rigmarole."

"We've already stolen it," the younger Claire observed. "We can't give it back and all is forgiven."

"What about Harry's buddy Strummer Edwards?" her father said. "He worked for that guy Dragna who butted heads with Mickey Cohen's crew." Cohen, the once king of the rackets in L.A., was doing time for tax evasion at a federal penitentiary in Atlanta.

"If this is a gangster cipher he might have knowledge of it," Nielson allowed.

"Why not?" her ex-husband said.

"Well, for certain Anita can't go asking Strummer behind Harry's back. Now, maybe after you and Harry make love the next time and he's in a mellow frame of mind, you can mention why you want to talk to his friend."

"Mom, please."

"It's those Redd Foxx records she's been listening to," her father cracked.

"And Moms Mabley," Nielson added.

Her daughter continued, "This is a problem involving a logical answer."

"Yes," the other two said simultaneously as they all stared at the coded journal.

"What about Del?" the father said eventually.

"Who?" his daughter asked.

"Del Standers," Nielson answered. "He was a Ritchie Boy in the war. These were men who worked in intelligence, code breakers, a lot of them of German-Jewish extraction like Del. They were headquartered at Camp Ritchie in Maryland, thus the nickname."

"But he was hounded during the bad times," the elder Claire added. "He might well be gun shy."

"Might be," Nielson allowed. "Or maybe he'd be up to the challenge."

CHAPTER NINE

It was late afternoon. Ingram sat at the bar top with Strummer Edwards in his off-the-books joint, the Stockyard. The name of the place was derived from a mural that was here before it was a bar and unlicensed casino. Along one of the walls, anthropomorphic pigs and cows cavorted about in a green field in suits, tuxes and formal dresses, several with open umbrellas to ward off the sun. There was a barn and silo in the background of the tableau where a bull in a bowler and rolled-up sleeves sat above a smoke belching tractor. He chomped a cigar.

"You figure to start doing this hawkshawing full time?" Edwards glanced at him sideways. Today, they were the only two in the bar.

"Better see if I make headway finding this dude first." He'd told his friend about the labels he'd found going through Tolbert's car.

"Uh-huh," Edwards drawled, having some of his beer. Both were drinking Hamm's. Edwards held the can in one of his expansive hands, two of the knuckles misshapen from a past of punching chumps in the head. Edwards, Ingram had observed some years ago, was a man of interesting contradictions. He could be flashy, but also had the discipline to invest. The Stockyard one of the material results of his foresightedness.

Everything about the bar was illegal except for the hookups for water, power and gas, and even those accounts were under false names. The enterprise was located on the second floor of a two-story building located on Hoover near the Coliseum. The bottom floor was occupied by Wertzendahl plumbing supply and the family owned the building. Walter Wertzendahl was the one Edwards dealt with in terms of seeing to needed repairs and the like. Ingram had an inkling that the Wertzendahls were getting a percentage of Edwards's action in lieu of rent as they certainly knew what was going on upstairs. But he hadn't previously broached the subject with his friend, and wasn't going to today.

"This might mean something," Edwards eventually said.

"What you got?"

"Seems a grip of furs got lifted from that Sabine outfit about two months ago." Edwards tapped his lit cigarette onto a glass ashtray on the bar. A thin pall of smoke hung over them, between the two and the recessed lights in the ceiling.

"I didn't remember anything about that in the news," Ingram said.

"Plenty of shit goes down ain't in them rags you run around for, Harry."

"You get a gander at these animal skins?" An image popped up in his head of Wilma Flintstone from the cartoon show wearing a saber-tooth tiger fur coat and a string of pearls the size of golf balls. The saber-tooth was somehow still alive and had a big grin on his face.

"I know they were for sale," he answered. "I know too that if it's the fella I'm assuming was behind the robbery, he talks smooth but carries a big knife if you dig what I'm saying. If the cat you're looking for is involved with him then you can probably save yourself unnecessary steps. Unless you want to put on your scuba gear and go diving off the Lido Pier where his body might be weighted down." He chuckled hollowly and took another drag on his cigarette.

"That kind of guy, huh?"

"M-hmmm."

"Hey, Strummer," a feminine voice called from behind the two.

They both swiveled around. A striking-looking woman stood in the bar's arched entryway. She was wearing white jeans and an off-the-shoulder puffy sleeve blouse. Ingram frowned, then his face cleared. She pointed at him.

"I know you," she said, shaking her finger.

"Sherry," Ingram remembered. They had met when Harry was looking into his Army buddy's death.

"Sherry Foster." She held out her hand, three loops of gold links encircling it. Ingram shook her hand.

"Sherry's working here these days," Edwards offered, stubbing out his cigarette. When Ingram had met her, she'd had a job at Dolphin's of Hollywood, a record shop in South Central where white and Black teens hung out. She was also engaged in certain other pastimes he'd needed to talk to her about. Edwards had connected the two.

"Good to see you again, Harry." To Edwards she said, "I came in early to finish up the inventory."

"Cool," her boss said.

"See you, Harry." She held up her hand, wiggling her fingers good-bye as she walked off.

"You too," he said.

Foster headed further into the establishment. This included a hidden entrance to the gaming area. It wasn't unusual to see a few white patrons in that part of the Stockyard, including once when Ingram and Claire were here, spotting Bette Davis with two bodyguards. She rolled craps that night with zeal.

"You mind laying the name of this high stepper on me?" Ingram asked when the two were alone again.

"No, I figure it don't make me no songbird to tell you that. His name is Gavin Rickler."

"His handle rings a bell."

Edwards looked over at him again. "He's been in the news a time or two."

Ingram wasn't going to press his friend. He finished his drink but didn't get off the stool. It occurred to him he could have another one on the house. The afternoon was getting long and why not be in a mellow mood, ruminating on what Mose Tolbert and Rickler were up to. He'd considered driving out to the Emerald Room, Rickler's establishment, but what would that accomplish? If he tried to brace the man, for sure his goons would happily give him a beat down. He wanted to be more clever than that. Too, he wanted to know more to go at Rickler any damn way on his home turf. He wasn't going anywhere, he'd be around.

"Fair enough. I better leave you to it." He started to rise.

"Meant to tell you, I ran into Shoals a couple of weeks ago. Was at the Olympic for the doggone wrasslin' matches." He winked at his friend. "Got this new chick who really digs them kind of physicalities. Gets her blood up, if you know what I mean."

"How's he doing?"

He lifted a shoulder and let it fall. "We said hi and bye, that was about it."

"Me and him having a falling out don't mean you two can't have a chat."

"He knows me and Josh know about him." He traced his finger through the condensation on the cold can and continued. "Lord knows as Granny used to say, I'm not one to cast stones, but there it is." He picked up his beer and finished it as well.

"'Preciate this, Strummer." He tapped the other man on the shoulder and got off the stool.

"Take it slow, pard'ner."

"The only way."

"Ain't that right."

Edwards grinned, firing up another cigarette and also rising. He shook his index finger signaling good-bye and made his office.

Back on the street, Ingram checked his watch and walked to the pay phone on the next block. The Disciples' stylized stalking cougar had been spray painted using a stencil on the phone booth glass. Lately he'd seen several of their declarations around town. Sometimes the words, WE'RE WATCHING, had been added. He got out his notebook and made a few notations, more material for his long-form idea.

This past December he'd raced past Edwards's blind pig in his car on his way to the Hacienda Motel, a no-tell motel on Figueroa. He along with several other newshounds had converged on the three-dollar-a-night place in response to the news that reached them over their respective police scanners. Rhythm and blues crooner Sam Cooke had been shot in the chest three times and died on the spot. From what was gathered, the shooting happened after a young woman he'd taken there, not his wife, had bolted out of the room, partly with her and his clothes, including his wallet which contained a goodly amount of cash. Angry, Cooke had banged on the door of the manager's office, supposedly under the impression the woman was holed up there in league with the manager. In turn the manager, a Black woman in her fifties, said she was terrified as this near-naked younger man, with only his sport coat wrapped around him, broke in screaming at her and she shot him in self-defense.

Lifting the handset off the hook, Ingram considered several rumors already sprouting in the community as to the true reasons for Cooke's death. One of them being that he was becoming more political in the songs he wrote and therefore had to be stopped before he riled up the downtrodden. He put a dime in the slot and dialed a number. When the line connected he said, "Figured I might find you in."

"What's shaking, Harry?" Wesley Crossman had been the last editor at *California Eagle* before it shut down last year due to declining revenues. While the presses had stopped rolling, the office was rented out for the desk space. Several reporters for the *Sentinel* were there as well as freelancers.

"Can I come by and dig through the archives?"

"Sure. Bring me a sandwich will you?"

"Pig foot and a bottle of beer?"

"A roast beef with some coleslaw on the side will do, Ma Rainey."

"Bet."

Cradling the receiver, Ingram stepped out of the booth as a prowl car pulled to a stop.

"Hey, you know what to do," the cop in the passenger seat said from the car. He was pointing the end of his nightstick at him.

"What's this about?"

"Less mouth, more following my orders," the cop said, exiting to the sidewalk. The one who'd been driving joined his partner.

Roughly, the first one pushed Ingram toward a wall, the nightstick jabbed him between his shoulder blades. "Spread 'em. You got warrants, wants, huh?"

"You ain't got nothin' on me."

"We got plenty on you, asshole," the second cop said. "Get your lyin' pictures in a special edition of *Life* magazine, huh, Ingram? The all fried chicken and watermelon issue?"

The other cop was patting him down and leaned toward his ear. "Any time, day or night, it could happen, Ingram. We say that camera in your hand was mistaken for a gun. Boom, there goes your head. Maybe you get a flat tire and when a duty-bound officer stops to render assistance, he has to put you down 'cause you went all apeshit what with your known hatred of the police." The odor of onions and cigarettes was on his breath.

"You about done, officer?" The contents of his pockets had been tossed on the sidewalk.

"Any goddamn time, Ingram." He tapped him in the back with the nightstick and the two departed.

Ingram bent over to pick up his items. When he straightened up, he saw an older woman with her shopping cart, the kind the elderly wheeled their shopping bags in. They exchanged a nod.

Returning his car and camera in it, Ingram then took a few pictures of what the Disciples had painted on the phone booth. He'd be damned if he was going to let the cops scare him or throw him off his game.

NOT LONG afterward, Crossman let Ingram in the back way to the *Eagle*'s offices on Central Avenue. He was an average height, slightly overweight middle-aged individual who in addition to his part-time job at the also weekly *Sentinel*, also freelanced with several of the same publications Ingram did. This included the digest *Jet* and *Dapper*, a Black men's magazine that recently had begun publishing more short stories. Today he was in his shirt sleeves and had his much-traveled pipe in hand. Ingram gave him the paper bag with his food in it.

On Crossman's desk were marked-up articles and photos with red crop marks on them. Idly Ingram sifted through them, noting the color death picture of a man's body laid out in the morgue, covered by a sheet. Regarding the discoloration on the corpse's neck, he had a notion of who this was. He picked up the photo, showing it to Crossman. "This Neal Atkins, the burglar?"

"Yeah. But you know I can't run that one. I got this Little League team picture, but he was a kid then." He tapped the picture of the smiling kids in their uniforms with his finger as Ingram regarded the shot. "Also got a mug shot, but that's not appropriate either."

"I hear you." Ingram put the photo back.

"I talked to the landlady where Atkins laid his head. She told me the cops had been there and tore his place apart on the day he died. Even busted into some of the walls."

"Looking for what?"

"That, among other issues, I'll raise in the article. There's also talk he may have been a jailhouse informant and was killed because of that."

"The cops won't admit he was."

"I know, but I have to raise it. Anyway, thanks for the grub, Harry. I realized when you'd called, I hadn't dirtied a plate since breakfast." He stuck the pipe in the corner of his mouth and Ingram closed the door. "What are you looking for?" he asked. There were two others inside, both typing away at their desks.

Ingram told him.

"Rickler, yeah," Crossman said, puffing a plume of aromatic smoke out of his mouth. "That's the fella runs a joint over in Gardena. A swanky card parlor called the Emerald Room. Bomb went off there once."

"Say what?"

Crossman continued, "Blew out some front windows but didn't do any real damage and nobody got hurt."

"Is he mobbed up?"

"Not like you mean. Maybe he has to kick back something to whatever there is of the mafia around these parts, but hell, this isn't New York."

"It is not."

"If anything," Crossman offered, "I'd wager he has ties to the downtown Caucasians. Drinking their lunches at the

Pacific Dining Car and lamenting you negroes going wild while playing snooker at the Jonathan Club."

Ingram searched through the paper's physical archives of bound newspapers and found the article that had run about the bombing at the Emerald Room in February of 1962. The Gardena Police Department at the time said the investigation was ongoing and they were receiving assistance from the close-by Sheriff's sub-station. He made a few notes from the piece and continued his research. In the Entertainment section from eleven months ago he found another small item about the club. It was about a young Japanese American woman winning the Miss Gardena beauty contest. The picture accompanying the piece showed a tall, wide-chested white man in a suit with a matinée idol smile handing a bouquet of roses to the winner. The caption identified him as local entrepreneur Gavin Rickler, a graduate of USC. That was the extent of what Ingram discovered in the archives. He rose, stretching, and put the bound newspapers back in place in order.

"Find anything?" Crossman asked when Ingram stopped by his open office door. The editor was leaning back in a swivel chair, hands tucked behind his head.

"Ah, you know, maybe a thread to something else. What do you know about Rickler's club?"

"I know it was started with an investment from Ernie Primm. This was after the war and Primm had visions of making Gardena a Vegas. He owned two or three of the card clubs in town and was looking to put up more of them. The other owners of course balked, so the deal was he decided to own a piece of a couple other places on the QT-like."

"That's where Rickler came in?"

He straightened up, taking his pipe off a short stack of galleys. "Yeah, I think he showed up in '58 or '59. He'd been a standout baseball and basketball star at 'SC several years before." He produced a pouch of tobacco and proceeded to pack a sizable pinch of flakes into the pipe bowl.

"The modern face of the casino owner," Ingram said. "Do you know what he did when he left college before he got to Gardena?"

His friend shook his head from side to side. "Sorry, no." Crossman was bent forward, putting a wood match he'd sparked onto the tobacco in his pipe bowl. He got it going and cocking his head to the side, offered, "'SC has an alumni magazine you know."

"Okay, might have to run that down. Thanks, Wes."

Crossman took his pipe out of his mouth and shook the stem at Ingram. "Whatever the heck it is you're up to, think about turning it into a true crime piece. Bob says he wants more of that too for the mag."

"Good to know," Ingram said as he started out. Bob was Robert Jeffers, the publisher of *Dapper.* Between trying to find Tobert, his preparation for his upcoming appearance on the Lomax show this coming Thursday and trying to get a handle on his picture-book project, he doubted he'd have time or the mental agility to do such a piece. But no sense telling Wes all that. Have to keep your editor happy, he'd learned long ago.

THAT EVENING he and Claire attended a fundraiser sponsored by the *Free Press* to raise monies for the Disciples in the lawsuit they were preparing to level against the city and the police department. The gathering took place in the Venice West Café, which was an institution in the Slum by the Sea. More than one Hollywood celebrity was milling about with the regular folk.

"That's Brando," Claire said to Ingram. There was standing room only inside the café and the crowd had spilled out onto the sidewalk on Dudley. Actor Marlon Brando was about two yards from them talking to a few others, his head back as he laughed.

"You sound kinda breathless when you say his name."

"Don't I?" Her eyes sparkled at him, and they kissed quickly.

"Hey you two."

"Hi, Gerry," Claire said.

"What's going on, man?" Ingram said to Gerry Tackwood.

"Boss has me out here covering the event."

Ingram smiled. "Make sure you get a great quote."

"Oh, I will." He had his portable tape recorder with him, its strap slung across his torso and the device down at his side. A police car rolled by, the two officers in the car eyeing the crowd, but the vehicle continued on.

Ingram said to his friend, "You know anybody over at USC?"

"A couple of adjuncts. Why, you looking for work there?"

"Harry's looking for a man who disappeared during the riots," Claire said. "Getting paid for it too."

"Well, look at you." Tackwood smiled genuinely.

"There's an 'SC angle," Ingram said. "I'm going to go over to their library to look through the alumni magazine but was hoping to talk to someone who'd been around there for a time about a connected guy named Gavin Rickler who went there in the '50s."

Tackwood nodded. "One of them I know might be of help. I'll ask."

"Thanks, Ger."

Inside, an older balding man in glasses had come to the front and raised his hands for the crowd to quiet down.

"That's Lawrence Lipton," Tackwood said. "I'm gonna slip inside."

"For sure," Ingram said.

Lipton was a poet and his novel of a few years ago, *The Holy Barbarians*, had made it known there was a beat scene in L.A. as there was in places like San Francisco and the East Village in New York. Ingram and Claire edged toward the entrance to better hear him.

"My fellow friends and ratfinks," Lipton was saying, "'cause I know you're out there among the real of us, you under the covers Parker G2ers and maybe even J. Edgar's goon squaders." The audience hooted, the sound filling the compact space. Lipton continued, "We come here tonight for as we know what went down not too many miles inland from here, while it was destruction, like what we did for war-torn Europe, we must enact a kind of Marshall Plan for our ghettos and under-privileged across the land of wealth and honey. As Art said in his newspaper, 'The negroes have voted!' No more money for A-bombs and money for milk and books. Tonight we can take that first step and bring it to the man like it's never been brought to him before."

Roars of approval again filled the room. After Lipton was finished, several other people spoke, including the lawyer for the Disciples and Dorrell Zinum. Art Kunkin, the

Freep's publisher, was the last to come to the front. His job was to make the pitch for people to dig deep and donate to the fundraiser. As he did this, several medium-sized tin buckets were passed around inside and out. It didn't take long for the buckets to be stuffed with cash and checks. At some point the patrol car that had been by earlier had returned and was now parked across the street, the two cops inside, smoking and watching.

"Good to see you again, Anita." The white man who'd stepped onto the sidewalk was in his forties, fit and tanned like a tennis player. He wore slacks, a stylish sports jacket and a turtleneck. His rugged features were complemented with sandy brown hair and sideburns, and his mustache was full but not bushy. He was the lawyer representing the Disciples.

He kissed her on the cheek and turned his attention on Ingram.

"Clyde, this is Harry, and Harry this is Clyde Kennedy, who is representing the Zinum family in their suit against the Police Department."

"Good to meet you," Ingram said.

They shook hands. "I've heard about you, Harry."

"Yeah?"

"From Dot. She's bragged on you even before your famous photo made you a household name."

"Then you must know Anton," Ingram said.

"That's right. We've known each other for about twenty years. Back when Anita and her sister were knee high."

"They babysat us a few times," she added, squeezing his upper arm. "He and Ingrid would have movie night and we'd watch Popeye cartoons with popcorn and candy because they had a projector. Clyde represented the cartoonist union local back then so could get us the films." Abruptly she stopped her reminiscing, giving the older man a solemn look. "I miss her too."

"Thanks, honey, so do I." He looked off as Dorrell Zinum had appeared and she was signaling to him. "Gotta go confer with my client. Let's get together soon."

She kissed his cheek. "We will."

"Looking forward to tipping a seltzer with you, Harry."

"Same here, Clyde."

When he was gone, Ingram looked questioningly at Claire.

"His first wife, Ingrid, died unexpectantly. Heart attack out of nowhere. She was pregnant at the time."

"Damn."

"It really knocked him on his heels, ya know? He dropped into the bottle for a time but with help from Anton, and my mom and dad and some other friends who didn't give up on him, he climbed back out. Somehow even when he was living in this threadbare apartment above a machinist shop, he'd managed to hold on to his law license. Anyway, he's been going to his AA meetings for more than a decade. Now he just lives for his work."

"He didn't re-marry?"

"No. According to Mom, he hasn't had any lasting girlfriends either."

"You know what them bluesmen says, whiskey and women done ruined my life."

In his ear she said, "And Bessie said she needed a hot dog for her roll."

"You should be careful how you tease me. Isn't it Be Kind to Veterans week?"

"You know by now I don't be teasing."

"How true."

Though the event was over, plenty of attendees were still hanging around. A set of bongos had been brought out along with a guitar. As the unmistakable odor of marijuana persisted, Lipton and a younger woman in white chinos, a striped shirt and a straw cowboy hat recited their poems to the improvised musical accompaniment.

"And the war birds haunt the skies over the rice paddies of the villagers," she called out, swaying to the bongo beat. The people standing around clapped or snapped their fingers in approval. "And the bombs they drop and their eyes flicker red as the jungle ignites and we must ask the reasons why and decry the excess when the poor can only look through the window and wonder." The young poet stopped swaying as the clicks of snapped fingers rose. Lipton held up one of her arms as if she were a contender who'd just won her boxing match.

Ingram and Claire moved away. Alongside the café was a narrow passageway swathed in near darkness. Her back against the brick wall, Claire hiked up a leg and wrapped it partly around Ingram as she used her hand to guide him inside her. At the moment she didn't notice that one of her heels was spiking a book on the ground that had either been discarded or somehow fallen from someone's grasp unnoticed. Though why they'd been in the passageway who knew. The title of the clothbound book was *The Ways of Tantra*, the words in worn gold leaf.

"I don't know what I'd do without you, Anita," he sighed.

"I'm so crazy for you," she replied as he thrust into her. She gasped with pleasure and gripped his shoulders, digging her nails into the material of his coat. "Now shut up and fuck me."

IN THE police car still stationed across the street, one of the uniformed cops continued making field notes of the observed proceedings at the cafe.

Those field notes, among others, landed on the desk of a captain in the LAPD's administrative offices, nicknamed the Glass House, walking distance from City Hall. The captain was in the intelligence division's command chain and reported directly to Chief Parker. He was a compact man with a broad face and broad chest. Like Parker, he was a decorated veteran of World War II, having seen action in the Pacific Theater. And like Crossman, he smoked a pipe, though he preferred a long-stemmed one akin to what a lighthouse keeper would smoke. He puffed away as he perused the reports. His phone rang and he picked up the handset.

"Yes," he said.

"It's me, Cap, Stevens. Everything's in place for the installation."

"Good. Keep me abreast."

"Oh yes."

The pipe smoker cradled the handset and continued reading. Classical music played softly on his radio.

CHAPTER TEN

Anita Claire stepped out of her house and paused on the walkway. She adjusted an earring and continued on to her car, humming along the way. Inside the house Ingram was also up but wasn't pressed for time like his girlfriend was. She had to be at the office early to help prepare for a town hall.

Taking his time, he checked himself out in his boxers and athletic T. He was pleased by the improving profile reflected in the mirror. While his stomach wasn't exactly that of a slim man—say like his TV workout buddy Jack LaLanne— it was not as pronounced as it had been two years ago. Once dressed, Ingram straightened up his area of the garage, turning on the police scanner. He also did several of LaLanne's resistance exercises, like modified push-ups. He leaned against his desk, arms extended, going down, then up, to a count of twenty-five. His office workout also included some jumping jacks and regular push-ups. The melodic voice of the female dispatcher filled the room as he exercised.

". . . Caucasian American, male, six feet two inches, last seen . . ."

". . . negro American, male with kitchen knife and small dog on a bicycle . . ."

". . . Unit 12-A, see the woman at 1425 West Olympic Boulevard, suspected bunco . . ."

While Ingram was tempted to grab a camera and dash out on more than one call, he'd decided he would keep on his primary task today. Well, he admitted, if it were a four-alarm fire or hostage situation, he might have responded. Done, Ingram turned off the scanner and, after washing a light coating of sweat off his face, drove off to the University of Southern California campus.

Twelve minutes later a Starbrite Carpeting and Services Dodge panel van pulled to a stop at the house. Two workers in gray striped overalls got out of the vehicle, both of them carrying metal toolboxes. One went around to the backyard while the other waited on the porch, continuing to smoke the cigarette he'd already been puffing on. The front door was opened by the one who'd gone around back. The two exchanged a few words and the smoking one took a last drag on his cigarette before dropping it onto the porch and grounding it out with his foot. The man picked up the dead stub and flicked it into the flower bed. He went into the house and quietly closed the door on the two of them.

AT THE Doheny Library on the USC campus, Ingram was directed to a recently acquired microfilm viewing machine. He was impressed—he was used to the microfiche-type viewers and had only seen one of these modern wonders in a magazine ad. To show him how to use it, the librarian loaded one of the compact film spools onto one side and threaded it through the center, which contained the magnifying glass and lights. She then connected the film strip to a matching empty spool on the other side. There were several gray-colored archive cardboard boxes of these film spools.

"Thank you," he said. She was somewhere in her sixties but was erect and svelte in a matching skirt and jacket. Her hair was pulled back, auburn colored streaked with white highlights.

"My pleasure, Mr. Ingram."

He looked at her questioningly.

"I recognize you from your picture in the newspaper."

He was still incredulous, as his picture had only been in the Black press.

She seemed to read the thought on his face, because she continued, "I'm not telling you anything you don't know about the political bent of this campus, but there is more going on here than what's let on. During the riots quite a few students came in here and more than one lively discussion took place. A lot of what was said reflected their upbringings, but there were a good deal of other opinions too. There are some students here who volunteer teach in the area, so they view the community differently." A reassuring smile creased her features. "You let me know if I can help you with anything else. Just ask for Claudia."

"I will."

"Be well."

She was about to leave and he said, "You've been here a while, haven't you? At the university I mean."

"I have."

"Does an alumnus named Gavin Rickler ring a bell? He has a card club over in Gardena. He was something of a big man on campus not too many years ago."

Claudia looked off for a moment then back at him, patting his arm. "Try the second box down from the top."

Ingram did as she suggested. He slowly scanned through the issues of the *USC Trojan Family Magazine*. Claudia had told Ingram the microfilm viewer, along with staff time to convert the back issues of the magazine, had been covered by a generous donation. From what he understood, the microfilmed monthly issues covered 1950 to now. Early copies going back decades lived on as hard copies and on microfiche.

In the February 1963 issue there was, as Claudia hinted, a brief bordered article on Rickler. USC had won the Rose Bowl that New Year's Day and the piece talked about Rickler hosting a pre-game party two nights before, not at his club but at a venue on this side of town. The Emerald Room was mentioned as well. Rickler, a standout athlete in his college years it was stated, had interests in other enterprises in the downtown adjacent area to the campus. Ingram laughed quietly. "Downtown adjacent" was the university's way of saying South Central where the institutions were located—albeit established when the land around here was untouched and on which horses pulling carts grazed. Concerned parents in the heartland paying for those hefty tuitions had to be reassured, after all. He wondered if letters had already gone out to prospective families assuring them the university had been safely guarded during the recent unpleasantness.

A snapshot accompanying the article depicted several people along with a beaming Rickler sitting at a rectangular table laid out with food and drink. His hair was light colored and he showed big teeth. The angle was such that the photographer must have been standing on a chair, Ingram estimated. Betty Payton was among those pictured. She had a big smile on her face and even given she was captured in harsh lighting from the flash, Ingram gauged she must have already had two or three servings of wine.

Time to see if he could get her to show all her hole cards.

Passing by her desk, Ingram spotted Claudia talking to two female students.

"Thanks again, Claudia."

"Looking forward to seeing you again."

"Same here." Outside he asked one of the colored gardeners who seemed to be perpetually trimming the campus's acres of greenery where he could find a pay phone. The photograph in the magazine on his mind, he made a call.

Betty Payton told him over the phone she'd be in town today to attend a lunch of one of her organizations at the Bullock's Wilshire Tea Room. At the upstairs entrance, the maître d' at the podium raised an eyebrow at him when he came up, but otherwise the older white woman's face remained pleasant.

"How can I help you?" she said.

He told her who he was here to see.

"Yes, Betty said you'd be dropping by. This way, please." As she moved, swishing sounds issued from her chiffon dress.

She escorted him past tables of other white women, some in fancy hats, dressed well for their high teas. A few quickly looked up at him and then murmured to their lunch companions, and others averted their gaze. A bemused Ingram was led to table where Payton sipped from a water glass.

"Mr. Ingram," the maître d' announced unnecessarily.

"Thank you, Greta."

The older woman nodded slightly. "Anything for you, sir?"

"I'm fine, thanks."

She went away and Ingram sat opposite.

"What's your progress, Harry?"

"I don't know how else to ask this, Betty, so tell me—are you part of a theft ring it seems your boy Mose and Rickler were up to?"

As she stared at him, a waiter arrived with a cart and made a production of pouring tea for Payton. He put the cup and saucer on the table. After he rolled his offerings away, she spoke. "I assumed the two were up to something like that, but I can assure you, I had no direct knowledge of what that was specifically."

"Was it Rickler who bailed out the business a few years ago?"

"You've been busy."

"All about what you paid me to do."

"Partly because of what people like Dorothy and Solly were going through, hounded by the FBI and all that and frankly his own drinking a result of the pressure he was under, Restoration by the mid-fifties was in bad shape. Mose owed money all over town. I offered to help him and I did."

"But that wasn't enough?"

"No. He not only needed someone to consolidate his debt but a signal to his less than legitimate creditors to get in line. A bank loan was out of the question."

"So how did he get to Rickler?"

"Through Albert Domergue."

"Related to Arlene?"

"Her older brother and something of a sharpie. I'm not sure about this, but my understanding was he was a silent partner in the Emerald Room. Apparently Domergue knew about Mose through one of the shady creditors. Mose told me that."

"And out of the goodness of his heart, he helped Mose out."

"Domergue and Gavin got a piece of the business. Like concrete, there's always need for building supplies." She sipped again. "And as you say, Mose and Gavin are up to, well, whatever it is they're up to."

Moving stolen goods around town via an already established trucks line made sense to Ingram. "What happened to Albert?"

"Died suddenly of a heart attack. After," she emphasized, "installing his sister to oversee his investment."

"And you're no stranger to the Emerald Room."

"True. It wasn't like some of us close to Mose didn't know about the arrangement. He'd invite us out there to the card club."

"Did Dorothy know?"

"Not the details, no."

"Yet you don't think Rickler brought harm to Mose?"

"Wouldn't that bring unwanted attention from the authorities?"

"You would think so. So far my impression is the cops don't seem to be asking around about him."

"What do you think that means?"

"Yeah," he drawled, weighing her words.

They talked for a few minutes more and he thanked her

for her time. On the way out a woman wearing a cocked hat with a veil regarded him. He winked at her and was gone. Betty Payton had come across as straight-forward in her answers. That she was in the dark about what may have sent Tolbert away or worse. He didn't think she was bird-dogging for Rickler. No, she was about her own interests, Ingram was sure.

LESS THAN two hours later, Ingram kept another appointment. He had been asked to take pictures of the body of Faraday Zinum being claimed by the independent medical examiner. The family's lawyer Clyde Kennedy was also present. He would accompany the body to where it was to be autopsied. As the dead man hadn't yet been embalmed to better preserve any type of evidence, the body had been kept in the Eternal Sands' refrigeration unit to retard decomposition. Ingram took shots of Zinum as he was wheeled out of cooling and during the process of shrouding his body. The young man was carefully wrapped in three layers of cloth. There was a solemnity to how Faraday was being handled and Ingram sought to preserve that dignity in his pictures. Faraday was then loaded into the cargo area of a station wagon.

"Okay, I'm off," Kennedy said to Ingram and Nakano. At the lawyer's suggestion, Nakano had filed a police report about the attempted arson of his business.

"Really?" Ingram had joked, "like the fox is gonna find out who's been eating those chickens. Fricasseeing them and whatnot."

Kennedy had replied, smiling, "Gotta have it on the record, is all." The three didn't believe the police would do any investigating of the incident.

Now, Nakano and Ingram gave a quick wave as the lawyer drove off in his Avanti, the convertible top down, trailing behind the station wagon.

"It's not sundown yet, but I could use a drink," Nakano said.

"You buying?" Ingram said.

"Sure as hell am."

They walked past several toadstool-shaped bonsai trees bordering part of the exterior. Back in his office, the funeral director opened a black lacquer cabinet with ornate images and Japanese lettering carved into its surface. He extracted a bottle of Crown Royal and two glasses and sat next to Ingram on the customer side, removing the whiskey from its distinctive purple with yellow piping drawstring cloth sack. He poured twin draughts a shade more than neat for both of them.

"Kenpai," Ingram said as they clinked glasses.

"Kenpai," Nakano said, returning the toast. He took a drink and leaned back, tension flowing from him visibly.

Ingram also enjoyed a taste. "How's Chris?" There were several framed photos in here of his eleven-year-old son, who lived in Hawaii with the boy's mother. He gestured the glass toward the son's beaming face in the shot taken on the beach two years ago.

"Talked to him last Sunday." Nakano swirled the contents of his glass about. "My plan is to get over there this winter. Apparently he's taken up surfing and is getting to be quite good at it. A regular Duke Kahanamoku. Helen even sent me a film of him." He adjusted the glasses bridging his nose. "I know I'm biased, but he looked impressive. 'Course I don't know squat about the sport."

Ingram only knew who Kahanamoku was because Nakano had previously told him about the Hawaiian surfing champ. "You worried he's gonna become big time on the waves and won't be following in the family business?"

Nakano was in the middle of a sip and choked a little, clearing his throat. "If I believed in the hereafter, I'd pray the boy runs far away from this," he held up his index finger, circling it in the air, "as fast as he could." He studied his friend. "The way things are going, you and Anita are probably going to have a youngin' or two running around. You want your son doing what you do?"

"I dig what you're saying." Ingram had more of his whiskey.

"You know what gaman means in Japanese culture?"

"Hmm," Ingram mused, "to endure the unbearable with patience and dignity."

"Yep," Nakano twanged. He set his glass on his desk. "The Buddhist says you can't do anything about a shitty situation, so let it go, don't let it eat you up. The wheel will turn eventually."

"You figure sometimes you need to put your hand on the wheel to turn it a little faster, Josh?"

"Goddamn right you do." Arms spread out from his body, he continued. "Look at this. How the hell I get here, huh?"

"It had to be done," Ingram pointed out. He knew why Nakano came to assume his current position. "You got responsibilities the rest of us ain't got, man."

"Didn't plan it that way. And I'm not so sure Strummer doesn't have a kid or two hidden away."

Ingram allowed this might be the case.

Nakano picked up his glass. "Duty and all that." They

each sipped their whiskey in silence. "Are we courting the ghosts of death? Didn't we see enough of that in the god-damn wars?" The former Army radioman got quiet.

"It's occurred to me a time or two." Despite knowing better, Ingram leaned over and poured another amount, less than before but enough to keep his buzz buzzing. He shook the bottle at Nakano, who held his glass out for another round. "But normally I don't have to deal with the grieving. You do."

"I put on a good show," Nakano said.

"If anything, I've tried to make peace with myself, getting a grip on the idea that death is a part of life."

"One giving way to the next," Nakano said, his voice barely audible, as if heard through the other side of a wall. He eyed his whiskey, which he held before him as if the liquid was truly an elixir from which knowledge could be obtained.

Ingram said, "Talk about what is, is, it's not like any of us is going to duck our turn when our time is up."

He glanced at a glass shelf to the left side of Nakano's desk. On this rested five differently designed urns for human ashes. Once upon a time he wouldn't have considered being cremated. A holdover from his childhood of infrequently attending church with his mother. Those old sisters stomp-ing and turning and twisting about in the aisles. They'd be in the thrall of the Holy Ghost, speaking in tongues as if their brains were invisibly wired to Martian language records by Berlitz. He supposed he'd been keeping his options open to be among the risen dead when the Rapture happened. But as Josh said, how did you cling to the paradise of the Great Beyond once you've seen what men could do to each other not in the heat of battle, but cold and calculating, like booby trapping a dead soldier's body so that when you went to get his dog tags, you were blown up?

What about his commie girlfriend? Ingram wondered, having more of his drink. Her an atheist who just knew dead was dead, no afterlife and no coming back as a cricket to be the best cricket you could be. What a comfort to be so certain.

"BROTHER REVEREND, you out of step," a slender man in his twenties shouted at Martin Luther King from the audience.

A woman in a fringed vest said, "Yeah, baby, this is about getting what's ours, not waiting for your pal Lyndon Baines to throw us another bone."

Anita Claire took this in from her position in the Mount Olive Redeemer church's all-purpose hall in the 10th District, which was Councilman Bradley's. King was among several sitting behind a portable table set up in front of the seated. He wiped a hand over his tired and worn face. This was not the first time since he'd returned to town to address the aftermath of the tumult in Watts that he'd been scolded by the residents in the press or one of these townhalls.

"My dear friends," King responded, "please give me the courtesy of hearing what I have to say. Just as I extend it to you. The Civil Rights Act is hardly a symbolic gesture of emptiness.

"More to the point," he continued over the din of steady grumbling, "we must use this time of violence and redirect our energies to moving forward, to materialize that which we have collectively fought so hard to make happen. We must move forward and not backward." He emphasized those words with several light chops of the side of his hand on the tabletop.

"Then tell Parker to stop calling us monkeys in a zoo," someone said. It had been widely reported that the Chief of Police had said those words regarding the rioters in Watts. The actual quote according to articles in the *Sentinel* and *Herald Examiner* was about rocks being thrown at his officers. "One person threw a rock and then, like monkeys in a zoo, others started throwing rocks."

"While you're at it," the slender man added, "tell them to get their boots off our necks or we gonna stomp on them."

Yells and applause rose, and Councilman Tom Bradley came to his full six-four height from behind the table, arms raised and hands gesturing. Claire noticed the sister and the Lutheran pastor who'd been at the memorial for Faraday Zinum sitting together in the audience. Dorrell Zinum and several other Disciples had entered the hall about a half hour ago and had taken up positions along the sidelines.

"Okay, folks, please, we're here to gather on-the-ground input and more than that formulate strategies to better our condition. We know you're frustrated. I'm frustrated," Bradley made another sweep of the room with his long arm. "All of us want redress to not only perceived injustices, but what has been documented in fact as to the unfairness we have suffered." He tapped his chest. "You know my story, as I know the stories, the journeys of every one of us here today from Texas, Louisiana . . . Alabama, for a better life. You also doggone know well we aren't giving you shuck and jive. We've come together today to redress and not simply spout pretty-sounding words."

This earned Bradley tepid claps. From where she stood in the back of the room, Claire watched several people turning to each other and conversing. His words had the impact of quieting the crowd some. Now Gus Hawkins spoke. He was a light-skinned Black man who was first elected to congress as an End Poverty in California candidate in the 1930s. His white colleagues were initially flummoxed that he sounded Black and talked about "us" in South Central.

In response to a question, Hawkins said, "I couldn't agree more, jobs and housing are irrevocably tied together. That's why I along with many others have been working to finally and fully overthrow these discriminatory housing covenants embodied in the likes of Proposition 14, a shameful unconstitutional law that passed last fall." The measure allowed property owners to openly discriminate in renting and selling.

"Passed by whitey," someone boomed to much laughter.

The morning wore on, marked by more discussion between the officials and the gathered.

"Here's a specific that you as our representatives can work on today," Dorrell Zinum said. "Have a sit-down with the cops to demand that they not to go crazy when we shut this city down for a one-day general strike, not only in memory of my murdered brother, but as a sign we are on the move and nothing's gonna hold us back." More applause and woops of joy went up. Bradley and King, sitting side by side, shared whispered words.

As of late, the Disciples for Community Defense had started to dress in recognizable attire, like the Nation of Islam members who were identifiable by their dark suits and

bow ties. Men and women wore dark blue jean jackets, slate
gray pants, black turtle necks and black work boots.

The gathered erupted. "General strike, general strike,
general strike."

Recollections of her and her sister's readings as teenagers
materialized in Claire's head. There had been less than a
handful of successful strikes of such size in the city. It had
taken a lot of effort and organizing to pull them off, like the
iron workers did in 1910. More than enthusiasm would have
to be utilized. And what would be the backlash if a strike
like that could be pulled off?

Again, Bradley signaled for quiet. "Let me say I will, post
this meeting, reach out to Chief Parker's office and demand
a sit down. Mind you, pulling off a general strike is monu-
mental, and that's not in our purview. But nonetheless, as
has been voiced today and at other community forums, police
relations with the negro community must be attended to.
For certain, more colored police officers need to be on the
force."

A round of boos echoed in the all-purpose room. Bradley
shook his head. Chants began again in support of a general
strike. Soon after, the hearing broke up and several members
of the press pushed in on King and the other speakers to get
their reactions. Conversely, Gerry Tackwood was talking
with members of the audience to record their take on the
proceedings.

"That could have gone better," Bradley said to Claire.
He'd re-established his normal placid expression. There was
sweat on his brow he dabbed off with a paper napkin.

"At least another riot didn't break out," she quipped.

Bradley surveyed the room as many people milled about.

In his even-tempered tone, he said, "Anita, you're my eyes and ears out here, so please do liaise with the good folks pushing for this shut down. Not trying to throw a monkey wrench in the works, peaceful protest is everyone's right. But this could lead to boycotts and who knows what all else."

"You're not asking me to keep a running tally of trouble-makers are you, Tom?"

His pencil-thin mustache might have twitched. "It takes one to know one, Miss Claire."

"Yes, sir."

Reverend King called him over to speak with a reporter from *Newsweek*.

"Have you been appointed the negro wrangler?" Tack-wood asked her with a smile.

"I know better than to answer that. Though it's not like Tom doesn't know about my past. When I first came onto his campaign a couple of years ago he showed me a file the Red Squad had on my parents."

"Huh? To show you what a decent guy he is, or was it a warning?"

"A little of both, I guess."

"Speaking of the cops, I'm pretty sure the Mexican-look-ing gentleman with the cookie duster over there is either a vice cop or a paid snitch for Parker's G-2." Parker was a decorated veteran of World War II. He liked to refer to the LAPD's intelligence gathering unit by the same designation the Army used for its intelligence division.

"How do you know that?"

"We've been tabulating various suspected undercover operatives, cross checking with real estate records, scuttle-butt and what have you. Initially it started because there was a homosexual writer for the paper, and he'd been compiling a file of his own, documenting busts of underground bars by undercover cops. Anyway, I'm sure I've seen that guy's picture as one of those."

"You plan to publish this?"

"That might bring way more heat than our little paper could handle. But I've also been trying to find out who heads up the intelligence squad. He would have to be a captain but there's several in Parker's inner circle."

"What about some buddy he was in the service with?" Claire questioned.

"That would make sense," Tackwood said. "They'd be loyal to each other and all that gung ho jive."

She further mused, "Or a detective he promoted for the job. A guy who'd done his dirt when he infiltrated a lefty organization back in the fifties."

"Yeah . . ." Tackwood agreed. "Pretty sure too, Parker is keeping files on politicians, heads of the assorted city departments and so on, like Stalin. The way Parker thinks, and I'm sure he gets buy-in from the business owners, he'd want to make sure he knows what the natives are up to. And set up the ones that can cause him trouble."

"You mean the Disciples?"

"They're up in his face and getting a lot of eager recruits coming through their doors," he pointed out.

Claire's stomach tightened. Memories of what her parents, allies and their friends had gone through when she was younger always caused her discomfort. How for various reasons relationships were destroyed when people who'd been there for each other over the years turned on each other. Or in some cases, pretend friends who'd gotten close, who you relied on, betrayed you because that was their job, to deliver you to the psychological guillotine, cutting you off from trust.

"You mention this to Dorell?"

"Sideways-like. When I interviewed her, I'd said how was she sure of who was who, that sort of thing. I was curious to see if they were aware that could happen."

"What did she say?"

"Said they've got a system."

"A rubber hose upside your head?"

Tackwood spread his hands. His eyes looked past her. "I see your boss is walking out. Let me see if I can get a quote from him for the Freep."

"Good luck with that. Send me your pictures from today of the one you suspect, okay? I'll try to look into him."

"Will do." Tackwood was already rushing over to the councilman.

After speaking to another staff member in attendance, Claire left the church, exiting onto Cochran Avenue. She had time before her next appointment as one of Bradley's field deputies, a meeting with the Greater West Adams Improvement Association, a grouping of Black and white residents and business owners. The topic was about a rise in prostitution in the neighborhood—due, apparently, to construction workers populating local watering holes in the area after dark. The terminus of Interstate 10, which stretched from Florida, would soon be complete. Locally, this part of the throughway was called the Santa Monica Freeway. The construction of the final leg, begun some eight years ago, had cut through the West Adams, after various properties were seized through eminent domain. Further west, where other colored folks and blue collar workers in the Pico area of the City of Santa Monica resided, had also been bulldozed over.

A job like hers required evening and weekend meetings, which for some put a strain on their love life or marriages. With Ingram, who at times kept his own odd hours, the two rolled with the inconsistent schedules, and as Claire had noticed, when they did have time together, they cherished those occasions. Back in her car, she drove toward Queen Anne Park, which wasn't too far away. This time of day what few children were here were infants and toddlers accompanied by mothers or babysitters. They squealed with pleasure on the swings and slides and in the sandbox. One kid, chunky but solid, stumbled through a knot of pigeons as they pecked the ground like a miniature Frankenstein. Disrupted, they flew up, whirling around him, darting into the air. He laughed with glee, sitting on his butt.

Amused, Claire watched him from a nearby bench, eating the sandwich she'd packed for lunch. Had Ingram looked like that when he was that age? If they had a child, would he look like that? Well, he'd be more golden hued. The idea scared and intrigued her. When she had finished her lunch, the sandwich, an apple and carrot sticks, she rose and threw the wax wrappings and paper bag away in a trash can. Rather than return to her car, she took her seat again on the bench. Weighing on her was her need to tell her boyfriend what she and her folks had been up to. Initially, when her mother had broached the subject of telling Ingram, she'd been resistant. But she also knew, as her mom had said, the longer she kept this to herself, the greater the fallout when Harry did find out.

"If anything, he'll probably be even more attracted to

you," she'd said the other day when they were in her father's granny apartment.

"Or be pissed off and dump me."

"Pretty sure Harry would understand your reason why you hadn't confided in him," her father had added. "And you can put it on us. We are justifiably paranoid about too many people being in on our secrets, given past consequences."

For two years, it had been Claire's notion that if she and her parents got busted, then Ingram wouldn't go down with them. "But now what with every damn cop on the force knowing who he is, they'd frame him anyway," she said.

"You're probably right, dear. But still, you can take the sting out by telling him we asked you to keep mum."

"A truth revealed with a lie attached," she'd observed.

"A little lie and a bigger truth," her mother had responded. "And anyway, we might need his help on the coded journal."

"You mean if Del can crack it?"

Her mother had momentarily seemed preoccupied then looked back at her. "That's exactly what I mean."

Refocused in the present, it was as if the sound of the children enjoying their playtime was reaching her through a wall of glass bricks. She felt the vibration of their presence as opposed to clarity in her ears.

Claire became cognizant of her breathing, visualizing the air as a light of indecipherable color or, more accurately, shifting colors. Her heart rate slowed and in her mind, she felt unmoored to the physical shell of her body. Her surroundings were available to her senses but she watched somewhat in a detached fashion, several children running and laughing after each other. They were moving like kids do, in no discernable patterns, circularly, serpentine and crisscrossing one another. She closed her eyes. In her inner vision, they were rollicking as if moving through deep snow.

Going inside, Claire concentrated on gathering her chi to inform her how best to tell Harry Ingram about her life as the Morning Bandit's henchwoman. It was as if she held aloft in her hand a multi-faceted spherical object so as to better examine its various sides, the probables of how Ingram might react to the news. Was determinism at play in our lives or were we truly free agents in what we did, unbeholden to the whims of fate?

"Want to share?"

Claire opened her eyes to a smiling face. The woman was about her age with dark hair and gray eyes. Claire found it ironic she was uncertain of this other woman's ethnicity—people were at times uncertain on what she was. She'd be asked, "Where are you from?" The woman was with the laughing boy who'd scattered the pigeons, who was colored. She was holding a smoldering marijuana cigarette.

"No thanks." She frowned.

"Don't worry, I don't get carried away and forget to take care of Billy. But a couple of puffs during the day helps keep me mellow, if you dig what I'm sayin."

The woman sounded Black but still Claire's hackles were now up. Paranoia or earned caution, given her fresh conversation with Tackwood? "I appreciate the offer, but I have to get back on the clock."

"Well," she said, eyes fixed on Claire, "maybe next time. We're here often."

"Okay." With that, Claire got up and walked to her car. Pulling out of the parking lot, when she righted her Valiant, she drove past a Starbrite Carpeting and Services panel van parked across the street from the park.

CHAPTER ELEVEN

The following morning, Ingram drove to the studio to do his interview. As he and Claire had discussed, the television appearance would help when it came time to try and sell his picture-book idea. After being let onto the KTTV lot, his name left at the guard gate, he parked and, per the directions the lovely-voiced Phyliss Lansdale had told him, entered the correct door. The Louis E. Lomax show ran ninety minutes and was on twice weekly. Ingram was to be on the first segment of the show. He found himself in a compact outer office, a Black woman no more than twenty-five behind the counter.

"Have a seat and I'll let Phyliss know you're here. Coffee or tea?"

"I'm fine, thank you." He sat as she spoke into an intercom. Among the framed pieces on the walls was a blow up of the cover of Lomax's book, *The Negro Revolt*. Another was a picture of the broadcaster and the assassinated Malcom X, killed earlier this year. Ingram was looking at the photo and reliving that day when the news broke about him being shot when a door to the inner suites opened and out stepped a six-foot-tall Black woman. He rose as she came over, offering her hand.

"Mr. Ingram. I'm Phyliss."

"Pleased to meet you." Phyliss was tall, dark-skinned and had an unlined, angular face. Her light-brown eyes seemed to have flakes of green in them. She wore what he'd learned from Claire was called sensible attire, adorned with a gold necklace and gold earrings, a bracelet and an ostentatious ring. Her skin tone offset by the gleaming metal was eye-catching.

"Come on back for makeup. I'll let Louis know you're here."

"For sure." He followed her inside, making sure to be cool and not stare at her backside, until they arrived at a doorless room.

"I'll leave you in Karla's capable hands and we'll fetch you in a few."

Nodding and smiling, he went into the makeup room as she strode off.

"Hello," Karla said. Surprisingly, she wasn't Black, but an older white woman with expertly coiffed gray hair and her own ornate gold ring. She indicated one of the black swivel chairs before a rectangular makeup mirror. On its vanity resided all sorts of powders and brushes. She clipped a satin cloth around his collar and went to work on him.

"That's some photo you took, Mr. Ingram."

"Sometimes I get lucky."

"Have them ofays been calling and harassing you?"

She said it so smoothly he had to refocus. "As you might expect."

"I heard that. Damn shame. Backward ass bastards." Her

fine-pointed brush paused next to his nose. "Excuse my French if you're religious."

"Not so much."

"I figured that was the case but you never know." She grinned and added, "Do one?"

He grinned too. "No, ma'am."

Soon she was done and as if she'd sent a telepathic message, less than thirty seconds later Lansdale appeared in the doorway to retrieve him.

"Thank you, darling," Lansdale said to Karla.

She did a small bow. "I live only to serve you, mistress."

"Um-hmm." She wagged an upright red-nailed finger at Ingram. "This way."

He said good-bye to Karla, who was lighting up a cigarette in a pearl inlay cigarette holder from another era. She waved at him as she began puffing away.

He followed Lansdale to the set. On a raised dais was a comfortable dark-colored club chair set at an angle to a three-legged wooden stool. Between the two seats was a microphone in a stand. A dull-colored curtain hung behind the dais. Strategically placed klieg lights lit the humble set.

"You take the padded chair, Harry."

Ingram did so. Two television cameras in different positions pointed at the set, each mounted on thick trunks that allowed them to be turned. A Black and a white cameraman stood behind their respective cameras. They had headphones on.

"Good to meet you, bother man."

Ingram looked over to see Lomax near him, having put a hand on his shoulder. He was a large-chested man in a gray suit with a white pocket square, black tie, starched white shirt and black glasses. He looked not so much like an incendiary journalist but a loan officer—albeit one with a hip outlook in those observing eyes. They shook hands.

"Let me palaver with my folks, then we'll get started. You parched, you want some water?"

Ingram could use a drink, aware his mouth was now dry. "That'd be great."

Lomax turned and called out, "Mark, can we get some agua for Mr. Ingram?"

"Coming right up, Louis," replied a voice from somewhere in the gloom beyond the set.

A plastic water pitcher and glass were placed on the end table by a slim Mexican American in white jeans with longish black hair.

"There you go, my man."

He thanked him as Mark withdrew, looking and sounding like a denizen of Venice to Ingram. Lomax returned, smoking a cigarette, a sheaf of yellow-colored papers in his hand. There were typed pages and handwritten ones as well.

"We go live in two minutes. Phyliss went over broadly what my questions would cover, yeah?"

"She did when we talked earlier today."

"I understand you served in Korea."

"Yeah."

"That where you traded in shooting with a rifle to doing it with a camera?"

Ingram cocked his head slightly. "Something like that. There was this cat from *Look* magazine covering us and damned if he didn't catch a bullet. Milo Costas was his name. When I got back stateside, I looked up his sister and offered to send her his camera." His face went blank. The memory hitting him harder than it had in some time. "We got to talking on the phone and it came out I'd been using the camera. She told me that was the best way to honor her brother. To keep using it with her blessing."

Lomax nodded his head sympathetically. "Man, that's great. I'll try to work that in if that's okay with you?"

"Sure." He hoped he wouldn't tear up if he got to tell the story on air.

"Thirty seconds, Louis," Mark called out.

"Thanks, daddy-O," he replied. Lomax walked away again to stub out his cigarette in a clear glass ashtray just out of the line of sight of the cameras. He then picked up a lapel microphone and attached that in place. The microphone was connected to a long insulated wire and he returned to perch on the stool, still holding his papers. He faced forward as he noted a silent countdown from Lansdale on her hand, who then pointed at him to begin.

"Good afternoon, my fellow citizens," Lomax said into one of the cameras. "The fires have been extinguished, the glass swept up and already Governor Brown has appointed his blue ribbon commission to ascertain the cause of the riot that lasted six days, property damage that's still being tallied and most significantly, the loss of lives . . . notably negro lives being the majority of the dead. While at least we have an effort from Sacramento to explore a way forward, from some quarters—and I'm looking at you in particular, Mayor Yorty—you hear the same old refrain, it's communists and outside agitators whipping up the minorities. That negros are anti-police. Well, today we're going to put those notions and their ilk under the microscope if you will, as our humble program has several guests lined up to talk about what so recently went down in our fair city."

Lomax paused to look down at his notes. He shifted on the stool, putting one foot on a rung. Ingram noticed his tasseled Italian loafers. "We'll have on a little later a representative from the W. E. B. Du Bois Club, a spokesperson from John Gibson's office, the councilman who represents the 15th District that includes Watts, and a surprise guest— one that's gonna blow your mind, I hasten to add." He turned toward Ingram, gesturing at him with the papers in his hand. "But right off the bat we're going to begin with a man who was on the ground, in the trenches as the happenin' happened. Harry Ingram is a name probably known to some of you, he's a local photo-journalist in the vein of Gordon Parks. Harry's work has been in this city's vibrant colored and white press, his images of the riots, if you will, also seen recently on Channel 5 and in the past nationally in *Ebony*, isn't that right, Harry?"

"One time," Ingram stressed, holding up his index finger.

Turning back face-front, a smiling Lomax continued. "But in particular, Mr. Ingram is here today because his now famous—or maybe it's infamous to some, like the authorities—photo of the demise of community leader Faraday Zinum by members of the Los Angeles Police Department has encapsulated in stark black and white what many of us, the so-called negro in America, has been campaigning about for years seeking redress. No," he said leaning forward, "we are not anti-police, we are, though, anti the police's abusive and dare I say murderous tactics in our neighborhoods. And yes, this show reached out to Chief Parker's office for their interpretation of this incident, but we were roundly rebuffed."

Swiveling back to look at Ingram again, he asked, "So, Harry, tell us what brought you out that day and what led up to the act you so boldly captured on film."

He'd prepared a flip answer, all about the need to document what the white press would miss. Sure, that was part of what brought him out then, but it wasn't the whole answer. "Louis, I owe it to the reporter whose camera I took it upon myself to inherit during the Korean War when he got killed covering us dogfaces. Milo Costas was his name and it wasn't like we were fast friends, nothing like that. But when it came down to it, when the action was hot, he didn't flinch so I can't either."

The segment lasted for nearly half an hour including breaks for commercials. When they were done, another set of commercials came on and Lomax got off the stool, arching his back and working his shoulders.

"Don't you find sitting like that uncomfortable?" Ingram asked.

Lomax had removed his glasses and was cleaning them with his handkerchief. "I do, and sometimes use a chair like yours." He put his glasses back on. "But I find when I'm doing a subject matter I really want to dig into like today's, being slightly discomforted seems to give me a sharper mental edge."

"Thanks for having me on."

"You keep doing what you're doing, Harry."

"You too, man."

"We'll get this bus out of second gear one damn day."

They shook hands again. When Lomax walked off to do his next interview, Venice Mark was at his side.

"This way, Mr. Ingram." The young assistant walked him

down a different path than the one he'd used to enter the
studio. "The surprise guest entered the building and will be
in makeup soon. Only a few get to see him without his mask
being put on."

"Why's that?"

Mark whispered, "He's LAPD, a negro gentleman who
patrols just outside of Watts."

"You mean he's still on the force?"

"That's correct, and he's going to speak out on not only
the riots but what it's like to be a minority cop." They were
snaking their way through gloomy hallways and came to a
brightly lit area where table saws and the like were being
used. Hammering and the assembly of several sets was going
on as Mark guided Ingram past the workers to a side door
with a push bar. He opened this and held it for Ingram.

"I dug what you laid down today, Mr. Ingram. I've read
a couple of your articles, you know."

"You mean in the Freep?"

"Yes, sir. Been thinking on a publication like that for the
gente. It's a new day for brown folks too, baby."

"Righteous."

They slapped five and Ingram stepped out fully in the
sunshine. Making his way back to his car, he felt elated from
his conversating with Lomax. He hadn't mentioned he'd lost
the camera in Watts and how for damn sure he missed his
Speed Graphic. Ingram realized he deliberately hadn't been
focusing on finding it so as not to be disappointed. Here he
was, looking for a missing man, and certainly a human
meant more than any object, but he was emotionally attached
to the camera while he remained detached about finding
Tolbert. But wasn't that how a detective was supposed to be?

Key in the lock of his car, Ingram considered, did that kind of mindset make him a dispassionate professional or a cold-blooded motherlover? Maybe, he concluded, getting behind the wheel, you can be both.

ENERGIZED FROM the interview and hungry, Ingram made it over to one of his favorite eateries, the Detour diner, which had come through the riots intact. Unless he was with Claire or someone else, he normally sat at the counter and did so today. Winnie McClure, co-owner of the establishment, wasn't around. Janet Burnham was behind the counter.

"How it going, Harry?"

"Not bad, you?" The waitress was a slim woman with high cheekbones and elliptically shaped eyes. Burnham was a few years older than Ingram.

"Trying to make my way." She reached below the counter, then put a paper napkin and utensils on it before him. "What's it going to be today?"

"Liver and onions and a lemonade."

"That comes with green beans," she said. Burnham made the notations on the top sheet of her order pad and tucked the pencil away in the pocket of her apron. She fetched a pitcher of water from where it rested under the order window and poured him a glass. She also clipped his meal ticket in place for one of the two cooks, then turned back to him.

"You get around, Harry. I saw your pictures in the paper from that young man's memorial. What you think about this general strike talk?"

"How'd you hear about that?" Claire had told him this had been chanted at the town hall she'd attended.

"I'm a wage slave, ain't I?"

"Damn, Janet, you better not let on to Winnie you been reading bootleg paperbacks by Karl Marx." He visualized the ones on his old lady's shelf.

"I have no idea who that is," she said seriously. "But we had us a lively discussion the other night with somebody from those Disciples for Defense or whatever those rabble rousers are calling themselves."

Then it clicked into place as Ingram remembered she was on a bowling team. "You mean over at the Holiday Bowl?"

"That's right. Well, what do you figure?"

"Can't say it's been much on my mind." He told her how he'd first heard about the call for the mass action, a term he'd learned from Anita Claire. "Sounded like it was people getting themselves excited, but there wouldn't be follow through. Like the usual."

She regarded him and said, "The riot was a sign these aren't usual times. Computers doing math, polio vaccines on sugar cubes. Rockets trying to get to the moon. Time to aim high it seems to me."

Ingram said, "It would take thousands of people, Janet. Bus drivers, handymen, nurses, all that."

"That's a lot of colored folks in them people, you know," she said.

"And take a lot of organizing," he said, using another term he'd come to understand.

"Okay, sure," she went on, "probably not like the March on Washington, but still. This guy Chet had us convinced a sea of Black faces could fill the streets in Watts. Carrying picket signs and speakers, real types who work with their hands, not figureheads like Dr. King, though God bless him for what he's done. Demanding fair hiring in jobs and putting a spotlight on the police. He pointed out if people like me talk to my circle of friends and fellow workers, then they talk to who they know, the idea spreads."

"You sure you're not in cahoots with Fidel Castro?" Ingram cracked. He noted the Chet she mentioned must be the lefty buddy of the missing Mose Tolbert.

"I know who that one is. But look here, Dick Gregory, it's time to get with the program."

"Hey, Janet, maybe you negro agitators could discuss your plans to take down the white man later and right now give me a refill, huh?" The older man who spoke held aloft his coffee cup, jiggling it.

"Hush up, Roger. Flapping your gums might loosen your dentures." Roger Kirk was a retired city garbage collector and a regular at the diner. She started toward him and said to Ingram, "It's about us having solidarity in a time like this. Right, Harry?"

"Yes, ma'am."

"You gonna be covering it, aren't you?"

"Oh, yes."

CHET HORNE let the bowling ball go just as his arm completed its downward arc, at a slight angle to his leaning body. The ball rotated as it whooshed along the lane, canting slightly to the right nearing the pins. All but two went down when the ball struck. The remaining pins stood next to each other.

"Man, that's something I wouldn't know about," Horne said as he picked up his ball from the return rack. "Anything funny about the money is not my department, brother."

They were in the Holiday Bowl on a Wednesday night.

Several of the lanes were occupied. Ingram sat with a beer and a half-finished hot dog with potato chips on a paper plate. He had to put on bowling shoes like Horne and everyone else, but had no intention of bowling. He'd bowled on leave in the service and was devastated to discover there was more involved than simply rolling a damn ball made of clay.

"You ever been to the Emerald Room with Mose?"

"Sure, a couple of times," Chet answered. Holding the ball just below his eyes, he sighted down the lane and then, assuming his form again, let the ball loose. It tore down the lane, a replay of Horne's previous roll. This time, the ball veered left just at the right moment, striking one of the remaining pins. In turn that pin knocked the other one over too.

Ingram nodded in appreciation of the man's skill. Horne was captain of the bowling team and this was his solo practice session before his team's game next week. Members of the Mighty Strykers represented several businesses, including Restoration Building Supply. Ingram hadn't told Horne about finding the tags for the fur coats. What he'd asked him initially was did he know if Tolbert had ever gotten a loan from any rough types.

"You saying Mose got money from that guy?" Horne sat in the plastic molded chair next to Ingram and had a sip of his water.

"Have you meet that gee, Rickler?" Two lanes over, two Japanese women were bowling and laughing and talking in Japanese.

"I remember seeing him there walking around, glad-handin' and so forth, making sure everybody was happy losing their money." He smiled at that. "But no, he wouldn't know me to say boo to."

"I know he knows Miss Betty," Chet added. "But rich white folks always know each other don't they? Now I ain't been there when she was there if that's what you want to know."

Ingram nodded.

"Look, man, believe me when I tell you I'm grateful to be punching a clock at Restoration. 'Cause different than other slaves I've had working for them crackers, this here situation has worked out better than I could have imagined. And I goddamn know you know what I'm talking about. So yeah, me and Mose get along fine. But do I think that one day I might own a piece of that cherry cream pie?" He paused, his own statement having surprised him.

"It could happen, Chet."

"Maybe when we get flying cars."

"From what I understand about Mose, he might be open to it."

"That the real reason Miss Betty sent you around, Harry? Maybe she does know what happened to Mose and he did run off with some big titty blonde and ain't come up for air yet. Your real job is to see if us coloreds are looking to take over. Eyes getting too big for our stomachs as the old timers used to say."

"I've been accused of a lot of things, but don't want hand-kerchief head as one of them," Ingram replied.

"For sure, soul brother."

Sipping his drink, Ingram made a pointed remark. "You all must be talking, though, what's going to happen if Mose doesn't show up."

Horne stood up. "Sure, there's been talk, worried talk if I'm being honest. Naturally we're wondering what's going to happen and if some Caucasian takes over is not, you know, of a mind like Mose, then what? But look here, don't you figure Miss Arlene might be part of this here equation you trying to put together in your head?" He turned to resume bowling.

Ingram took another bite of his now cold hot dog, chewing and mulling over what Horne suggested. Horne bowled several more sets, including three strikes in a row. When he sat back down, Ingram continued, "She knows the numbers but she don't know how to palaver with customers like you. She don't know the trade."

"But that works, 'cause some of them gray boys I got to deal with in those peckerwood places like South Gate tolerate me since they know I represent Mose. What they gonna say if Mose really isn't around? Or Miss Betty and her investor pals throw in the towel and sell off the business to the highest bidder?"

"That could happen too," Ingram conceded. He'd called Doris Letrec, the office manager of Galton, the process server company he did work for. She was well-versed in legalese and he'd asked her how long did a person have to remain missing before they were declared dead, at least in California.

"Presumed dead is the term," she'd said. "And it's five years. But," she'd continued, "there could be any number of clauses in an agreement your missing man has with this woman who hired you and her fellow investors. He doesn't own the assets outright, does he? That is, is he paying them back a loan on a monthly basis and they would have to seize the goods?"

"Don't know," he'd said.

"You might want to look into that."

In the bowling alley, Ingram watched Horne for nearly another hour before he was done, intermittently asking him a few more questions about Tolbert but learning nothing else of use to his search. He did tell him that the employees were looking to meet in the next two weeks if Tolbert was still missing.

"Figure to put a letter together for Betty and the rest?" Ingram asked.

"Good idea," Horne said, wiping a thin sheet of sweat from his face with a paper napkin.

Outside, the two said their good-byes and Ingram stood there for a moment, taking a black cigar out of his pocket and biting off the end, lit it. Off to his left he heard a sound and turned his head. The two woman who'd been bowling together were walking around the corner of the building on the coffee shop side. They had their arms around each other and it was obvious that they hadn't noticed Ingram some yards away. The two paused by the side of a two-toned Rambler. One put her arms around the other's neck and they kissed passionately. Ingram turned away and was glad he didn't have to disturb them by walking past, as his car was parked on Crenshaw. He puffed away cheerily as he drove off, imaging what the two women would be doing later. Ingram toyed with the idea of tackling writing a paperback with the title *Bowling Alley Lesbians*. Hell, it might be a runaway hit.

Driving and smoking, the window on the driver's side cracked to let out the fumes, he wondered if Anita had paperbacks of those type of women with women novels among her collection. He hadn't noticed any but it wasn't as if he'd memorized the titles, though their lurid covers always made an impression. Ingram would damn sure remember a steamy primary colors illustrated romp with a shapely woman undressing another shapely woman.

Also, Anita traded books with her friend Judy Berkson. A side notion occurred to him; he hadn't seen Berkson in the company of a man when she'd been over to their house, and she was a frequent visitor. Had they talked about anyone she might be seeing? He couldn't remember. Berkson wasn't a bad-looking chick, and what if, he lustfully speculated, she was secretly a model for women loving women covers?

Distracted, Ingram had to hastily apply the brakes so as not to plow through a red light. Maybe he should pull over to a gas station and splash some cold water on his face in their bathroom. The light turned green, and Ingram accelerated, managing to tuck his voyeuristic longings away, at least enough to safely navigate the city streets. When he got home, he didn't share his lascivious imaginings with Anita Claire. She was sitting on the ell of the couch, her legs tucked under her, sipping coffee and reading a book.

"Hey, sweetie," she said, not looking around when he came through the front door.

"Hey yourself." He was behind her, looking down at the book, scanning the words for a moment. "You're really getting into this." It was another book on philosophy.

"Could be it's just a fad." She looked up at him and reaching up, put a hand around his neck to pull his face closer. They kissed.

"I'm going to have something a little stronger."

"Make me one too," she said, stretching.

At the rollaway bar he poured vodka and tonic into two

slim cylindrical glasses. Above this on the wall was a poster mounted on stiff backing. It was a close-up photo of hands holding a sax, the long fingers working the keys. While the musician's face was intentionally out of focus in the background, Ingram knew it was Coleman Hawkins. Superimposed over part of the image were the words, "Jazz speaks for life. The Blues tell the story of life's difficulties . . ." The quote and the shot were from last year's Berlin Jazz Festival. The words were from the speech Martin Luther King had given at the event.

He left the glasses on the cart and in the kitchen removed one of the two aluminum ice trays from the freezer and released the frozen cubes. He put some of these in a small bowl and returned the tray to the freezer. As he set the divider in the sink, another fantasy whirled to life in his head.

Playboy Ingram was dressed in a silk smoking jacket and had a pipe sticking out of the side of his mouth. Not that beat up thing Wes Crossman smoked, but a sleek model as befitting a with-it bachelor like him. In the next room not only did his lady love hunger for his presence, but the two other women from the bowling alley were there as well. They wanted to experiment with the both of them all night long. This lustful male indulgence of course called for the three women to be dressed in short robes and lingerie. He laughed out loud, shaking his head back to reality.

"What's so funny?" Claire asked from the other room.

"I realize I'm living the *Dapper* life. Two-gun private eye by day, lady's man by night."

"Yeah, you are."

He returned to the living room. He tinkled ice into the

glasses and handed one to Claire, who'd put the book aside. As was their custom, he removed his shoes and sat next to her on the couch. They clinked glasses and each sampled their cocktail.

Setting his glass onto the coffee table, Ingram said, "How was your day, darling?"

She told him about it, including the encounter with the woman at the park.

"Maybe she was a beatnik," he offered.

"I don't know, there was something off about her. Too friendly."

"Trying to set you up for a bust?" Flashing back to the two in the Holliday Bowl parking lot, he added, "Or trying to pick you up."

"Hmmm," she considered. "Your turn."

He told her, and when he'd finished his recap, he stretched. "Feel like eating out tonight?"

"Where?"

"Lim Fu's?"

"Part of your man-about-town lifestyle, huh?"

"You damn right."

They walked to the restaurant and were able to get a booth. Its dark wood and red velvet wall and sounds of ice tinkling in patron's cocktail glasses made for a sultry cocoon against the mundane beyond. Having hot tea and their appetizer of fried shrimp, Ingram said, cognizant to maintain a conversational tone, "I've been rolling this over, but seems I should take a look inside Tolbert's house."

"You told me Betty doesn't have a key."

"I did say that." He dipped his shrimp by the tail into some hot mustard.

From the look on her face, it took her a moment to absorb the import of what he was saying. "Oh, Harry, is the risk worth what you might find . . . if anything, which is more than likely the result."

"There's a reason the cops always search a person's place. They haven't in this case, according to Betty."

"Doesn't mean they haven't and didn't tell her," Claire said.

"Good point. Though why wouldn't they tell her? Worried he might get in touch with her, and she tells him they did?"

"Like they want to catch him?" she said.

"When Ben was killed, I found useful information in his room. And nobody let me into his either."

"Find out more about him and Rickler?"

"Don't know until, you know."

"Harry, this is different. Ben was a jazz musician living among the natives, no better than Johnny Otis as far as the police were concerned. That's what you gonna tell them when they snatch you off to jail? 'Cause what if the cops are watching his place?"

"When I was over there, I didn't spot anybody staking out his pad."

"Isn't that the idea, you don't stick out?"

"I think I'm hipper to their ways than the average cat. But this is a chancy move." Ingram took another swallow of his drink. He said slowly, "What if you were my lookout?"

She chucked her hand under his chin. "Silly boy, now you're getting somewhere."

"It'd be better if we did it in the day."

"Not in the dead of night, with less eyes on us?"

"If I'm prowling through the house at night, someone might see my flashlight shine from underneath a shade. Also, with the daytime, the better the odds are his neighbors are at work."

She considered this for a moment and said, "As robbers say, sounds like you already cased the joint."

"I did," he admitted. "He lives in View Park."

She frowned. "From what you said about his forward thinking in his business, funny he would live in an area that fought to keep itself white."

"Betty told me he inherited the house from an aunt who was ailing. He took care of her as her only family out here. She didn't have any children of her own, so he was the golden-haired child who took her to her doctor's appointments and what have you. From what she says, he was one of the whites who wouldn't sign a petition that got passed around to keep a colored doctor and his family out. Apparently he argued with his neighbors for being behind the times. At one point 'Nigger Lover' was spray painted on his garage door for his efforts."

"A few more of us have moved in there, Harry. I know a family who's migrated from West Adams. You don't think one of his resentful neighbors bashed in his head and he's lying in his house on the shag carpet?"

He held his hands apart. "Only one way to find out."

She said, "Won't we be noticed?"

"You'll be in the car and—"

"Nix on that," she interrupted. "I'm in all the way."

"Who's going to keep lookout?"

A small smile on her face, she said, "Judy can."

"She works during the day. What makes you think she'll

go along with this?" Berkson had a job in a tile factory in Huntington Park.

"I know her. She's a solid sender, as they used to say. I also know she's got plenty of sick days piled up thanks to her union contract."

Ingram folded his arms, considering the offer. "Okay, but she's gotta be cool."

"The coolest. That girl has done some shit."

Lesbian cover model came to mind as well as the inescapable conclusion that some of the stuff Berkson had been up to must have included Anita. Vodka tonic at his mouth, he remarked, "Gotta admit her being white is less likely to call attention. I mean, in the right light them hillbillies in the hills might think you was one of them, but you know."

"Smart ass."

"You think she could do this on Thursday? Say at ten in the morning? I've got a few things I need to buy tomorrow, including gloves we best be wearing."

"I'll call her right now." She got up and went to the pay phone inside the restaurant in the alcove on the way to the bathrooms. Claire pushed in the door and sat inside, closing it again so as not to be overheard by a passerby. She dialed her friend and after pleasantries asked her bluntly, "Judy, you up for a little crime?"

She listened to her answer, grinning broadly. "Yeah, me and the old man are gonna be in on this," she joyously told her. "Like Bonnie and Clyde." Another pause as Berkson replied and then Claire answered, "Who you tellin'?" She guffawed loudly and after saying good-bye, returned to the booth. Their main courses had been served.

Ingram was eating and making a list of items. A melancholy descended.

"What?" she said, noticing.

"The stuff we'll need," he began, "I'd have gone over to Shop Rite to get the items."

"You and Shoals haven't spoken to one another since then."

"Nope." He resumed making his list and forking in a heaping of chicken chow mein.

"Judy'll be at the house nine-thirty bright and early on D-Day, sarge. Are we going to use disguises?"

"Sounds like a good idea," he said. "What are you thinking?"

"We're going to have tools with us, right?"

"And we don't try and hide that."

"Exactly."

"We'll need to get some different license plates. I'll steal them before light on Thursday."

Claire cocked her head at him and said, "You have a devious mind, Mr. Ingram." She winked at him across the table and ate with pleasure.

Ingram gave her a wary look. Was she enjoying the idea of committing burglary too damn much he wondered, leaving the rest of his chow mein untouched.

CHAPTER TWELVE

The morning they broke into the missing Moses Tolbert's home, they took two vehicles to the address in the low hills of View Park—less than six miles from their house. The place was up a winding street ending in a cul-de-sac. Ingram and Claire arrived in a pick-up truck borrowed through Edwards. Ingram parked it in the driveway. Berkson arrived in a convertible two-tone DeSoto, the top up, and parked two houses away, her car pointed toward the only way on or off the street. In a scarf and sunglasses, she sat behind the steering wheel, pretending to be regarding a street map she'd unfolded.

Tolbert's house was a one-story stucco home with a front bay window partially obscured by an impressive grouping of poinsettias. Compared to some of his neighbors, whose homes were Spanish Colonial Revival, a few spanning two lots with balconies on the second-stories and pools out back, his was humble but well-cared for. The paint still had its luster and there were no cracks in the outer walls. Apparently the gardener had still been caring for the lawn.

"This way," Ingram said, gently guiding Anita by the elbow toward the garage.

The couple were dressed in work clothes, worn khakis and light blue cotton shirts, Ingram carrying a toolbox. Claire wore a floppy hat on her head, her hair bunched up inside of it. She hadn't put on earrings. But even in these loose unflattering clothes, Ingram was certain even a casual observer could see she was a woman. The house was on a slant and constructed in such a way that the living room was over the two-car garage which was accessible by a driveway. There was a padlock securing this. He asked Claire to stand so as to partially block him from view while he used a pair of bolt cutters to sever the padlock's loop. He put the ruined lock in the toolbox and swung the garage door upward.

Ingram flicked on the light switch. As expected, there was no car in here, though there was an ink blot of an oil stain on the dusty concrete indicating where Tolbert's car would normally be parked. Where a second car might be parked was a woodworking workshop. There was a bandsaw and several pieces of furniture in stages of either being repaired or fashioned from the ground up. Ingram noticed back issues of *Look* magazine stacked on a work bench.

"Lower it?" Claire asked, her hand grabbing the small length of rope attached to the garage door handle.

Ingram nodded in the affirmative. Past a water heater, he stood toward the rear of the garage at a hollow-core door leading into the house. The door was locked but he knocked it loose with a ballpeen-hammer after one blow.

She came over next to him, indicating the door. "When you checked out the house before, you figured this would be the way in."

Ingram put the hammer back in the toolbox. "I looked up the floorplans downtown, too."

"Aren't you the clever lad." Claire pulled him close and reached a hand down the front of his pants, taking a hold of his stiffening member. "I should give you a reward."

"You should, but we better keep our mind on business."

"Spoilsport."

"One mission at a time, soldier."

They kissed and she reluctantly let him go. Ingram took a moment to clear his head, then removed the gloves he'd tucked in his rear pocket. He put them on, as did Claire. They entered the kitchen. The air inside was still, a mustiness to the place from it being closed up going on three weeks. A used dish, saucer, coffee cup and utensils were in the sink. A thin layer of grease had congealed in a skillet on the stove. No trace odors from whatever had been fried could be detected. Somewhere deeper into the house, a clock ticked. Clearly there had been no recent human occupants in here.

Ingram began looking through the drawers. He found a few coasters with the Emerald Room's name on it.

"I'll check the mail," Claire said.

"Okay."

The living room was a step-down off a circular foyer. Mail was dropped into a receiving box attached to the wall beside the front door. Claire lifted a latticed metal gate to retrieve some of the mail. The rest had overflowed out of the receptacle and was spread across the pavers. She gathered all of this and went into the living room, sat down and looked through what she had. There was a gas bill and one for the water and power. She set these aside and continued to glance through the letters and so on. Ingram joined her.

"Find anything personal?" They'd previously discussed

looking to find a handwritten letter written to Tolbert maybe from a lady friend or any type of friend who might be a lead to where he was.

"Doesn't look like," she said. "Mostly it's other business mailers like a new kind of forklift or wholesale prices on florescent bulbs. These must be duplicates of what comes in at Restoration." She went silent as she continued sifting through her pile, which included *Jet* magazine.

"Hold up, check this out." She held up an invitation-sized envelope addressed in feminine script. It was addressed to Tolbert but no return address. The postmark was August thirteenth, the second day of the riots.

"We've already committed burglary, open it," Ingram suggested.

Claire did. Inside was a piece of paper torn from a spiral-bound notepad folded in half. She opened it up to reveal a brief note thanking Tolbert for his donation to the cause. It was signed "Dorrell."

"That's consistent with what we know about him," she said as she refolded the note and put it back in the envelope. When Ingram didn't respond, she looked up at him from where she sat in a padded chair. He was looking at a painting over the fireplace.

"What?"

He pointed at the modernistic piece. "Pretty sure that's recently done."

"You mean because of that building on fire in it?"

He stepped over to the painting. "I saw it being painted during the riots."

Claire joined him to gaze up at the artwork. It was in oils and contained realistically rendered sections along with fantastical imagery such as the floating eye with its energy crackles that Ingram recognized. There were depictions of people, some it seemed protesting, and among the imagery was a riveting depiction of a policeman siccing a German shepherd on two young Black men, the dog straining its leash as it attacked.

Ingram stepped closer. The over-large teeth in the snarling animal had words painted on them in red such as CONTROL and JAIL. Swiveling his head slightly, he said, "I'm pretty sure the building on fire is 77th Station." He turned to grin at her, "Your kind of art, huh?"

"Don't you forget it, baby." She leaned her head forward. "Can you make out the signature?"

"Deebeck," I think. "But that cat I saw painting this wasn't Dutch."

"Massa could have been," she said seriously.

Ingram displayed a wan smile. He retrieved a small camera he'd brought along from the toolbox and began taking snaps of the painting. "This has gotta mean Tolbert knows this dude. Unless he was passing by later like I did and had to buy this."

"And they'd probably seen each other on the thirteenth, if not later."

"Now, Betty says Tolbert disappeared during the riots."

"You think this painter might know where he is?"

"Looks like I should ask him, if I can find him."

Claire said, "Just to be thorough, we should check out the bedroom."

"Yes, ma'am."

There were several more pieces of art in the bedroom, including three carved masks along a wall and another painting by Deebeck. This one was a portrait of a dark-skinned Black woman with regal features.

"Maybe he's his patron," Claire observed.

Ingram was standing behind her and began nuzzling her neck. He gently moved a hand onto one of her breasts. She put her hand over his, moaning slightly as he pressed against her.

"If you're starting something, Mr. Ingram, you better damn sure finish it."

"I think we've got time."

As they shuffled toward the bed she said, "Should I tell Judy to go?"

He was about to answer but was cut off by two short bursts of a car horn—Berkson's signal for them to be on alert.

"So much for that." Claire broke away and walked fast along the short hallway. Ingram followed. Before they could look outside there was a knock at the door. Momentarily the two went still, looking at each other. He was pretty sure it wasn't Berkson or the police as they wouldn't knock.

"We better answer it," Ingram said and strode to the door and opened it wide. An older man and woman, both white, were standing there. They both wore glasses and the man held a shotgun crossways over his torso.

"What are you doing here?" the woman demanded.

"We were sent over by the service," Ingram answered calmly. Idly, he wondered when the gun had last been fired.

"Andrew and I saw you two park in Tolbert's driveway, and once we could see who you were, we discussed what to do. I wanted to call the police, but he said, well, maybe that wasn't necessary."

"Him being how he is with you people," Andrew added.

He glared at Ingram and looked past him at Claire, muttering, "Told her you was a woman."

"But we're both in civil defense and praying on it, figured we should make sure," the woman continued. She had gray curly hair and her glasses had a golden chain attached to the stems. "You two were hired to do some work in his house, is that it?"

"That's right," Claire said at Ingram's shoulder.

"What kind of work? He hired you directly, did he?"

"Retiling and patching up a few water spots," Ingram answered.

"Yeah?" Andrew said. "Show us, right, Deb?"

"Right," Deb agreed.

"What's the problem here?"

Husband and wife turned to see Judy Berkson walking up. She'd removed her scarf, combed her hair and was taking off the sunglasses as she approached.

"Who are you?" Deb asked.

"Our boss," Claire answered smoothly. "She's a manager of the service."

"That's right," Berkson agreed, falling into the role.

"You have a card?" Andrew had turned toward her, the shotgun still held at the ready.

"Sure," Berkson said.

Ingram and Claire remained blank faced but then showed surprise at the derringer Berkson produced from her purse. Acting quickly, Ingram snatched the shotgun from Andrew's hand.

Berkson jerked the derringer toward the doorframe. "Get inside and keep your yap shut unless you want to catch a bullet."

The open-mouthed couple complied. The door closed on them.

"What do you intend to do with us?" Deb said.

"Let's go to the bedroom," Ingram suggested.

"You heard the man," Berkson said.

Together they went into the other room. Ingram pointed at the closet. "Get in there and don't come out for half an hour. Our accomplice is watching the house."

Deb regarded Berkson. "Imagine a wholesome-looking young woman like yourself in league with these two devils."

Berkson replied, "Think about what we're up to after-hours."

Deb gasped.

"What a friend we have in Jesus . . ." Andrew began singing. He had a pleasing voice.

". . . All our sins and griefs to bear . . ." Deb joined in.

"In you go," Claire said, clearly trying not to laugh.

They went into the closet holding each other. She closed the door on them as the two continued to sing the old hymn. Ingram lodged a chair's back under the knob and the three quit the bedroom.

"Will they be able to get out?" Berkson said. "They're pains in the asses but still I don't want them to starve."

"Some Ma Barker you are," Ingram sighed. He went back into the bedroom and quietly removed the chair. He could now hear them in prayer on the other side of the door. He'd put the shotgun aside in here. He picked it up, cracked the barrel open and removed the buckshot shells. He considered sticking them in his pocket but settled on putting them in a little round trash can in the corner. On top of the pile was an old newspaper and other crumpled-up pieces of paper. Ingram reached below this so the man wouldn't spot the shells and encountered a solid object. He took the paper away to look at what he'd encountered. Then, he put the shells on the bottom of the can and put the papers back on top. Ingram crept out, returning to the living room.

"Look at this." He showed what he found to Claire and Berkson. It was metal, cylindrical, and had a mesh circle in one part and wires trailing from it. The two women shared a knowing look.

"That's a listening device," Claire said. "Is it transmitting?"

"Don't they have to be plugged in, wired to the electricity? Look at these loose wires."

"Yeah, but there's been all kinds of advances with transistors, Harry. Satellites, dry cell batteries and whatnot." She picked it up and gingerly examined the thing. "How'd you find it?"

He told her.

"Where did Tolbert get it?" Berkson said.

"Good question."

Claire said, "Is he snooping on his employees?"

"Or being snooped on?" Ingram countered.

Reflecting on her parents' experiences, she said, "You think the phone is wiretapped?"

"Good question."

He followed her to the phone and she picked up the handset, listening. She cradled it again. "Didn't hear no clicks."

"Like you said, there's been all kind of advances. Maybe them taps is silent these days."

Ingram grinned as the ever-cautious Anita wiped non-existent fingerprints off the phone with her gloved hand.

"Guess we go out the front," she declared.

"We should make it look good in case anybody else is curious."

As Ingram had suggested, when they exited Tolbert's house, Berkson resumed her role as the manager for the unspecified service.

"Get on over to those apartments on Avalon, would you?"

"Yes, ma'am," Claire said as she got back in the pick-up. Berkson returned to her car. Soon Claire and Ingram were driving away on the street, passing a woman on her porch tending to several potted plants on her stoop. She looked up at them as they went past, descending the hilly street.

Back at their home in the flats of the Crenshaw district, the three sat around the glass patio table in the back yard.

"Here's to close calls," Berkson toasted, holding her half glass of beer aloft.

"Salud." Claire clinked her portion of the beer she'd shared with her friend against Berkson's glass and Ingram's bottle of Eastside Old Tap. Ingram had also set out a bowl of potato chips. He had placed the listening device next to the bowl.

"You always carry that pop gun around, Judy?" Ingram asked. "Or is it you Bolshevik broads are always ready for a showdown?"

"No mercy for the enemies of the people, comrade. Anyway, I don't have no rugged hunk like you for protection, Harry. Us single gals got to take care of ourselves." She sipped some beer and added, "Though what's your buddy Strummer up to these days?"

Claire made a face. "Sheet."

"He don't go for white girls?" She batted her eyes.

"He goes for anything in a skirt," Ingram replied. "Doing his best to get 'em out of those skirts."

Claire said, "Just like you used to, baby?"

Ingram chuckled and drank some of his beer.

Berkson asked, "You think this artist might have an idea where Tolbert is?"

"I'm figuring whoever Deebeck is, he's not having shows in galleries. If he's a friend of Tolbert's, he might know something. I plan to go over to the apartment building where I saw him on the roof. If nothing else, I can ask folks around there if they know of him."

"And what about the Emerald Room?"

"What's that?" Berkson said.

She explained the connection between Betty Payton and Gavin Rickler.

Berkson said to Claire, "Why don't we go out there and check it out?"

"Just you and me?"

"Hell to the yeah."

"I'm not cutting you two in on my fee," Ingram said, only half-jokingly.

"I'll get it out of him," Claire said in a stage whisper. The two women laughed.

"Now look here, Nancy Drew and Miss Marple—" Ingram began.

"Miss Marple, how dare you," Claire said in mock indignation.

"Whatever. From what Strummer says, Rickler isn't to be played with, derringer or not."

Claire told him, "You take care of the streets, Harry Ingram, me and my girl can handle this, checking out a card club. Anyway, with your sudden notoriety and your picture all in the papers, he might know what you look like."

"So what?"

"So, you don't learn anything even if he thinks you're there trying to do a story on him and he don't cotton to that. 'Cause if there's one lesson I've taken away from the FBI's techniques it's that it's all about gathering information from various quarters."

"Okay. Y'all hang around, do a little gambling so you fit in, dig?"

"You mean us being chicks he won't suspect anything?"

"You said it, not me."

"Dog." Claire sneered. Then, taking on a more serious look, she said, "What if Rickler was spying on Tolbert?" She tapped the listening device. "Was he worried Tolbert was somehow getting the best of him on one of their shady deals, like with the fur coats?"

"And Rickler retaliated when Tolbert found out?" Ingram folded his arms, mulling the notion over. "All the more reason for y'all to take this serious."

Berkson gave a slight nod. "We do, big daddy."

Claire glared at her. "You broads better watch yourself around my man."

They both cracked up.

Ingram asked, "You know if you're gonna blend in, you might have to come up with more than a ten spot to keep up."

"I got it covered, honey," Claire said.

"I know how much you make working for the city," he said.

"Got me some mad money, sweetie."

Ingram and Berkson regarded her.

"What, I'm frugal. I'm'a stake you, Judy."

"Really?"

"No jive."

"Fine by me," her friend said.

"You sure?" her boyfriend said.

"Not a problem. Besides, we ain't gonna lose."

"Every sucker's famous last words," he said.

"I'd say something dirty but we have company." Claire grinned.

"Time for some bones. Huh, Harry?" Berkson said, also smiling.

Ingram broke out the dominoes. They played several rounds into the late afternoon while finalizing their next moves.

IN HIS office at the Stockyard that evening, Strummer Edwards was on the phone with a man named Clovis Mitchell. Edwards knew if it came down to it, Mitchell wasn't to be trusted. But he'd come through on his end as long as it was about business and making his cut.

"Let's just say the folks I represent will pay well for the return of this . . . ledger."

"Them white boys in the back room," Edwards said. He wasn't sure how it was Mitchell got hooked up with the Jonathan Club types to be their glorified errand boy. It must have been when Mitchell attended Pepperdine College.

"That's one way of referring to them," Clovis said.

"How much?"

"You could name a sum."

"Twenty grand finder's fee."

"Possibly. Understand it's in code, so you wouldn't be able to go around trying to get a higher bidder."

"I play fair and square."

"I know you do. That's why I dialed you."

"Why do your . . . associates think this stolen ledger, as you call it, can be found on this side of town?"

Clovis paused before speaking. "They think the Morning Bandit is Black."

"Read he's always masked up, including gloves, cap and whatnot."

"The bank guard the Bandit shot was a retired cop in Maywood. He was talked to in the hospital and said he was sure from the way the Bandit swore and ran he was—and these were his words, I was told—a jig." Mitchell chuckled.

Edwards also snickered. "I guess a peckerwood cop in Maywood would know."

THE FOLLOWING day, Ingram cruised back to where he'd seen Deebeck on the rooftop of the apartment building in Watts. Along the way, he reflected on the two sides of Chet Horne. Horne was the manager of a business which relied on small-time capitalists for their livelihood yet was about shaking things up in his off hours with that letter to Betty and Mose's other investors. Ingram supposed those aspects weren't counter to each other. Wasn't it about workers controlling the big gears, being able to turn them as opposed to getting ground up between them? Now who was sounding like a Bolshevik?

Getting closer to the apartment building, Ingram noticed two Black men sifting through the debris leftover from the

recent fires and destruction. The detritus included busted-out window frames, torn loose and melted accordion gates
and several neon signs, some of which were intact. He recognized one of the men, a tallish individual with a beard.
Ingram pulled over and got out.

"Hunting for anything in particular, John?" He had his
Canon camera with him and began taking a few snaps of
John Outterbridge, a sculptor and teacher.

"Hey, Harry, how you doing?" Outterbridge had two
nearby shopping carts partially filled. He smiled at him and
continued looking about.

"What are you figuring to make from all this?"

"I don't know yet but me, Noah and a few others figured
we'd scavenge through the refuse before the city got it
together to come down here and bulldoze all this wonderful
found material away." He referred to the second scavenger
further down the block, Noah Purifoy. Like Outterbridge,
he was a sculptor and proponent of using what might be
termed junk to make their assemblages. Ingram'd photo-
graphed a show of these artists' work last summer.

"Give me a hand, will you?"

Ingram set the camera on a car's hood and went over to
help him lift a door off a small pile of rubble. They set it
aside. Revealed was a diamond-shaped glass ornament.

"Gold," Outterbridge exclaimed, picking up the artifact.
Gingerly, he set this in one of the carts atop his growing
collection. He turned, frowning at Ingram as the photographer clicked off more shots. "Where's that old-fashioned
shutter box of yours?"

Ingram told him it had gone missing after he was beaten
by the police.

"Damn shame," Outterbridge said, hand on the back of his neck. "What I mean is the blue boys vamping on you and the lost camera."

"I had that thing for more than ten years."

Outterbridge remained silent.

"I'll let you get back to it," Ingram said. "But say, do you know a painter who goes by Deebeck?" He told Outterbridge what little he knew about the artist and described the painting he'd been working on that day. Ingram pointedly did not mention that he saw the completed piece in a home he broke into.

"No, but sounds like I should be following this cat. You looking to do an article on him?"

"Not exactly, but I would like to talk to him. I was on my way to where I last saw him during the riots."

"Sorry I can't be of help."

"No sweat. I'll see you, John. Make sure you invite me to the opening when you're done creating your masterpieces." Ingram picked up his replacement camera.

"For sure." After shaking his hand, he returned to his task and Ingram took off again. Shortly he arrived at the address where he'd seen Deebeck and parked once more. Exiting the apartment building was a man in jeans and fringe suede vest with big gold buttons. There was no shirt underneath the vest. He held a conga drum by a hand. Ingram reached him as the younger man got to the bottom step of the covered porch.

"Excuse me, but do you know this artist who goes by Deebeck?"

"The rooftop artist," the other man said, jerking a thumb upward.

"That's him. He lives here?"

"Naw," he said, setting his drum down. "I think he knows somebody in the building who maybe gave him a key or something 'cause he was always up there day and night. We even had a little setup there a month or so ago."

"Set?"

He did a quick riff on his drum. "Music and words, wine and some Mary Jane, if you dig what I'm saying." He snapped a finger at Ingram, pointing at him. "You don't smell like cop."

"I'm the opposite. Did Deebeck put this shindig on?"

"He was there like several of us were. It was cool, ya know?"

"But you don't know who he knows here?"

He hunched a shoulder. "See, I'm just falling through myself, I don't stay here either. Well, sometimes I'm here overnightin' on my buddy's couch, but sometimes I'm not."

"Would your friend know who knows Deebeck?"

"Could be. But the dude's at work right now. Putting on them bumpers at the Ford plant. He'll be off work later. But he also might be stopping at a gin joint so who knows when he might roll through. Plus this stroke you're talking about, Deebeck, he hasn't been around for a while. Leastways I'd always see him when I came through, and I ain't seen him lately."

"Like how lately?"

"Couple of weeks, I'd say."

Ingram assessed that. "Do me a solid. When you next see your friend, give him this, would you?" Ingram wrote his name and phone number on a page in the steno pad he had in his back pocket. He included that he was a reporter for the *Sentinel*.

The drummer read the note, folded the paper in half and tucked it away in his front pocket. "I'll do that. You know you might also ask the folks starting up the new coffee house."

"Around here you mean?"

"Yeah, think they're gonna call it Watts Happening." He pointed eastward. "They've been meeting at the park since after the brothers and sisters got done. Can't say they're over there now, but that's what I know."

"'Preciate your time."

"Keep on, keepin' on."

"Hell yes."

The conga player picked up his drum and strapped it around his torso. He walked away drumming and humming. When Ingram got over to Will Rogers Park on 103rd Street, on two of the outer walls of the brick gym were the words BACK OFF, BLACK STAFF. Inside, he found a female Parks and Rec worker there using a push broom to sweep the scarred, much in need of replacing wood floor of the basketball court. Several of the gym's windows high up in the cinder block walls had been broken out during the unrest. Apparently, the message to would-be arsonists must have worked, Ingram mused, given the structure was still standing.

After he told the sweeping woman who he was, showing her his press credentials and suggesting to her he was working on a story, he asked about the people meeting to plan the new coffee house.

"They mostly meet out on the benches," she said. "Can't say I know when they'll be here next, but if you come back a time or two, I'm sure you'll find them."

"You know any of them?"

"Tommy Jacquett," she offered. "He's a friend of my big sister and he's been talking about all sorts of ideas including a music festival." For the first time, she looked over at Ingram. "I'm in a singing group and he said he'd feature us if the music thing happened." She kept sweeping and he followed her. She reversed course to push the dust, bottle caps and what have you into the tidy pile she'd been accumulating.

"Ever hear of an artist calling himself Deebeck?"

She stopped sweeping, throwing her head back and laughing. "Now he's crazy. Been knowing him since we was at Markham." They continued her circuit of the floor.

"Junior high you mean?"

"Uh-huh. That boy was painting and drawing even then. He'd do pictures of all kinds, a lot of cars 'cause he was around them all the time. Donnie drew his teachers, dogs, cats, garbage trucks, made up stuff from the stories he was always reading about spaceships and whatnot."

"You said his name is Donnie?"

"Yeah, Don Beck. Everybody calls him Donnie."

"He live around here?"

She shook her head. "No, not since he dropped out of high school. But I heard he's been showing up lately to do some of his painting. His grandpa is still around though. Got a junk shop he's been owning since my mom first moved here. Really, he raised Donnie."

"His last name is Beck too?"

"Uh-huh. His shop is called Treasure Chest or something like that. I haven't been there in a while." She walked off to get a dustpan and returned.

"I got it," Ingram said, hunching down to hold the pan so she could sweep the trash onto it.

"Thanks." Twice she filled the dustpan and dumped the contents into a metal trash can out on the floor.

"You know where his grandfather's shop is?"

"On Avalon, not far from Charley O's."

"The burger stand?"

"That's right."

"You've been a big help." He turned to go.

"When you do your article, try to mention us, my group I mean. We're called the Charlarettes. I'm Jerri with an *I*."

"I'll try, Jerri with an *I*."

"See you."

Ingram didn't like fibbing to her so maybe he would try and write an article mentioning them. Afterall, it seemed Donnie "Deebeck" Beck was on the rise as a painter. But first Ingram needed to locate him and ask him about Mose Tolbert. After leaving the park, he stopped at a Thrifty's drugstore and checked the address for Beck's shop in the Yellow Pages chained to the pay phone booth inside the store. It wasn't called the Treasure Chest but Treasure Island, though it was on Avalon. He arrived not ten minutes later.

The shop was tucked between a boarded-up dress store and a sales and service concern called Drayton's Vacuum Cleaners. The storefronts occupied the first floor of a larger building with apartments on the second floor. There was evidence of flames having scorched the exterior, but that appeared to be the extent of damages, Ingram observed. The display in the window of the elder Beck's business was a scene out of any number of pirate stories he remembered reading as a kid. There was an artificial beach sloping down to plaster relief waves of icy blue water. Plaster starfish and crabs were on the fake sand and there was a treasure chest lying on its side that held the type of goods offered in the store.

The tableau was composed of Lionel train cars, reminding Ingram of a set he had as a kid his mother got from Sears & Roebuck. There were Red Rider and Super Car metal lunch boxes too, Tiffany lamps that had to be fake ones, he reasoned, various typewriters and a set of World Book Encyclopedias that he concluded must be twenty years out of date. Standing looking at the Island's offerings, he wistfully remembered when he and Shoals Pettigrew were in grade school. The two friends imagined that once they'd made their submarine, the *Fantastic*, they would sail the world for adventure and the gold doubloons they'd surely find in sunken galleons.

Ingram tried the latch to the shop, but it was locked. He went back to the window to press his face closer to the glass to peer inside. He expected the shop would be cluttered, but it seemed Beck the elder kept his assortments of castoff goods orderly. He knocked on the glass but got no response. Ingram entered the vacuum cleaner shop next door. A man of medium build and medium height, darker than him with a clean-shaven head, was watching a largish woman work a Hoover vacuum cleaner back and forth on a rug tacked to the otherwise barren floor. She was cleaning up a swath of dirt Ingram figured had been laid out by the proprietor for this demonstration.

"What I tell you?" the man said. He had a squeaky voice. He wore a drab shop apron with several pockets in it. Screwdrivers and other types of tools in those pockets.

"You're a wizard, Mr. Drayton," the woman enthused. "I just knew this machine was on its last legs." She shut off the vacuum cleaner and Drayton said to Ingram, "Let me help Mrs. Cullers get this loaded in her car and I'll be right with you."

"Sure," Ingram nodded. He took in the compact space filled with spare parts while Drayton and his customer went out front and down the street. The repairman soon returned.

"What can I do for you today?"

"I was wondering if you'd seen Mr. Beck around lately."

Drayton took a moment to assess his visitor. "You some kind of bill collector? Looking to lay some papers on him? Something about you." He trailed off and he took out an opened pack of Pall Malls from his shirt pocket. Shaking one loose, he gripped the butt end between his lips and withdrew the smoke. Pointedly he didn't offer one to Ingram.

As an omission would serve him better, he replied, "I'm a clicker and looking for his grandson, the painter." He showed him his press credential. Keeping the notion of withholding information alive, he hoped Drayton would assume he wanted to find Deebeck for an article.

Drayton, who'd lit up, removed the cigarette from his mouth and blew out a stream as he held and studied the laminated press pass. Often when he flashed the damned credential at the cops, it seemed to be more an invitation to bar his way than let him through.

Drayton handed it back and said, "He went fishing."

"You mean none of my business where he is?"

Drayton chuckled. "For real. A couple of days ago he headed out to Diamond Valley Lake to get him some trout."

"He can afford to just take off like that?"

"Len got hisself a pension from them years as a brakeman on the Santa Fe. He makes enough selling his treasures, as he likes to call 'em, to pay the rent so he can keep tinkering and fixing."

"That go for you too? And is Len short for Leonard?"

"Yeah, something like that," he said, chuckling. "His real name believe it or not is Leonidas."

"He was a Greek king or some such," Ingram stated.

"That's right," Drayton answered. "His mom was a lover of the classics, the way he tells it."

"When do you think he'll be back?"

Drayton let a shoulder lift and fall. "He probably won't be back until the weekend. He camps out there and reads those books of his by lantern, enjoying his pan-fried fish and sips of brandy. Peeing on a rock. Hell, he might never come back," he added wistfully.

"You ever go out there with him?"

Drayton gave him a lopsided grin. "Maybe if I was out there lazin' against a tree waiting for a fish to take the bait, my own thoughts would worry me."

Ingram sympathized with that notion. "How about Donnie, have you seen him around?"

"Not lately. But he sometimes helps out his grandpa in the shop." Anticipating his next question he added, "Seems to me I'd heard Len mention Donnie was living somewhere in the Hollywood area but don't quote me on that."

"Well, thanks for your time. I'll be back around."

"Sure, man."

As Ingram walked out, coming in was a jowly individual with a gut hanging over his belt. He was pushing a vacuum cleaner and whistling.

"Hey, Rich, might of burned out the motor this time," he called to Drayton.

"Bring it on in, Oscar, let's check it out," the proprietor said cheerily. Harry identified with the repairman's can-do attitude. Though as he meandered toward his car, he did wonder, could he be both a crime photographer, as a few articles had referred to him, or could he turn his shoe leather skills learned as a process server into being a kind of detective full time? Or was he just fooling himself thinking that if he found Tolbert, people would be clamoring for his services? Didn't you have to take a test or something like that to get a private eye license? What about an office? It tickled him to imagine Anita sitting at a desk intercepting would-be clients, grilling them as to their troubles before they could get in to see him.

He dug out a flat dark brown cigar and freeing it from its cellophane wrapper, lit it. He leaned there against his car, contemplating. For several minutes he stayed that way, watching the smoke from his crooked cigar drift away like a soothsayer, as if there were signs to read in the various random shapes of smoke. Achieving no such revelation, he left Drayton to the joy of his work. What if that was the sign he was looking for? He was handy with tools. Open a camera repair shop and do portraits and wedding pictures on the side. Yeah, that was it. He drove along with the driver's window down, letting the smoke from his cigar trail behind him. On his radio's news station, a breaking news report started. The incendiary comments by the masked officer had been broadcast on the Louis Lomax show and already the backlash had begun. Chief Parker was being interviewed from his office downtown.

"Let me assure the law-abiding citizens of this vast and varied metropolis my officers serve that the underhanded comments from this supposed member of my department are lies and falsehoods. Why do you think he was masked?" Parker added in an indignant tone. "Because clearly he is not a colored member of my ranks. In fact, it wouldn't surprise me that once we unmask this charlatan, it will be discovered he might very well be a member of one of the subversive groups fomenting the recent hoodlum rioting."

The news reporter asked, "You're saying positively, Chief, that the person who said, among other charges, there's a double standard in terms of advancement of white officers versus negroes and Mexicans, is not an officer?"

"Yes, emphatically yes," Parker responded. The radio signal crackled and buzzed for a moment as Ingram went under a freeway overpass. "As I've said several times before, we live in a cold war climate that engenders hot emotions like what was on display in Watts less than a month ago. Emotions that are being fanned by these malcontents and dare I say, agents of . . . other concerns."

"Agents of other concerns, Chief? What do you mean exactly?"

"It will all be detailed at the close of the investigation into this scurrilous matter. In fact, now I'm going to ask you to leave my office as I'm going into a meeting with my command staff. Let me repeat that I will be getting to the bottom of this and appropriate heads will roll."

Parker's chair could be heard over the air scraping along the floor as he pushed back from his desk. Ingram felt sorry for the colored cops under Parker. No doubt anyone having put in for a sick day, an appointment at the dentist, or off on vacation when the broadcast aired would be under suspicion.

Ingram chucked the smoldering stub of his cigar out the window and rolled on.

CLAIRE ANSWERED the call on the second ring. She was sitting at her desk in Councilman Bradley's field office on Washington Boulevard. "Anita Claire," she said pleasantly.

"Is this the Sears tool department?"

"No it isn't." She identified who she was and the office.

"My apologies. Got my numbers mixed up. Thanks for your time."

"Of course."

She hung up and returned to typing up her notes. When she took her lunch break later, she drove to the dead drop her parents and Del Standers had worked out. Given what they'd experienced in the heyday of the FBI hunting reds under every other bed, they'd agreed to use the tried-and-true methods of communicating. The supposedly mistaken phone call was Claire's cue that there was information for her to be picked up. She arrived at The Pantry, a twenty-four-hour eatery downtown on Figueroa. She parked in their lot and, inside, found a seat at the counter. Every kind from fast-talking insurance salesmen, harried secretaries, beefy Water and Power workers to guys just released from jail ate there. After ordering, she went to the lady's room. There, taped behind the paper towel dispenser, was a folded note. She read it twice then flushed it away. Back at the counter, she ate lighter than usual. Her stomach aflutter at what she'd read.

That night at home, Claire dressed for her night of espionage at the Emerald Room. "Have you seen my necklace, Harry?"

She was in her underwear seated at the mall vanity in their bedroom. Ingram came up behind her as she adjusted an earring. One hand on her shoulder, his other hand reached down, gently massaging the front of her lacy black panties. She inhaled sharply and bit his arm playfully. She had just taken a shower and her wet hair was wrapped in a towel.

"Is it here, baby?"

"Keep looking," she encouraged him as he eased his finger off her clit and slipped it inside her.

They kissed and moaned and continued their love-making there at the vanity, eventually winding up on the bed. By then Ingram had taken off his trousers and shirt, down to his boxers and A-shirt as she led him there by his erect member.

"Think we should try that drawing we saw in the book?" she suggested. They lay side by side on the edge of the bed, Claire working her hand up and down on him as they kissed and nuzzled.

"Which one?" he asked eagerly.

"Let me show you." She had him lay on the bed, and slipping off his boxers, she left his undershirt on. She in turn got nude. When she got on top of him, she was facing in the opposite direction.

"Oh, that one," Ingram gulped.

Claire was inspired by *The Ways of Tantra*, the book she'd found outside the Venice Café—after a heated encounter, as they were about to have now. How had that book been there right then? Left by two others in lust and love? Should she in turn leave it somewhere else in the city?

"Ohhh," he said. That was the last articulate utterance from either of them for some time. Finishing, the two gasped and parted.

"That was something else," Ingram blew out air.

"Um-hmm."

In her recent readings on Buddhism, Claire'd encountered mentions of tantra, which was a way of achieving higher spiritualism. Part of that concerned the practice of tantric sex. Not simply for pleasure but as a way to unlock portions of the mind and body connection, as the book found by the café extolled, which included as a number of drawings demonstrating the numerous ways bonding through intimacy could be achieved. She was feeling connected.

Claire righted her body and kissed his chest. The towel had come undone from around her wet black hair, and now partially dried, it cascaded down around her face and onto his torso. Claire pulled away and laid her head on a pillow.

"Excuse me a second."

Ingram got up to visit the bathroom. Claire looked over to check the time and noticed the necklace she'd been looking for. The jewelry was partially hanging in the drawer of the nightstand. She rolled over to it, sitting up in the process. She heard the toilet flush through the closed door to the bathroom and Ingram returned after washing his hands.

"Did you put this here?" She jingled the necklace toward him.

"No. It's not like I been slipping out at night wearing your jewelry."

"Don't bother me if you do," she said absently. She got up

to get dressed, first putting on the necklace. It was gold and silver, an Art Deco-style ornament set with an emerald gemstone in its center.

Ingram reveled in the vision of her naked body, dark hair framing her composed face, the necklace on her reflecting light. He also began getting dressed. "Don't you usually keep that one hanging off your mirror?"

"Yeah," she agreed.

"Then you must have moved it."

"We didn't go anywhere lately," she said.

Ingram considered this. "Did you wear it when we went grocery shopping?"

She cut her eyes at him. "Right, along with my stilettos 'cause the man behind the meat counter gives me that prime choice when I wink at him."

"Who is he, I'll kill him."

"I'm serious, Harry, I didn't move it."

"I do it all the time, Anita. I pick up a lens figuring I'm going to use it then set it down when it occurs to me to use a different one. Just the other day I looked all over the garage for my wide angle one and only when I came back in the kitchen found it sitting on top of the breadbox." He gestured. "You could have strapped me to a lie detector and I would have passed with flying colors. I had no memory of putting it there. See, when you start to put on a few years, all that information gets crowed in the brain. There's only so many thoughts you can keep up in here at any one time," he said, tapping his forehead with his finger.

"Zip me up, Rip Van Winkle."

Laughing softly, he did so, her back to him, she holding her hair up. Once he was done, she let her hair back down and for a moment, they stood close together, his hands on her shoulders.

"You two pistol packin' dames keep your cool tonight," he said. "The mission is only to observe."

"Roger, Wilco."

Ingram put an arm around her upper body like a wrestler delivering his signature move. He squeezed and let her go. Turning, she gave him a peck on the cheek. Back at her vanity, she checked her fresh lipstick and dabbed a bit of perfume behind her ears and upper shoulder area. She started to exit.

"Bye, honey."

Wagging a finger at her, he said, "All right now."

He watched from the porch as she got in her car and gunned the engine to life. After, he went into the kitchen, got some ice cubes and made a drink. He turned on the television and clicked the channel selector, coming to a show he'd occasionally watched, *Voyage to the Bottom of the Sea*. As this was the tail end of summer, reruns were on until the new season of shows next month. Tonight's story was already in progress. As far as Ingram could tell, the *Seaview*, the futuristic-looking submarine the main characters sailed in, had been captured by a flying saucer that crashed in the ocean. Admiral Nelson, commander of the sub, was now confronting the space alien in his saucer.

The spaceman, it seems, was able to change his appearance and had transformed himself to look like the admiral. Ingram mused this must have been done to make Nelson feel more comfortable? Wouldn't he worry this meant the alien could kill him and sneak about his ship? Anyway, the alien tells him the Earth is doomed unless the star traveler can leave our planet. Ingram wasn't quite sure why that would happen, but he kept watching. At the next break in programming, commercials came on. The cowboy tough Marlboro Man moodily smoked his cigarette on the open range. And the animated Charlie Tuna was yet again disappointed when his suicidal desire to be boiled alive, chopped up and canned for StarKist failed. Ingram got up to make himself a sandwich from leftover cold meatloaf.

He justified his additional intake of food this evening given tonight's meal with his lady love had been of the vegetarian variety, eggplant instead of meat in the lasagna. He wasn't, though, going to have a beer with his sandwich.

"Don't worry," Claire had said, "we're not giving up barb-que pork ribs. But figured we might could use the variety."

"Isn't that what green beans are for?"

"It's not bad, right?"

"Pretty tasty," he'd said and meant it. But the good Lord in his infinite wisdom made him a carnivore. The sandwich was heavenly. Soon, though, he checked the time on his watch. He hoped the two Bolsheviks were doing all right.

IN GARDENA, Claire reached into her purse. She pulled out several twenty dollar bills and counted out a hundred for her friend, who eyed her as she did this. They were in Judy's parked car.

"You weren't kidding about mad money."

Claire resisted the impulse to tell her how she'd come by the money, helping her folks rob banks. "We can get change inside at the cage. Unless you're feeling sporty and plan to go at the big timers."

"I'll stick with the cosmetologists and truck drivers."

"As will I," Claire agreed. They stepped out of the car, Berkson locking it, and walked across the well-lit parking lot. Three armed security guards on bicycles patrolled, weaving between and around the vehicles.

The Emerald Room itself was a long, low one-story building with an off-center covered entrance. This had a curving green neon snaking around its quadruple support columns leading upward to the name of the place spelled out in gleaming, arching three-dimensional pulsing script bracketed to the roof of the broad portico. Dwarf majesty palm trees bordered the expanse of the asphalt parking lot adjacent to the casino. Entrance to this was accessible from three sides with the main driveway off of Rosecrans, the wide roadway the casino faced.

Claire opened one of the double doors for her friend and the two women entered the facility. They were greeted with the unmistakable aroma of stale cigarette smoke combined with the desperate sweat of gamblers too long at the tables. The hallway they walked had high wainscotting and was lined in lush green flocked wallpaper. The wall-to-wall carpeting was a deep red color and the overhead lighting offered muted yellow illumination.

Claire and Berkson entered the establishment proper. From what she knew of how the place was configured, this was the main room, and there were two more. Where they stood now was for the hoi polloi. They were at a railing bordering the goings on and you had to step down from this rise to where the tables were. The tables weren't round but octangular, covered in forest green felt with the card club's name in the center. Padded chairs like what you'd see in a hotel encircled each table. Their covering was the color of the carpeting, though in here the flooring was scuffed hard-wood. Should a chip fall on the floor, it would be easily seen.

A few patrons leaned at the railing, smoking and drink-ing, eyeing the tables with hopeful intent. On one side of the room was a rectangular chalkboard. If it was a busy night like a Friday or the weekend, your name would be written here, often times your lucky nickname, to wait your turn. But tonight, there was no one at the chalk board as several tables on the floor were not at capacity. Some of them were sans any player at all. Light snacks were laid out on folding tables on the periphery. The second room beyond was for live acts from comedians to singers and bands. These were not headliners who might have a gig at the Cocoanut Grove several miles away, but some of them had a local following.

The third area was where the serious bettors came to play. This was also where the poker tournaments were held. Sev-eral waitresses in starched white shirts and black skirts of demure length brought drinks and took away empty glasses on round silver trays. Also moving around or stationed at specific spots were the security guards in business suits. That they were armed was evident as some let their coats flap open revealing the butts of guns in shoulder holsters. Probably a reminder not to get greedy, Claire reflected. The Morning Bandit, if he already hadn't been pressing his luck, would be a complete fool to try and take down a score in the club.

"Synchronize our watches?" Claire said to Berkson.

"I'm'a try that table over there," she said, nodding toward one off to the side. There were four people at it, two men and two women. One of them wore cat eyeglasses and had a beehive hairdo. One of the men looked old enough to be a World War I veteran. He had on a canvas fisherman's cap, and his lean frame was clothed in baggy attire. The muscles in his face were taut and his hands didn't tremble as he handled his cards.

"The old fella reminds me of a kindly uncle," she added. "That's gotta be a sign."

"Sure it is."

"Damn right."

Berkson gave Claire's hand a squeeze and went to the cashier cage to pay for some chips. The club charged a small percentage to do the buy-in, and at the end if you had chips to cash in. They also made money on the drinks and that you as a player paid a fee to play per hand, calculated by how long you sat at any given table. Unlike Vegas, you didn't play against the house but against the other players.

Claire took her time to wander about in another part of the large room. Like a floating lagoon, a pall of cigarette smoke hung over people's heads, the image reminding her of the smoke that had risen over Watts. Along the walls were several framed reproductions and blown-up photos including a horse racing scene and Van Gogh's *Wheatfield with Crows*. From out of one of the doorways came a man with a distracted look on his face. He was followed by Gavin Rickler, who was holding a glass of amber liquid and ice cubes. Rickler was a presence as she expected, blond and dark eyed as Harry had described him. A minor plutocrat surveying his domain. He hadn't said a word, but her impression of him was that of an appliance salesmen. He concentrated on you just long enough to make the sale, then would move on. Claire moved past them without breaking stride, but lingered to try and overhear them.

"Don't sweat it, Uke, those psalm singers will cool down."

Rickler put a hand on the other man's shoulder. He was Japanese American, probably mid-fifties with close-cut, graying hair. "They're still licking their wounds, but like the kicked dog they are, they like to growl while huddled in a corner." He leaned toward his ear. "They'll take the scraps." His displayed a practiced smile.

"It's my nature to worry, Gavin." The man, Uke, looked around the room. "The holy rollers are still on a tear."

"If they got laid more often they'd be so much calmer," Rickler replied, a serious cast to his face. Then his bemused appearance returned. "But who would go for their sour pusses?"

Uke allowed a thin smile to come and go on his face. "I'll be in touch."

"Yeah, man." Rickler clapped him again on the shoulder. Uke headed toward the exit.

As Rickler turned, he glanced at Claire, who pretended to be interested in a round of Texas Hold 'Em being played at a table to her right. He paused for a moment, studying her profile, then, taking a sip of his drink and whistling, continued through the doorway, presumably returning to his office. She had no idea who Uke was, but she did know about Proposition E backed by the state's attorney general, Stanley Mosk. The measure sought to ban all poker clubs in the county. Gamblers looked up long enough from their cards to vote the attempt down, resoundingly. Claire went to the cashier and purchased forty dollars' worth of chips. Sitting at the table she'd been hovering around, she realized Rickler's comment about "scraps" could mean Uke was his bagman. Maybe he was supposed to deliver a bribe to whatever religious group was currently making noise. She made a note to check recent back issues of the *Daily Breeze*, the local paper that covered this part of what was called the South Bay.

"Hello," she said as she began arranging her chips.

"How you doing?" an older Black woman said. A cigarette bobbled in her mouth as she spoke. She was dressed as if in church and Claire estimated could be here was where she did her most devout praying. "I'm Viola."

"Anita. Pleased to meet you. Looking forward to playing."

"Guess we'll see."

"Ain't that the truth," she said.

"Dealer rotates and calls the game, and three times around for bets and declares. We've also all agreed on dollar limit on raises." The man who delivered these rules flatly was white, long faced and droopy eyed. Effortlessly, he shuffled the cards with his leathery hands. He was dressed in worn workingman's clothes, including a light windbreaker with an embroidered image of a micrometer over a capital *C* insignia. "If you want the all ins, there's a few over there where you can scratch that itch." He pushed the shuffled stack toward the player on his right so they could cut them.

"I'm fine," Claire said. She guessed the man was a machinist, given the symbol on his jacket.

The dealer grunted as he picked up the cards and said as he did so, "Hold 'em."

Claire was dealt her two down cards, both kings. She did her best not to show her excitement. Forty-five minutes later she was up by ten dollars. Given the humble stakes at the table, and that two of the players often folded on their third card, she considered she was in high cotton. She looked forward to bragging to Ingram. Looking across the room again to eyeball Berkson, she saw a familiar face at the railing. It took her a moment to recognize Betty Payton. Instinctively, she started to raise her hand and call out to Payton but stopped herself.

"Baby, you don't have to ask for permission to go to the ladies' room," Viola joked. "This here ain't Mississippi. Almost, but still, sheet."

"Thought I recognized someone, but I was mistaken," Claire said. Payton was walking parallel to the railing and hadn't spotted her. Good. She didn't want to be singled out in case Rickler saw them together. One of the suited security guards stepped up to the rise and Payton talked to him. He nodded and turned his head and disappeared through an archway. Claire frowned. If he was going to tell Rickler that Payton was here, she assumed he'd come this way. But maybe there was more than one way to reach the boss's office.

One of the other players, a Filipina also of a maturing age, laughed heartily as she tossed a chip onto the small pile of them, seeing the raise. "Me and my old man were coming through this town in Texas once and we stopped at a café off the highway to use the facilities and get something to eat," she said. "We go through the door and them dried up old Confederates didn't know what to make of us. I was too dark to be Chinese and my boyfriend is all a mix, including Guatemalan and Iranian on his mother's side."

She laughed again, winking at Claire. "They were so confused. They finally settled on us being some kind of Mexicans from deep in the jungle or some damn place. They didn't mess with us and we ate in peace."

"Damn right," the cussing church woman said. She put in a chip and the play continued.

The guard came back through the archway. Payton was standing at the railing, a glass of water having been brought to her by one of the waitresses. The guard gave her a high sign and she went through the archway.

When the final round of betting came, Claire said, "I'm out. Be right back, don't sell my seat." She tossed her cards onto the felt and rose, scooting her chair back quietly. Rickler had taken the trouble to have little pieces of cloth glued to the bottoms of the chair legs. Claire went over to Judy Berkson and leaned close to her ear.

"That was Betty Payton," she told her. "See if you can do a little eavesdropping. I'm trying to not let her know I'm here. They must have gone back to Rickler's office."

"Okay," she said. As Claire turned away, Berkson gathered up her chips and put them in her handbag. "Be back in a few, but you don't have to hold my seat for me."

"Whatever you say, sugah," the woman with the beehive said. The only name she'd given the group was LaRue.

BERKSON PAUSED once she was back on the rise. She didn't want any of the guards seeing her go through the archway. When they were looking elsewhere, she ducked through. She found herself in a gloomily lit hallway, the duplicate of the one leading to the main room. Berkson went along, her footfalls absorbed by the carpeting. She arrived at a bend and took the turn. Now she was in yet another hallway that was shorter than the first, and at its end, split two ways. With her eyes now adjusted to the dim lighting, she saw stairs on her right leading down. She went to the left, figuring this was a way to Rickler's office. Creeping forward, she could hear muffled voices ebbing through a polished wooden door. Berkson concluded the door must be oak. It appeared quite substantial. Having no choice, she put her ear to its surface.

". . . the hell, Betty. I don't know what to tell you. As I've assured you, I haven't touched a hair on Mose's head and have no idea on anyone else doing him harm. The operation was running smooth. Fact, we had another score lined up when the riots broke out and he went missing."

Her response was incoherent to Berkson. She could only hear Rickler because he had a baritone voice and was using volume to make his point.

"Look, I understand. It's damn sure in my interest to keep the business running, too. What if I slot a guy to be the figurehead so it's a white face to calm the accounts. But he'll report to you, and you keep Chet as the right hand man, since he knows what's what. Shame a colored man can't take the reins, but that's the way it is. We didn't make the world like this."

Betty spoke again. Berkson shifted slightly, setting her hand against the door, and it creaked. That sound in the stillness of the hallway was like an iceberg cracking and splitting in two.

"Shit," she breathed. She turned and sprinted down the hall, her back to the door audibly opening behind her.

"Hey, who the hell are you?" Rickler yelled.

She kept running and rushed down the stairs another level. Returning to the main room was a sure way to get caught. She reached the bottom and found another hallway, Rickler on the stairs behind her. There were two doors on either side. She tried the nearest one, but it was locked.

"Nowhere to go, lady."

Berkson turned to face Rickler. Right behind him was one of his guards, who must have heard the commotion.

"What are you doing spying on me?" Rickler demanded, stepping closer.

"I was looking for the exit."

"Bullshit." He took her roughly by the arm and with his guard, muscled her up the stairs and back to his office. When they passed the open archway, she could see several people had gathered to see what was going on. She didn't see Claire.

"Take her back to the office," Rickler told the guard. "I need to smooth this out."

"Okay, Gavin."

The guard didn't manhandle Berkson but stayed on her close to guide her to their destination. Rickler went out on the main floor to assuage the patrons. Berkson listened. "It's okay folks, just a sneak thief trying to get cute." She assumed his vacuous smile was once more on display.

Payton was gone from the office when Berkson was ushered inside. It was well-appointed and included a small couch, comfortable chairs, a wet bar, hi-fi set up with a tape recorder and several pieces of art including a modern art statuette that looked like a twisted part of a jet's landing gear on a shelf. There was a bathroom she could partly see through an ajar door.

"Sit down." The guard indicated the couch.

Berkson did as instructed. She sat alertly, knees together, hands on them. This way, she reasoned, he would see them shake due to her nervousness. Rickler came in. He closed the door to his back and faced her, taking her measure.

"Dump out her purse, Tim," he said.

The guard took it off her lap and, at the desk, emptied it out by turning it over. The poker chips, her wallet, derringer, lipstick, a comb and a couple of other items not as serious as the gun tumbled onto the blotter on Rickler's desk.

Tim, a man with a barrel chest and recessed eyes, picked up the derringer, grinning. "What'd you plan to do with this pop gun, sweetheart?"

"A single woman can't be too careful," she said.

"The wallet." Ricker held out his hand and Tim handed it across. Scornfully he tossed the derringer back on the table.

Rickler snapped the wallet open and, thumbing through the contents, soon extracted her driver's license. He studied it for a few moments, looking up once from the picture on it to her, then back to the license. "So, Judith Eleanora Berkson, why the hell are you here?"

"My old man," she began, concocting a lie just as quick as she could spin it. "He's running around with this barmaid."

"You working for Mosk?" Rickler demanded.

"What?"

"Don't play dumb. The state attorney general and his psalm singers still got their noses in the air about card clubs. You snooping for them, trying to get dirt on me?"

"No."

His eyes narrowing, he stepped forward. "You're lying. And you're going to tell me the truth."

"Fire!" came a yell from elsewhere.

"The hell now?" Rickler said as again someone yelled fire, louder this time. "You watch her," he told Tim and left his office in a trot.

"I gotta pee," Berkson said. "You two scare me."

"Pee then."

She jerked a head toward the bathroom. "Come on," she pleaded, her leg bouncing up and down. A beat, then, cocking her head, she said softly, "You can watch me."

Tim had a hip hitched on the edge of the desk. "Yeah?"

"I'm your prisoner, aren't I?"

He looked toward the office door, which was open.

"Your boss is taking care of whatever's going on out there." She stood up, hiking up her skirt a few inches and reaching her hands under the folds.

Tim came off the desk leering. "Oh . . . shit."

She moved closer to him, turning her face up at him invitingly. He gaped and she shoved him and in the next motion twisted about, scooping up her derringer.

"Teasing whore," he growled, leaping for her.

Operating more from nervousness than reflex, she yelped and hit him twice on the bridge of his nose, causing him to falter. This wasn't like her bluffing those two nuts at Tolbert's house. Tim was dangerous. Knowing full well she couldn't shoot him, she turned and rushed into the bathroom, slamming the door. Fortunately, it had a lock.

"Get your ass out here," Tim yelled, jiggling the knob and pounding on the door. This door wasn't like the one to the office. Three times he rammed his shoulder with his bulk behind it and each time it gave some on the hinges. The third attempt tore it lose though it hung halfway in and halfway out of the doorway. Tim bulled into the bathroom just in time to see Berkson's lower legs and feet dangling over the toilet through the small sliding glass window there. Leaping across the compact space, he grabbed for her and came away with a handful of the material of her skirt.

Bellowing, he roared out of the bathroom as he couldn't fit through that window.

"Get back here, goddammit."

Outside, head and body aimed toward the ground, Berkson was surprised again when hands were on her from behind. She decided she'd better do some punching and started swinging awkwardly.

"It's me, Judy."

"Anita!" she said jubilantly. She alighted on the asphalt upright. She had a ragged slit up the side of her skirt where Tim had torn it.

"Let's go," her friend said.

"Hold up, you two." One of the parking lot guards peddled up fast on his bike at the same time a car screeched onto the lot—driving straight at the guard. He sought to unholster his weapon and Claire whacked him hard in the jaw, knocking him to the ground. She kicked the gun away. Two other guards were peddling furiously from different directions, converging on the spot.

"Let's get the hell out of here," Ingram shouted from behind the wheel of his station wagon.

Berkson already had the rear door open. Tim was running toward them too, gun out. Ingram had his .45 in hand and sticking his arm out of the window, shot it into the air. Tim dove for cover. The car roared away, clipping a parked Plymouth Fury on the way off the lot.

"Wow," Berkson gulped.

Claire said, "That was close."

"Glad you were here for backup, Harry," Berkson said.

"At first he was gonna sneak follow us," Claire mentioned. "Typical man's thinking."

"But she sussed out what I was planning," Ingram added. He'd turned off his headlights and was taking back streets. They weren't being tailed.

Berkson put her hand on his shoulder. "Either way, glad you were here, Harry."

He looked over at Claire. "Partners gotta watch out for each other, don't they?"

"You set the fire?" Berkson asked.

"Shit yeah," Claire said proudly. "There's a pantry off the kitchen for snacks and stuff, I was hoping it would give you some kind of distraction."

"He's got my damn driver's license."

"Can't worry about it now," Ingram said. Havin' served his share of papers in Gardena, Ingram was familiar with its side streets. He parked on a darkened avenue and they passed the time guessing song titles from incorrectly remembered lyrics. They then snuck back to the club to retrieve Berkson's car. Fortunately, there were still a number of vehicles parked on the lot.

FROM THE kitchen at their home, Claire obtained three white cups and a bottle of chilled sake in the refrigerator. Back in the living room, she poured the rice wine into the cups. Ingram had been drinking the stuff since service in Korea. They had decided it was safer for Judy to stay with them tonight and soon, she returned from the bedroom wearing Claire's polka dot pajamas. Claire was dressed in her other pajamas. After clinking their cups together in a cheers, the two told Ingram what they'd been through and what Berkson had managed to overhear.

"The way it sounded," Claire concluded, "Rickler must

have bankrolled that fur robbery like Strummer hinted at and was in partnership with Mose Tolbert."

"And Betty too, it sounded like," Berkson added.

"This probably wasn't the first time. Tolbert's business has four trucks. I guess they use them to move the stolen items around," Ingram said.

Claire asked, "You think the manager, what's his name, is in on the deal?"

"Chet Horne, you mean? Probably. And a couple of others at the place too, I'd bet."

"Including the bookkeeper?" she added.

Ingram had more of his drink, lifting both eyebrows.

Claire said, "Betty came to you because she thought Rickler had harmed Tolbert and wanted to know if that was so. But it doesn't seem she was worried about her own safety."

"More about the bottom line," Berkson observed. "She must help finance some of these heists for her cut of the operation, as Rickler said."

Claire and Ingram exchanged a nod. He then said, "If Rickler didn't go after his crime partner, why did Tolbert disappear?"

Both women exchanged blank expressions.

"Anyway, it's beddy-bye time for all of us," Claire said, yawning as she rose and finishing her drink. "You know where the blankets and stuff are."

Berkson was also on her feet. "Thank you two."

"You know we're not going to let anything happen to you, Judy." Ingram had halted in the doorway leading to the master bedroom.

"I know, Harry. But I can't hide out forever."

"We'll work it out," he said. "Goodnight."

"Night."

The guest bedroom of the house, on the opposite end of the hallway to the couple's bedroom, contained a rollaway bed. When they were discussing the events at the card club, Claire had gone in and unfolded the thing. The bed was already made up with sheets and a blanket, and she'd added a pillow. In the room were a few taped and stacked cardboard boxes in a corner, five framed prints of painting reproductions leaning against the wall and a compact closet behind an accordion door.

In her dreams that night, Berkson was running away from bike-men who were part wheels with their clothed torsos and heads sprouting from where the handlebars would normally be. She ducked into a Victorian mansion she'd seen in *Jane Eyre*. Like the twists and turns she and Claire had taken that night to reach her car, she had to get through a maze, the walls moving and reforming at new angles to each other. Eventually she got to a room lined in velvet, a heart-shaped bed in the middle with golden curtains glimmering behind it.

On the bed, Ingram and Claire were making love. At some point they halted, bodies slick with sweat. Her friend beckoned to Berkson and she joined them happily.

When she awoke from her dream before light, she'd been blushing. She'd only been able to compose herself after several splashes of cold water on her face.

CHAPTER THIRTEEN

Ingram awoke to Claire propped up on an elbow. Her face close to his, an odd expression on it. "Yes, dear?"

"I have to tell you something. And I'm taking the coward's way out, figuring you won't blow your top with Judy in the house."

"Okay . . ."

"You know about the Morning Bandit gang?"

A soft knock at the door interrupted them. "I'm going to make us breakfast," Berkson said from the other side.

"Thanks, sweetie," Claire called back. "Let's eat first," she said to her boyfriend.

Getting out of bed, Ingram regarded her evenly. "Sure."

She smiled sweetly. He continued to the bathroom.

The three ate heartily in the nook in the kitchen. Their guest had cooked up link sausage, poached eggs and toast. Coffee too, of course.

Patting his middle Ingram said, "Gonna have to double up on my workouts, Judy."

"Me too," Claire added, sopping up some yoke with a piece of toast.

"You two are the best," Berkson said.

"I'll swing by your pad a little later today, Judy, and take a gander."

"Thanks, Harry."

"You stay around here for today, okay? The neighborhood I mean," Claire mentioned.

"Like I said, I can't hide out forever, Anita. I'll get another derringer and take my chances. And really, I could move for peace of mind. Better yet, get myself a .38 for real peace of mind."

"Damn, Judy, one step at a time," Ingram interjected. "Both you chicks are getting a might too bloodthirsty, ain't ya?"

"You know you like it," Claire said.

Ignoring the truth of what she said, he replied, "Anyway, seems to me we might be able to give Mr. Rickler bigger things to worry about."

"What, you figure on doing a fire bombing of the club like what happened before?" Claire said. The eager cast to her face suggested she wouldn't mind making that happen.

"Nothing that drastic." To Berkson, he asked, "But lend me your keys, all right?"

"Sure," Berkson said.

They finished eating while continuing to discuss whether it was more than just these heists that Payton was part of with Rickler and Tolbert. Though this probably meant Chet Horne was part of it too, Ingram pointed out.

"The bug is part of this," Claire said.

"Partners spying on each other?" Berkson wondered.

"Deebeck also being scarce is not a coincidence," Ingram stated.

Gulping down the remains of her second cup of coffee, Claire kissed Ingram on the mouth good-bye and Berkson on the cheek. She left as the other two cleaned up the dishes and whatnot.

"What you guys want for dinner?"

"Don't sweat it, we can get some takeout or step over to my joint, the Detour."

"Harry, please, I insist. I have a couple more days off, and you two have stuck your necks way out for me."

"It's the other way around, isn't it?"

"I suppose it's mutual. Me and Anita did get a kick out of last night's escapade."

Ingram had heard that kind of talk back in the Army. Greenhorn soldiers would be charged after a firefight, having come away unscathed. But that next time the Reds were shooting at you and the guy you'd gone through basic together with was talking to you and then he wasn't because his brains had been blown out. A different perspective settled in after that.

Berkson touched his arm as they stood at the sink. "Smoked turkey legs, yams and green beans."

"Sold."

"Damn right."

After saying good-bye, Ingram went into the garage and grabbed his binoculars. He used them at times when out in the field on a story hunt or not so long ago serving papers to check out the scene. Then, unlocking the gate to the backyard, he departed along the driveway.

HAVING A morning to lounge around, Berkson went into the living room. She wondered could two women shack up with one man? Even if one of them was white? What would the neighbors say? What would Anita say except punch her in the face? Berkson grinned, amused by her wanton notions. As a way to break the ice on the subject, she might ask Harry if *Dapper* would be interested in that kind of article—knowing damn well the publisher would be. She'd met him once at a party she went to with Harry and Anita.

Berkson took a book from the shelf by historian Philip Foner. It chronicled the struggles of the Fur and Leather Workers Union in the 1940s. While currently she wasn't a member of a manufacturing union, she'd nonetheless lately been considering what it would entail to become a labor organizer. Like Claire's, Berkson's lefty parents had introduced her early on to campaigns for equal rights. She tuned the radio to the classical music station. Putting her feet in slippers, also borrowed from Claire, on the coffee table, she started to read.

About an hour later, the murmuring of voices brought her out of her reading. She looked up to see through the picture window two men in overalls coming up the walk. One of them was smoking. Bookmarking her spot, she got off the couch and went to the door. Neither Ingram nor Claire had told her anything about workmen coming.

"Yes?" she said after opening the door.

The men looked startled. One was smoking, a double bandage on his chin.

"Is Mrs. Ashby in?" the other said.

"You have the wrong address," Berkson said.

"Sorry to bother you, ma'am," the second one said. "Let's go," he said to his companion. He took a long pull on his cigarette and held the smoke in until he was several feet away.

Berkson watched them walk away quickly. They got in a

Dodge panel van marked STARBRITE CARPETING AND SER-VICES. After she was sure they had gone, Berkson returned to her book.

INTENTIONALLY, INGRAM had made it seem there wasn't much need to be concerned about Rickler knowing where Berkson lived. In actuality, he assumed the card club owner would send at least one of his men to keep watch as he'd want to know if the eavesdropper was working for the church groups. He was not disappointed in his guesswork.

Berkson's second floor apartment on East 79th Street in the Florence-Graham area was not far from where she worked as a tile-cutting machine operator at Millard Tile and Works in Huntington Park. He'd parked his Falcon station wagon down the block and reconnoitered with his binoculars as best he could before approaching her door and going inside. He spotted several white men but they either drove or walked by. Then one pulled up, parked and got out.

Indoors, crouched down at the side of the window looking down on the street, Ingram watched the white fella who was sitting in the Chrysler Imperial. He'd come to the door and knocked, but he hadn't answered, and the man returned to his car. Spying on him walking away, Ingram noted the drape of the man's sport coat on his broad shoulders. The guy sent by Rickler was a bruiser and Ingram needed an advantage over him. The curtains were partly closed, a thin gap between the material. In this way, Ingram could straighten up and move back without being seen. The only way in or out of the apartment was the front door, so sneaking up on the man wasn't possible. Going out the only door would send the watcher scurrying. Considering what to do, Ingram settled on his plan and stepped out of Berkson's apartment.

He took his time on the landing, heard the door opening and closing on the Imperial. The bruiser jogged across the street.

"Hey, you, hold up," he shouted, a hand in the air.

"Me?" Ingram said, coming down the steps.

"Yeah, who the fuck are you?" the enforcer asked as he started up the bottom step. It was Tim from the parking lot last night.

Ingram swung, whacking a small frying pan upside the more muscular man's head. Tim went backward off the steps and onto his back. Ingram pounced, his foot jammed sideways on the struck man's chest. Tim tried to rise and this time got hit in the forehead with the pan for his efforts.

"Motherfucker," Tim gurgled, his eyes unfocused and voice thick.

"Tell Rickler I know about what he and Mose are up to."

"The fuck you do."

"Listen, hotshot, I know the swag from heists your boss bankrolls are moved around in Restoration trucks, I also know those two are burning the candle at both ends. Stealing and selling real furs and using the labels on bootleg ones too." Just as Ingram heard his own words, he locked on to a notion about Betty Payton. The tough glared at Ingram. Odds were he didn't know any of this but he'd report back to Rickler, which was what Ingram wanted.

"I don't give two shits about any of that. But if a hair on

Judy's head should be mussed 'cause of you or one of your playmates, then hell will rain down on Rickler." He lifted his foot off the man's chest and took a few steps backward, ready to use the frying pan again.

"Take it easy, Jackie Robinson." Rickler's man sat up on the lawn, a hand rubbing his throbbing head. "You've made your point."

A few neighbors had come out to see what was up, from a distance.

"What Rickler needs to be doing," Ingram concluded, "is helping find Mose. If he wants to be useful and not a stone in the road."

Ingram went back up to the apartment to return the frying pan and open the drapes wide. The tough got off the ground and weaved his way to his car. He retrieved a flask from the glovebox and took a swig. Thereafter he shook his head vigorously for several moments, coughed harshly and keyed his car to life. He was gone by the time Ingram exited the apartment and walked to his car. Pleased with this morning's outcome and that apparently no one had called the police on him.

That evening at the house in the Crenshaw District the three enjoyed the meal Berkson had prepared. They also had white wine with their dinner as they discussed what had happened earlier today.

"That's not coincidence," Ingram said. When Berkson had told them about the carpet cleaners and their Starbrite marked truck, Claire said such a truck had been near the park where she'd eaten lunch the other day. And Ingram remembered her story about being approached by the stranger at the playground with an offer to break the law.

"It occurred to me when I was at Safeway," Berkson said, "both cars weren't in the driveway and mine was parked on the street. That's why they figured no one was home."

Claire put down her fork and got up from the table. She gestured for the two to keep talking.

"I guess they're a burglar crew," Ingram said.

"Yeah, could be, Harry."

Claire held up a note she'd written on in block lettering. I THINK WE'RE BEING LISTENED TO.

Ingram stared at her, not sure what to say. Berkson was also silent. Claire spoke into Ingram's ear.

"Could be I've had too much wine tonight but the necklace not being where it's supposed to be, the device in Tolbert's house and now the carpet cleaners . . ."

"Okay, we better make sure," he whispered.

She nodded assent. Searching, they kept talking, but about innocuous subject matter.

"We should go to a Rams game this year," Berkson said.

"Good idea, Judy," Claire answered.

The three knew a bug would need to have an electrical connection. Found inside one of the lamps in the living room was a listening device identical to the one they'd taken from Tolbert's home. They also found another microphone gadget in the lamp in the bedroom on Ingram's nightstand. The third device was planted inside the electric clock in the kitchen. Along the way, Ingram took pictures of the exposed bugs with a small camera that was nearly silent when he pushed the shutter button. Done, they spoke in the middle of the backyard in case they'd missed anything. Ingram brought his flashlight.

"Our phone is probably tapped," Claire pointed out.

"For sure this isn't Rickler," Ingram said. "It's the same ones spying on Tolbert."

"It could be the FBI but I'm betting it's Parker and his intelligence division," Claire said. "A lot of them are left over from the Red Squad. They're trying to get dirt on you to make the Zinum suit go away, Harry. Spread the lie you faked the picture somehow too, I'm sure."

"Let's not forget who you work for, dear. I'm sure the chief don't mind keeping tabs on uppity darkies and those that work for them."

She put a hand to her mouth. "Those fuckers heard us when we were having sex."

Berkson put wide eyes on her.

"Dirty bastards." Inwardly, he didn't feel embarrassed but wanted to keep the peace and not seem anything but indignant.

"Hope it made 'em jealous," Claire huffed.

"We should keep the devices where they are, you know."

"Why?"

"If we take them out, they'll know."

"But we've already talked about the Starbrite truck," Berkson pointed out.

Ingram said, "The dining room isn't bugged so maybe they didn't hear us, or at least hear us clearly."

"Screw those chumps," Claire said.

"But now we know and they don't know we know, we might be able to use that to our advantage."

"How do you mean?"

Ingram explained, "Like you said, Parker and Hoover will use lies and disinformation to tar and feather the ones they want to make look like idiots so no one believes them."

"Some people were harassed so bad they killed themselves," she said gravely. "Driven out of their jobs or off of their church committees." She trailed off, then added, "Not sure what all we can feed them, Harry, that will trip them up."

"Not sure either. But let's at least leave them be for a couple of days."

"But now we have to try and act normal. They've already heard us talking about Tolbert and Rickler." Claire paused. "Is that why he disappeared?"

"He doesn't tell Rickler?"

"Could be he didn't want him getting mad and sending a leg breaker to see him like he tried with Judy."

"Maybe it's that or maybe there's more to it. Tolbert has also been involved in left causes."

A chill rippled through Claire. "Your buddy Hoyt and his Providers might be part of this. It's not a crackpot fantasy that there's ties between the capitalists and the police who represent their interests."

"We can't go getting paranoid," Berkson said.

Ingram said, "Yeah, can't imagine a hardass like Parker taking orders from Winston Hoyt or any damn body."

"A suggestion from him could have been all it takes after a round of golf or getting a rub down after a steam at the Jonathan Club. Assuming they have a steam room there, but I wouldn't know, being Black and a woman, neither of which is let in there."

"Uh-huh," he agreed.

A silence stretched between them until Claire said, "Well, fine, shit, this has got me all riled up and I do want to see if we can put one over on these fat cats and their lackies."

"Go on with your bad self, Emma Goldman," Berkson said. "Guess I better get home and search my place too."

"You want us to follow you home?" Claire asked. The three began walking toward the back door off the kitchen, talking as they did so.

"The Starbrite boys are sneaks and I'm feeling confident Mr. Rickler got the message," Berkson said.

"When you get home, take a slow spin around the block first before going in," Ingram said when they were in front of the house. "Anything looks funny, you hightail it back here."

"I will," she said. This time she did give Ingram a smack on the cheek and Claire a quick kiss on the lips.

The couple stood arm in arm, waving on the lighted porch as Berkson drove away. Back inside, the two went into the bathroom off their bedroom and closed the door. They'd searched the lone overhead light fixture and two electrical outlets so were relatively certain there was no listening device in here. Claire sat on the lid of the toilet and Ingram on the edge of the bathtub.

"Something else you better know, 'cause now with this business . . ." She trailed off.

"I'm listening." They both kept their voices low.

"I'm part of the Morning Bandit gang."

He stared at her and finally responded, "You and your folks."

She nodded. "Kind of hard to explain how it all started."

Ingram remembered his conversation with Charlie Sutton, a man who knew her father. This was a couple of years ago, while he was looking into the death of his army buddy Ben Kinslow. He'd talked to him when he'd been tasked by

Anita to find a missing diary written by Judy Berkson's father naming names. To hopefully make sure it was lost but not stolen by the FBI. Ingram had debated then about mentioning the conversation to her and didn't at the time as he'd ultimately dismissed what Sutton told him: that Solly Claire was the Morning Bandit. Now, he did tell her, finishing with, "Like them old Bolsheviks, your pops was pulling down scores to strike a blow against the moneyed class, huh? Bonnie and Clyde and Che Guevara." Ruefully, he shook his head. Ingram was surprised he wasn't that surprised. He also recalled the money band in her mother's car.

"At first it was just him. We got involved to protect my dad. Now not for nothing, it's brought Mom and Dad closer together again."

"The family that steals together," he quipped.

"Mom is great for casing the banks," she said proudly. "Nice white schoolmarm-looking lady."

"And you the pistol-packing backup."

"Shotgunner, but yeah."

"Naturally you three goddamn revolutionaries are carrying out orders from the ghost of Lenin." He laughed too loud.

Indignantly, she replied, "We've gotten money to ANC, Harry. We ain't bullshittin'."

"I know. But even without whoever listening in on us, it's crazy dangerous, Anita. I mean shit." He pointed at the bathroom door and what lay beyond.

"We decided after our last close call to quit."

"Good."

"But . . ."

"Don't be shy now."

She told him about the codded notebook. "Mom and I took the book to a friend of theirs, Del Standers. He'd been a Ritchie Boy during the war."

"Who were they?"

She explained who they were and that Standers was one of the group. She added, "We kinda hedged it was a notebook left behind by Mickey Cohen or his accountant."

Ingram nodded. The bank they'd robbed was in Maywood, not far from Boyle Heights. Though he had a nightspot on the Sunset Strip, the gangster kept a place in Boyle Heights where he'd grown up. "But it's not?"

"It's dynamite, Harry. Del cracked the code. This book details all sorts of transactions by the Providers. Going back years."

"Fuck," he whispered, trying to take this all in.

"I'd been wrestling with coming clean, Harry. But now knowing what the logbook is, I had to tell you." A pause and she added, "Talk about bad timing."

"Look, we got no choice. We gotta deal with these bugs and Tolbert first. After that, if we're still around, we get on the book."

Claire got up and so did he. She hugged him tight. "It's a lot, I know."

"It's you and me, baby. Right down the line."

Claire kissed him like a woman long alone in the desert. In their bedroom the two tried not to be too self-conscious. After a few minutes of sounding stilted, they settled into their natural patter. Sleep, though, was elusive for both.

FINALLY, CLAIRE was able to achieve slumber. Ingram eventually dozed. Yet as he descended into a deeper state,

Seoul City Sue, the Arkansas born white woman propagandist for North Korea, invaded his dreamscape once again. She would broadcast over radio and her recordings would be heard over public address systems telling the GIs their wives and girlfriends were seeing other men. Or she would question, why were negro soldiers fighting for white Uncle Sam, a country that would not recognize their sacrifices back home?

Ingram stood at the end of the driveway. Seoul City Sue came out of the garage workshop. She was curvy like a *Dapper* model, in a silk dress, showing thigh through a slit up its side. A cigarette smoldered from the end of her ivory inlaid cigarette holder. The propagandist was giving orders to two hulking flunkies like out of an EC horror comic book. The goons carried boxes of Ingram's photos.

"Hey, that's my stuff," he objected. He moved to stop them. "Put that down."

"Back off, Yankee," Seoul City Sue warned.

"The hell you say."

Seoul City Sue pointed her fist at him, index finger extended, and a gun winked into existence in her hand. She shot him three times in the chest. After that, Ingram slept peacefully.

CHAPTER FOURTEEN

Claire and Ingram went through their normal routine in the morning, making sure to close the bathroom door for some sense of privacy. As he shaved, it occurred to Ingram that like Dorothy Nielson, Betty Payton probably cased the homes of the swells she palled around with. Had to be Rickler using Tim and whoever ripped them off. Lining his and her pockets. That was old-fashioned greed, not about no redistribution of wealth.

Dressed, the two went into the kitchen and had a light breakfast.

"The more I think about it, I bet Mose went off on a bender." Ingram slurped his coffee.

Claire said, "What are you gonna tell Betty?"

"That she should accept the truth," he said. There was a two-day-old edition of the *Herald Examiner* folded on the table and he quietly tore off a piece. Using a pencil, he wrote a note and slid it across to her. "What else is there to do, right?" he said.

"I guess so." Claire read the note asking her to call Judy Berkson later from a pay phone to see if she'd found a bug. Claire nodded. He asked her what she had planned

today and she provided their listeners with a bland itin-
erary.

Outside, like otherworld versions of denizens of the Donna
Reed Show, Ingram quickly kissed Claire on the lips as she
walked toward her car to leave for work while he stayed home.
He waved at her as she departed. Before turning back, he
scanned the street, hoping he wasn't obvious doing so.

Inside the house, he went through and out to the garage,
turning on one of the goose-necked lamps. There was power
in here and they hadn't searched the place last night. If one
of the cops' eavesdropping doohickeys had been installed,
there weren't too many places to hide it. In addition to several types of lamps, there was his portable radio. He
unscrewed the back of the radio and the plates on the bases
of the lamps. He soon was satisfied there wasn't a bug in the
garage. He turned on the radio to the beginnings of a
Dodger game and took a seat in one of his mismatched
chairs. Two of them he'd found discarded at the curb and
the other two bought at Goodwill.

He wanted to light up a cigar but, given the photo chem-
icals in here, not a wise idea. He wondered why the cops had
come back to the house. Their devices were already in place
so was the idea they wanted to put one in here? Had one of
their bugs stopped working? Or was something even more
nefarious their objective? Ingram stayed with the game for
the first two and a half innings, then turned off the radio
and went into the kitchen for a glass of water. He answered
the phone on the second ring.

"Hello?"

"This Harry Ingram?" a gravelly voice said on the other
end. The man sounded older.

Ingram told him it was and the caller continued. "I'm Len Beck, heard you came around to see me."

"Yes, sir. Are you at your shop now?"

"Sure am. I understand you were looking for—"

"Not to cut you off, Mr. Beck, but I got something boiling over on the stove. Look, I'll be right over, okay?"

"Uh, sure."

"See you soon."

Ingram hung up. Just in case eyes were watching the house, he took a few beats as if taking care of his emergency. After leaving his house, he considered doubling back to see if the carpet men showed up, but decided to get to Treasure Island without further subterfuge.

He arrived to find the elder Beck in the middle of a negotiation with two women over the price of a scarred credenza.

"You understand this is for the church, Len," one of them was saying.

"I do, Delphina, that's why I'm only asking a fair price."

"Seems high for the condition this is in," Delphina's companion said. She put a hand on the credenza, causing it to tilt to and fro. One of its legs was shorter than the other three.

Beck wore bowline glasses with thin lenses. He had a receding hairline of salt and pepper hair and a trimmed snow-white beard. He moved easily though he might be sixty or seventy some odd, Ingram estimated. Beck hitched his thumbs in the corner of the pockets of his worn dungarees. "Tell you what, I'll even up the legs and see what I can do about the finish." He waved a hand over the piece of furniture like a magician about to perform an act of conjuring.

Delphina regarded the other women and to Beck, said, "You got a deal, you 'ole smooth talker you." They shook hands. Ingram, who'd worn his snap brim hat, touched the brim as they went past and on out of the shop.

"You must be Mr. Ingram."

"Harry is fine."

"You took that picture, didn't you?"

"I did."

"You gonna make Donnie famous like you?"

"Can't guarantee something like that, Len, if that's okay to call you that."

"It is. Give me a hand with this."

Ingram gripped the opposite end of the credenza Beck had taken hold of. Together, they carried it toward his work area, but he indicated he wanted the piece over toward a corner.

"We're gonna flip it over," he said.

They did this so he could get at the legs.

Ingram resumed. "I plan to put him in an article I'm looking to write about Watts in the weeks following the riots. I talked to an editor at the *Nation* who has some interest. But I need to send him an outline first."

"They been around since the *Crisis* magazine."

Ingram was impressed the old man had it on the ball. "Yes they have." The *Crisis* was published by the NAACP. "But I'm going to put all my cards on the table, Len. I also want to talk to your grandson because I believe he's friends with Mose Tolbert and I'm trying to find him."

The older Beck had begun the process of unscrewing the legs from the bottom of the credenza. He squirted a measure of WD-40 where each leg was flush with the base to cut through the accumulated rust and grime on the threads. He talked as he worked. "I recognize that name. Seems Donnie mentioned this Tolbert was gonna help him get an art show together 'cause he knew those kind of people. You lookin' for this fella to be in the article too?"

"He's definitely a fan of Donnie's work. I've seen one of his paintings at the man's home—a while ago, I mean."

Now Beck used an adjustable wrench, closed its jaws on the leg. He'd first wrapped part of the rag around the leg to protect the threads. He twisted, grunting, and the leg turned. "Last time Donnie was by he said he had a gig, that's what he called a job, like a jazz musician, taking him out of town for a few weeks."

"He say where or what the job was?"

"Oh, that boy is always talking about who shot John and his big plans." He paused, having gotten the second leg loose. "Though when it comes to getting the work, he's no joke. He's done jobs for the props department over there at them Paramount studios." He motioned in the air. "Did these buildings like what you see in New York on big sheets of glass. He showed me the photos of him working. Said the photographer who worked for the studio did them and laid a few prints on him."

He looked over at Ingram. "You ever do that kind of work?"

"Can't say I have."

"Anyway, Donnie said it was some sort of play or, hell, I'm not sure. I think he also told me it was in St. Louis."

"He say when he was coming back?"

He took the last leg off. "No, but that's not unusual. He's what you call footloose and fancy free. Meet some chick and that cat may not be back for half a year."

"You remember when he left?"

He carried the legs to his worktable. "Must have been the second, no third day of the riots. That Saturday I guess it was. Friday he'd stayed overnight with me in the shop making sure I was okay and them angry soul brothers weren't gonna torch me to cinders. Guess it helps I've been here since Hector was a pup and I knew them young'ins out in the streets since they was running around in knee pants."

Ingram didn't figure that was a coincidence, given Tolbert was last seen that Friday. Was one man responsible for the disappearance of the other? They went away together or suffered the same fate?

"Do you know if he got a call about this job on Saturday?"

Beck gestured. "No idea. But he called me late on Saturday to say he was heading out of town."

Lacking an immediate follow-up question, Ingram glanced around the workspace. He chanced upon a loose pile of periodicals such as *Ebony* and even a several months old issue of *Dapper* near him on a stool. There were several letters atop the stack. Ingram keyed in on who the top letter was addressed to.

"Your grandson gets his mail here?"

The older Beck was measuring the credenza's legs, jotting down the lengths. "The stuff he wants, yeah." He paused, holding one of the legs before his eyes as if examining a rare gem. Offhandedly he added, "He wanted to make damn sure I looked out for a check he was waiting on from some more studio work he'd done. Wouldn't be the first time I had to send him money once he called me." He shook his head. "Damn sight better than how his long-haired beatnik buddies treat him. Doing work for nothing 'cause it's for the people. Sheet." He chuckled.

"What beatnik buddies?"

"That newspaper he draws for sometimes, the *Free Message*."

"The *Free Press* you mean?"

He snapped his fingers. "That's it. A young white dude for the paper was around here interviewing me and some others about the riots."

That had to be Gerry Tackwood. "Donnie's done work for the paper?"

Beck pointed to the pile. "Some of his drawings have been used in it. He keeps them when they get published. For his portfolio, he called it. Go ahead, take a gander."

Ingram searched through the pile and came to a folded-over tabloid sheet. It was an article by Gerry Tackwood about discriminatory apartment rental practices in West L.A. which included an illustration. The ink and wash drawing was of a giant white hand spread before a black couple and their two small children. It was signed Deebeck. Checking the date, Ingram saw this had run a month ago. On the back side of the sheet was part of a piece he'd written. Bemusedly, he concluded if his own head wasn't up his ass so much, he would have noticed this before—hiding in plain sight from his ego.

Rearranging the pile, he noticed a certificate of merit he'd initially sifted past. He read it. "Donnie played on the Little League team you sponsored."

"Yes, sir, heck of a shortstop."

"Neal Atkins played on the team." He recalled the photo Crossman had of the youths in his Little League gear.

The older Beck shook his head glumly. "He did. He was quick, could steal a base like Maury Wills. Too bad he didn't stick to that kind of . . . taking."

"You know if they kept in touch?"

"Can't say for sure but it wouldn't surprise me."

"You've been a lot of help, Len." He put his card on the letters. "If you hear from Donnie, let him know I'd like to talk to him."

"Sure thing." Beck was clamping a pair of vice grips on the threads of one of the legs.

Ingram left him to his work and drove off to look for a pay phone. He found one two blocks over and called Tackwood. Not at the Freep office but at his home, a courtyard apartment he'd been to with Claire for a party on the border with Culver City.

"Hello," a female voice answered.

Ingram asked for Tackwood.

"He's not here right now. Can I give him a message?" she asked.

Ingram was curious as to the identity of the mystery woman but kept it professional. He told her who he was and asked that Tackwood call him this evening at home if possible.

"He has your number?"

Ingram relayed that he did and she informed him she'd give him the message. He next drove to the Galton Process Services and Legal Papers offices on Grand Avenue, not far from the downtown courthouses. He parked on its compact lot and entered. Along one wall several padded metal chairs were aligned. On one of the chairs sat a beefy man in khakis and flannel shirt reading over papers he was holding in both rough hands. His face was clouded and intermittently he mumbled a curse word as he read.

"Hey, stranger," Doris Letrec said, looking up from her typing on an Underwood, removing her cat-eye glasses on a chain. She was the office manager and her desk faced the street.

"Hey yourself," he said.

A pony wall had recently been installed past the chairs the length of the room. Ingram pushed open its gate and stepped to Letrec's side. The beefy man regarded this, then returned to his reading.

"You stop by for work?" she asked. "Got a couple of hot ones."

"Not today, sorry, but I'd like to use the back room."

"Of course, Harry, go right ahead."

The door to Letrec's right was inset with pebbled frosted glass and a set of drawn blinds. As he started past her desk, that door cracked open the bare minimum width to allow the face of a white man to appear in the sliver of the opening. The eye was as pale blue as a washed-out sky.

"Hello, Harry," the eye's owner said.

"Tremaine, how's it going?"

"Shoulder to the wheel, old son, shoulder to the wheel." The door closed slowly and clicked back into place.

A wry smile on his face, Ingram turned his head to Letrec, who mirrored his expression. He continued on, pouring himself a cup of coffee from the new-fangled coffee maker. Tremane Galton was the owner of the business. Born in Britain, he'd lived in the States going on some thirty-odd years. He was agoraphobic, yet managed to drive from his house in Frogtown to the office at least three days a week.

Ingram walked past a row of file cabinets to an unmarked door in the rear south wall. He stepped inside and closing the door, pulled the string on the bare light bulb overhead. In here were all types of aged ledgers. These assorted record books were kept in order by year on two shelves. In particular, he wanted to look at the listings of building permits, business licenses and property taxes issued by this city and several surrounding municipalities. This private accumulation of public information, usually requiring visiting various city records offices, was handy to have in one place when tracking down errant business owners who didn't want their entanglements known.

Ingram first looked up the Starbrite name. A main reason he'd come today was to confirm what he and Claire suspected, that there was no listing for such a company, having already looked in the White and Yellow Pages. He found no legal reference in terms of a property tax bill or business tax record in Los Angeles, nor when he checked through a few cities' records in the vicinity. He was convinced the supposed carpet service was a disguised police operation.

He next looked through the records for Tolbert's business but as he suspected, neither Rickler's or Albert Domergue's names were on the older property records.

If someone looked at the property tax records for Whitehead's grocery store, only Arthur Yarbrough's name was identified as owner. In reality, Ingram, Josh Nakano and Strummer Edwards owned a percentage of the market. This was delineated on an agreement signed by the three of them, its original held in a safety deposit box. Legally, if his blind friend wanted to squawk and not pay them their cut each year, or short them, Ingram understood Yarbrough would have the upper hand. But each trusted the other and too, unsaid was that neither Yarbrough nor Ingram were looking to get on Edwards's bad side. Both had discussed this after a few sips in the grocer's back office. They were damn certain Edwards had eliminated more than one unfortunate from the face of this troubled world.

Wanting to be thorough, Ingram also checked the Emerald Room's records, but his search didn't yield anything out of the ordinary. Ingram reminded himself he could get lost following the dusty trail of who Albert Domergue was and all his holdings. Still, he felt he should do some nosing about him if only to ascertain his relationship to the bookkeeper. All the more reason, he concluded, returning the hand-printed record binders to their proper location, to have that talk with Betty Payton. Yawning and stretching where he sat at the table, he stood again and returned the ledgers and binders he'd been looking through to their respective locations on the shelves. He clicked off the light and stepped back to the main room. Letrec wasn't at her desk and the man who'd been reading and grousing was long gone. He looked at Galton's door and considered knocking on it to say good-bye. The office manager returned from using the restroom and smiled at Ingram.

"Find what you were looking for, Harry?"

"Found something." He'd wetted a paper towel from the water cooler and was using that to clean out his empty cup.

"One breadcrumb at a time for the bloodhound." She retrieved several file folders from her desk and walking past Ingram, patted him on the shoulder. "Good to see you again."

"Okay to use the phone?"

"Of course." He called Gerry Tackwood and was glad he found him at the Freep's office. They talked some. When he was finished, he said to Letrec, "Thanks, Doris."

"Hope to see you around, Harry."

Ingram left the service and drove over to the Detour diner. He was pleased to see Winnie McClure behind the counter. She hadn't been here the other week he'd come through. McClure was a heavyset woman with a handsome face and reddish-brown hair. As usual she had it styled short and straight, a pixie cut like childhood drawings he recalled of Peter Pan in story books. As it was past the lunch rush, only a few patrons were present. He sat in a booth.

"What'll it be, Harry?" McClure said coming over.

"Water for now. Meeting a guy for a late lunch."

"Okay."

He studied the miniature chalkboard on the wall for today's specials. He could handle those smothered pork chops and greens. Having and wanting to keep a girlfriend like Anita Claire though had made him more conscious of his waistline. Not that she was a shallow person but in all ways he wanted to impress her. He almost cackled, deluding himself that he somehow impressed her when he damn sure knew it was the other way around. Too, he better get to his fighting weight, considering what all was coming at them.

Tackwood arrived and Ingram waved him over. Tackwood sat opposite.

"Thanks for meeting me," Ingram said.

"A free lunch is a free lunch." Tackwood also studied the specials.

McClure came back, pad at the ready. "Gentlemen?"

"I'll have the pork chops and greens," Tackwood said.

"That comes with macaroni and cheese," McClure said.

"Fantastic," Tackwood enthused.

Ingram gave in and also ordered the same, but no macaroni. Double up the workouts for sure, he vowed.

"Mm-hmm," she said, writing down their orders. "Y'all want cokes or 7 Up with that? Got fresh squeezed lemonade too."

"I'll stick with water," Ingram said.

"7 Up for me," Tackwood said. "Before we get to your thing, check this out, I was working on my article when you called. Yesterday I had a meet with my contact at the 77th. Following up on Atkins supposedly taking his own life in lockup." Neal Atkins's reported suicide in custody had been covered by the white press, spurred by Crossman's article speculating foul play, which had run in the *Sentinel*.

"You don't buy the informant rumor and that he was done in by a fellow prisoner?"

"Do you?"

Ingram said evenly, "Smells like a cop fairy tale to cover their tracks."

McClure brought their drinks and set out utensils. She went away again and they continued talking.

"I agree. My guy tells me he talked to Atkins earlier that evening. He knew him slightly from the streets. Atkins had been scooped up on an outstanding warrant during the rebellion." Tackwood had his hand on his plastic cup of 7 Up and ice but didn't drink from it. "He said that Atkins was looking forward to getting out and was in good spirits. The warrant was for unpaid parking tickets, not a thing to kill yourself over."

Ingram nodded agreement.

Now Tackwood had some of his soda. "My guy was working down the hall from where they were holding Atkins. Not, I hasten to inform you, my stalwart colleague, in the general lock-up with the unwashed."

The usual holding tank at 77th was a holding cell in the basement where everyone from drunks to women's shoe sniffers were crowded into initially upon being booked. Ingram'd taken plenty of pictures of the inhabitants there. "You're saying they put him in isolation for a reason?"

"I'm saying my guy was ordered away from his usual duties round about eight that night. He was told to go over to Records and Identification at Central to deliver several boxes of records."

"Getting your guy out of the way, you mean?"

"Seems like."

Ingram considered what his friend was saying. "He was the masked man on Lomax?"

"Yes," Tackwood admitted quietly.

"But he's not a cop. There's no standing guard at the tank. Only he's invisible." Ingram snapped his fingers. "The janitor, they're always cleaning up vomit, piss and who knows what all else down in holding. He overhears them paddy cops talking all the time. That's who Atkins would talk to."

A pause, then, "Pretty good, Harry. That's right."

"Parker must have checked sick days and whatnot to his appearance on TV. He won't find him 'cause he probably doesn't clock in to work until late afternoon."

"Exactly. No one suspects him. Lomax agreed to go along with the dodge to better protect him. But what he talks about is accurate."

"You're not gonna out him in an article?"

"Of course not. But that's what I've been wrestling with, how to write this without giving him away."

They kept talking and their food arrived, Ingram nodding to McClure who once again returned to the racing sheet. "By the time my guy got back to the station, Atkins's body had already been taken to the morgue's meat locker. Now when I find this out, I go over to the morgue to see if I could worm my way in to take a gander at the corpse. Atkins had already been cremated, and the ashes interred at Evergreen."

"Definitely not the protocol." Ingram and Tackwood both knew the rule at the morgue: hold the body for a year, as attempts would be made to find the next of kin. Only then, if unsuccessful, would the departed be taken care of, and the ashes buried at the County's potter's field section amid the acreage of Evergreen cemetery in Boyle Heights.

"Why would the cops want to murder a lightweight like Atkins?"

"Still trying to figure that out. But I know you feel it like I do. The uprising has not only lit a spark in the ghetto but put a fire under the cops too. Everybody knows which way the wind is blowing."

"You got that right," Ingram agreed.

"I've been talking with Dorrell Zinum and a few others about this, my fears are for sure Parker would step it up in terms of keeping watch on the natives and whatnot. Did Anita show you my shots from the town hall and I pointed out this cat to her? The one I said was suspected of being a snitch or undercover cop?"

"She did," Ingram said, cutting off a piece of meat. "It

relates to what I wanted to ask you about. I'm a little gun shy talking over the wires these days. Including the *Free Press*'s phones."

His friend weighed that as Ingram told him about finding the listening devices and the Starbrite cover the intelligence squad used.

"See," Tackwood said, gesturing with the end of his fork at Ingram before plunging it into his macaroni and cheese. "That photo of yours, man," he said over a mouthful. He swallowed and added, "I've been nosing around, hearing about a few men and women advocates on our side of the fence suspected of being in cahoots with Parker's G2 one way or the other. I've also Ided a couple of undercover narcotics officers along the way."

"Yeah . . . ." Ingram sighed. He recalled a story his late friend Ben Kinslow had told him. Kinslow, because he was white, had been let go in a bust at a club that snared two black musician friends of his for a couple of marijuana cigarettes. The one who ratted them out to the narcotics squad was the colored drummer.

Ingram told him what Crossman had relayed about the cops searching Atkins's apartment. "Still, we could be trying too hard to connect them dots, Gerry."

"Maybe," Tackwood allowed. "But it does seem awfully convenient that Atkins winds up dead. And here you are being bugged, which means you're not the only one. Who knows where those Starbrite trucks have been."

For a while they both ate in silence, consumed by their own thoughts. Eventually Ingram asked, "So what's your next steps?"

Tackwood reached into his back pocket. "Check this out."

He took a folded piece of paper out and handed it across. "I'll be covering this for the paper."

Ingram unfolded the paper. It was a flyer announcing a "Be-In" at the Fifth Estate coffeehouse where the *Free Press* had its offices in the basement.

"Kind of a cross between a 'Happening' and a 'Teach-In,'" Tackwood said, bemused.

Ingram nodded. "Teach-Ins," he knew, involving among other aspects discussions of direct action techniques, had started earlier this year around anti-war protests at the University of Michigan. The name inspired by "Sit-Ins" at lunch counters by those involved in the struggle for civil rights. The flyer stated there would be various discussion leaders, including a representative from the Disciples, along with poetry and live music and art. The lettering was artfully done and designed as if issuing from the flute of a snake charmer sitting cross-legged toward the bottom of the page.

Ingram noted the name of the artist. It was Deebeck. Ingram asked Tackwood if he knew him since he'd done other work for the paper.

"Art knows him, not me," Tackwood said.

"Think he'll be there?"

Tackwood hunched a shoulder and spread his hands. "There's always a few painters at these things, man. Dolling up chicks in bikinis, face painting and all that."

"Mind if I keep this?"

"Be my guest."

Ingram tucked the flyer away. "G2 will be at the Be-In too, you know."

Tackwood touched two fingers to his temple. "Maybe we

can get the transcendentalists to use their mind waves to detect them."

Ingram chuckled hollowly, like a man who'd had a good steak before his appointment with the guillotine. He supposed a reasonable person would have a knot of dread in their stomach, given the import of his and Tackwood's discussion. Instead, he was hungry for the food before him and ready to confront what was sure to come. Finding Tolbert was part of the answer.

CHAPTER FIFTEEN

Toward the evening, Ingram and Claire stood in their living room and talked about their day for the benefit of their listeners. Thereafter, they took the day's mail out back with their beverages to the patio table. An adjustable light attached to the house provided light on the patio. They'd searched it for a listening device. Being out here was a normal thing to do given the day's warmth was yet to dissipate. Among the selection of mail was a business-sized letter from Betty Payton. Claire used a nail to open the flap. She removed the folded-in-three-sheet of crème colored paper and the check encased within. Unfolding the sheet, she regarded the amount on the check before handing it over to Ingram.

He whistled, appreciative of the thousand dollars Payton had paid him. "Damn."

Reading the handwritten note accompanying the check, Claire said, "She says she heard from Mose. He's down in Puerto Vallarta. Thank you for your efforts." She put the sheet aside, the script on it neatly handwritten in blue ink. "That's a pretty nice payout, Harry. Maybe I ought to try this gumshoe hustle." She grinned, imagining them a version of Nick and Nora of the Thin Man movies she'd seen on television over the years.

"You'd be good at it." He tipped his bottled beer at the letter. "Of course you know this is bullshit." He drank some of his brew. "It must be because of Rickler. I'd suggested to his goon to produce Tolbert." They talked in their normal voices, assuming they were unheard or at the most muffled from the devices inside their home. To be doubly sure, they'd left the radio on inside at a higher volume.

"And he can't?" Claire wondered.

"I think it means Rickler didn't put the snatch on him. Tolbert went away on his own."

She waved the check. "And this?"

"You heard her that night. Betty may be all help the downtrodden, but not so much when it affects her bottom line. She's satisfied him and her are cool, that they can go back to their little schemes."

"And you don't mess with Rickler and therefore create another problem what with being concerned about attention from the attorney general. You gonna talk to her?"

"I'm'a cash her check. But no, what for? She's heard from Rickler enough to figure out I know what she's up to." He shrugged. "Who am I to judge?"

"Yeah," she drawled. "Mom's going to be disappointed in her, though."

Ingram touched her arm. "This isn't about Betty now. We're the ones the cops bugged."

She nodded slightly.

"Let's go over to the Cloverleaf and you can buy me a proper drink."

"How about an order of onion rings too?"

They both rose. "They don't serve 'em and anyway, you'd only eat two."

She patted her butt. "Gotta watch my figure."

"Don't worry, I'm watching it." Ingram reached out and drew her close, nuzzling her neck. He pulled her tighter, grinding against her as he became erect. She pulled away, holding his hand.

"Get a move on, Ingram, I'm thirsty."

"You sure know how to deflate a guy."

She laughed and walked toward the house. Ingram followed her.

The actual name of the bar was the Lucky Clover, and it was on Broadway not too far from the *Herald Examiner* newspaper, which was at the intersection of 11th Street. The watering hole had garnered the nickname Cloverleaf because the location once upon a time had been the end point station for the Yellow Car trolly. In that era the bar had served the trolly operators, mechanics and other workingmen. Yet as freeways crisscrossing one another came to symbolize the dominance of the car in the Southland, the watering hole had acquired the moniker.

"I say we rip the bugs out and write an article for the *Sentinel*. Probably get you back on the Lomax show."

Ingram replied, "The cops will say we planted those bad boys." He and Claire sat close in one of the booths. A cocoon of smoke, clinking glasses and muted laughter filled the bar. The Supremes "Stop! In the Name of Love" played quietly on the jukebox.

"There has to be a way we can authenticate the listening devices," she countered.

Ingram nodded. "Not exactly electrical do-dads you could buy at Zodys."

She leaned toward him, touching her forehead to his. "Exactly." They smacked a kiss loudly.

"I know you want to take it to the tools of the capitalists, but maybe you better run this past your boss first."

She stuck out her bottom lip. "Now who's ruining the mood."

"Just being practical."

"Shit," she retorted. "Tom is going to want to do some sort of look into this on the quiet like, pussyfoot around and whatnot. That would take too damn long."

"How about we disconnect the one in the bedroom? I take it to some dang engineer or another to write up his assessment of the device." Since they'd discovered their home was being surveilled electronically, they'd been going to a motel on Western to make love. "Our secret audience might not think too much of that. One or two of their bugs probably crap out regularly."

"Then do the article?"

"I could leak it to Gerry for a piece in the Freep. Or for that matter, go to Louis Lomax directly."

"That could work," she allowed.

Time passed and they left the bar and headed to their parked car. As they were approaching a driveway, a car zoomed from behind them and blocked their path. Two cold-eyed white men in sport coats got out of the vehicle, a Ford Fairlane. There was an adjustable spotlight outside the passenger side window of the Ford. This was turned to shine in their faces.

The one closest to the couple was momentarily backlit

and his shape reminded Ingram of the dead hoodlum named Wicks. The man he'd killed in cold blood. Claire noticed his intake of breath and tightened her hand over his.

"Hands on the wall," the one closet to them said.

"Fuck off," Claire said.

"You got a mouth on you, gal." He stepped closer. Along his jawline was a several days old gash. "You best be keeping it shut."

His partner, also white, stepped from around the driver's side. He flashed a detective's shield. "Police. Now do as we say." He tucked his credentials away.

"What's this about?" Ingram said.

"It's about you being a colored snoop." He shoved Ingram. He was taller and had a build like a linebacker for the Rams.

"We better do as they say, Harry." Ingram knew she was worried her boyfriend was going to strike the man.

"Yeah, Harry, listen to your mulatto pinup girl. Being half-white, she might know a thing or two." The plain-clothesman with the chin injury snickered.

Slowly, Ingram put his hands on the wall.

Chin Injury gestured. "You too, sweetie. And hand over that purse."

Claire complied.

The bigger one began patting Ingram down while the other dumped the contents of Claire's purse on the hood of his cruiser. Her lipstick rolled off onto the sidewalk.

"Asshole," she muttered, looking over her shoulder.

He then put his hands on her hips.

"Get your goddamn paws off of her," Ingram said.

"Or what, boy?"

"Or I put my foot so far up your ass you'll spit polish."

"Harry . . ."

The one with the wound began to ostensibly search Claire again. All emotion was drained from her face. The other cop put a hand on Ingram's shoulder as he flinched. The detective also reached his free hand under his coat.

"Ain't this some shit?" a female voice said. "The fires are barely out and Parker's gray boys still act like they own us." She was a slender woman with big glasses. Another woman and a man flanked her. Customers from the bar.

"Get back inside or you're spending a night in jail," the plainclothesman near Claire warned.

"That supposed to scare me?"

"These colored broads, the fuck is in their Wheaties these days?" He turned from Claire. Pedestrians across the street had stopped to look as well. Three of them stepped off the curb, one of them pointing.

"Hey," the taller cop said in a low tone, "The idea was to do this quietlike."

"Yeah, so?" his partner growled.

"Take your head out of your ass, Stevens. You want the wagon over here? Then you explain how it went," the one on Ingram retorted. He then said in a low voice into Ingram's face, "Consider seriously switching up your career, Ingram. Wedding pictures and bar mitzvahs, that sounds about right, don't it?" He clamped a hand on Ingram's upper arm. "Nothing you can do to bring Zinum back."

Ingram glared back at him.

"Let's get the fuck out of here."

More people were gathering in front of the Lucky Clover, Clyde Hampton the bartender among them. The taller one got back behind the wheel of the Ford. His partner stood with his back toward the passenger door, staring down the clientele. Reluctantly he also got back in the car, the engine running. The unmarked car backed up in a lurch. Rear tires screeching, the car was righted, and the two policemen drove away.

"Sure want to thank you folks." Ingram had an arm around Claire's shoulders. Both were shaky.

"No sweat," Hampton said as he came over, smiles going all around.

When the couple returned home, they systematically removed all the listening devices, being careful not to damage them. Finished, they went to bed, holding on to one another. When Claire finally went to sleep, Ingram untangled himself from her and removed his .45 in the drawer in the nightstand. He put the gun under his pillow. He double-checked the door locks and spread pages from the newspaper at the thresholds of the front door and the one off the kitchen. Back in bed, every night sound brought him fully alert until daybreak.

CHAPTER SIXTEEN

Ingram and Claire held hands as they made their way toward the Fifth Estate. There were a goodly number of Black folks at the Be-In, distinct from other such gatherings that tended to be mostly white folks. Familiar faces such as Lawrence Lipton and Art Kunkin, publisher of the *Free Press*, a sponsor of this event, were also here. Several other organizations were co-sponsors, including the Disciples for Community Defense and even Ascension Grace Lutheran. Mark Schmeling, the pastor there who'd spoken at the memorial for Faraday Zinum, was billed as one of the discussion leaders. In addition to the Fifth Estate coffee house, the parking area beside the building had been blocked off for use for the event. Tents and colorful canopies had been erected there and other activities were taking place. The gathering even spilled over to the currently empty storefront next door.

Because this section of the Sunset Strip was technically an unincorporated area lying between the cities of Los Angeles and Beverly Hills, sheriff's cars of deputies were stationed about along with some from the LAPD. A block west of the coffeehouse and one and half blocks east were closed to traffic. People milled about in the cordoned-off roadway.

"Our coordinated efforts are paying off," a speaker was saying at the standing microphone. He wasn't a youth but a middle-aged, muscular white man in a wrinkled suit in need of a visit to the cleaners. He wore an open collar shirt and held a few rolled-up sheets of paper in a beefy hand. "Know that the head of my union, Harry Bridges, leader of the 1934 west coast longshoreman strike, has given full-throated support, which also means material support, to our brothers and sisters, be they in the ghetto, the barrio or here in bourgeois West Hollywood." He laughed, raising both his arms and shaking his fists over his head, crumpling his papers. Whoops and cheers filled the room. He continued as the adulation faded away. "We did it then and we can do it now. It's not just in Montgomery and Natchez that the cries go up for justice and equal treatment. In the shadow and signifier that is Watts, we must have it here in this our home. General strike, general strike . . ."

The chant was taken up by those in the room, "General strike, general strike!" was repeated over and over. Ingram had his hand around Claire's waist and the two danced some as they also took up the slogan. The labor representative stepped away, waving to the crowd as he exited the establishment. As a young woman in braids then came to the microphone, Ingram and Claire started for a side door to check out what else was going on. Nearby stood Pastor Schmeling studying his notes in preparation for what he was going to speak on. He and Ingram exchanged a nod.

"Over there," Claire said, pointing at one of the canopies in the parking lot. Several people were gathered around checking out a man painting designs on bikini-clad young women of various hues and ethnicities, some of whom were fruging in between getting adorned. The beat was provided by another woman in jeans and a fringe top percussing on a set of bongos. She had masking tape around a few of the joints on her fingers. A rectangular piece of carpet had been laid down to protect the asphalt underneath from spills. Yet even as the women moved about, Deebeck twisted and contorted with them, meticulously working his brush while depicting flowers and fire breathing dragons on skin.

"Well, all right," Ingram muttered. "He did show."

Claire looked at him, then back at the painter. "That's Deebeck?"

"Yep."

The two remained there, waiting for a break so Ingram could talk to Deebeck. At some point all the women had artwork on them, including peace signs, ankhs and slogans like "US Out of Vietnam" and "Freedom Now." Donnie Beck stripped off his shirt and he too was painted upon by a few of the women. There was a lot of laughter and applause and the conga drummer finally took a rest, rising and bowing to the praise. Ingram and Claire approached him.

"You must be the guy who visited Papa B." Beck was wiping his sweating brow with a small towel. He gestured to one of the cameras draped around Ingram's neck.

"I am," Ingram said. "And I'm looking for Mose Tolbert."

"Yeah . . . why?"

"This was great, Donnie." A lithe woman in a polka-dot bikini, a brilliant flame painted on her, clasped him by the shoulder and gave him a big, loud kiss.

Smiling, Ingram said, "Maybe we should talk privately."

Momentarily Beck studied Ingram, then said, "See you in a minute, Annette." She winked at him as he walked off with them.

Ingram introduced Claire and added, "Tolbert was bugged by the cops' intelligence boys, and so were we. They run around disguised in carpet trucks."

Beck studied them. "You the one that took the picture of the soul brother's murder?" He'd put his shirt back on, though he hadn't buttoned it. He dug in his pockets and produced a slightly crumpled pack of Camel cigarettes. "Got you some attention."

"Unwanted," Claire said.

Beck offered the pack to the other two, who declined.

Ingram asked, "You were friends with Neal Atkins, weren't you?"

"That's right."

"What do you know about what happened to him?"

A bent cigarette hung from Beck's mouth. "You know about him too?"

"His suspicious death has been in the news."

"His eyes got bigger than his stomach," Beck said.

"Meaning he was ambitious about what?" Claire said.

He turned slightly and cupping his hands, lit his cigarette.

A piece fell into place for Ingram. The image of those two breaking into the liquor store, the cops too busy all over the place to catch anyone who was organized and methodical, like Atkins. He was killed in custody. The cops had worked him over and apparently went too far. A sneak thief wouldn't get that kind of attention unless they wanted something back.

"He stole something important to the cops, the

intelligence boys, didn't he? Damn sure more than just a fur coat or color TV set. Come to you with it and you went to Tolbert because it was that heavy."

Beck blew smoke into the air. "You spinnin' out some wild shit, man. You been enjoying the Mary Jane around here?"

"Hardly."

Claire was looking off and put a hand on Ingram's arm. She said to Beck, "You came out of hiding to check the temperature, didn't you? See what kind of heat might still be on you?"

"Figured you was the brains of y'all's outfit."

Ingram said, "You got that right."

"What's in it for me if I maybe know about those Starbrite trucks you mentioned?"

Ingram said, "We don't know. But for damn sure it's about people like us being under their thumb."

Claire added, "What were the riots about if not striking back?"

Beck took a deep drag. "Look here, I'm gonna keep on enjoying this here hootenanny." He flicked the cigarette away. "I suggest you do too."

Ingram and Claire exchanged a look but didn't say anything to try and stop him. After he left, Claire said, "Will he get in touch?"

"Hell if I know, baby."

"Then I guess we dig the scene."

"Righteous."

They held hands and walked about. "See that Mexican gentleman over by the tent where the transcendental talk is happening? He was at a town hall in Watts I was at. Identified by Gerry as an undercover cop. An infiltrator. He's shaved his mustache, but I recognize him," Claire said. The tent she referred to was of some size and had a sandwich board set up near its entrance with the words Metaphysics Lounge written on it along with the times of several activities. Later would be tarot readings and a session about aligning one's chakras.

"I recognize him from the pictures Gerry sent. Chances are there's more than just him mixing in here today," Ingram said, echoing what he'd said to Tackwood.

Ingram peeked inside the Metaphysics Lounge. The attendees were sitting cross-legged on a carpet in the process of meditating. Their guru at the head, an older, quite tanned white guy in striped pants and a fringe vest sans shirt, murmured a chant. At intervals he tapped a small gong next to him with a puff-headed mallet. Ingram stared hard, surprised to see Arlene Domergue the bookkeeper among the enlightened. He wasn't surprised to also see Sister Violet O'Shay in there, too. She opened her eyes and smiled at him. He smiled back and moved along.

At some point, the two checked out different offerings. Claire went into the other building to hear a math professor, a Freedom Summer participant, discuss a mathematics initiative aimed at kids in the ghetto in town. Ingram wandered around taking pictures along with other press people in attendance. He and Tackwood ran into each other and talked. The latter was sipping coffee from a paper cup under the midday sun.

"Snapped a couple of shots of your cop buddy on the sly," Ingram told him. "The one you'd pointed out to Anita before."

"Lay a print on me when you develop your pics."

"Y'all ain't really considering running them in the paper, are you?"

Tackwood smiled, "One never knows . . ."

"Do one," Ingram finished, the line from a Fats Waller song. "I'm going to lay these on Dorrell. Have her circulate them among the leadership before the big rally."

"I heard that," Tackwood said.

The day wore on with more speakers and various workshops like one on community organizing. During one of the planned breaks, a female fire eater entertained, as did a stilt walker dressed as the banker in Monopoly complete with a monocle. He juggled papier-mâché mortar bombs, the kind seen in cartoons—a cannonball shape and color, with a fuse. The banker carried more of his bombs in a gunny sack slung around him. Occasionally he'd toss one of his bombs at a person and they'd wilt to the ground after making an explosion sound. Each bomb had a different country or financial scandal painted on it in white lettering. Ingram got a shot of one of the bombs as it came at him. The Congo was written on the rough textured sphere.

"Hey," he said to Claire when he found her again. Late afternoon lengthened the shadows.

"Hey yourself," she said, kissing him.

People were gathered in the parking lot and the event concluded with talk about the general strike. Dorrell Zinum spoke, along with others representing campus organizations, staid groups like the NAACP and so on. From what was said, there had been a good number of meetings and outreach creating momentum for the city-wide shutdown planned for the Friday two weeks from now. At one point

Ingram talked to her to tell her about the suspected under-cover cop.

"Could be he's just a snitch or could be he's worse."

"Looking to put a frame on us," she said.

"You'll have them tomorrow."

"Thanks, brother."

"For sure."

Ingram and Claire decided to leave before the last speaker was to come to the mic. As others had done, they'd parked some blocks away and walked slowly to the car. It was dusk and the barricades had been removed blocking Sunset in front of the Fifth Estate. In Ingram's station wagon, he yawned as he sat behind the steering wheel.

"Long day, huh?" Claire massaged his upper shoulder briefly.

"Ain't that the truth. But damned if it wasn't—"

"Energizing. Makes you feel good that progress can be accomplished."

"Yeah," he agreed.

He started the car and drove off. More people were on the sidewalks, leaving the Be-In. They were smiling and talking, the positive vibe emanating from them as well. Claire put her head on Ingram's shoulder as he drove, her hand on his upper leg.

"Be careful, young lady."

She rubbed his crotch. "Oh, I will." But not wishing to distract him, she removed her hand even as he stiffened.

"I suppose it's for the best," he sighed. "Keep my mind on driving."

A deep chuckle rumbled in her.

By the time they got near their house it was dark and Ingram had on the headlights.

"Harry," Claire murmured, half-asleep, "I need you to tuck me in, baby."

"Damn sure plan to do it twice, the good Lord willing." Brow furrowed, he muttered, "What the heck is a Helms Bakery truck doing out at this time of day?" Ingram remarked as they neared their house and the two spotted the distinctive vehicle. It had just turned the far corner of the block.

"Maybe it broke down earlier?" Claire wondered.

Ingram slowed, beginning his turn into the driveway. A bright light invaded the inside of the Falcon.

"The hell?" Ingram said, his foot off the accelerator as he couldn't see anything through the windshield. An engine roared.

"Harry, what's happening?"

Ingram was reaching across her to unlatch the passenger side door. Their combined weight popped the door open as the squarish Helms truck rammed into the driver's side door. The screech of metal wrenching filled the evening as glass exploded everywhere. Out they tumbled onto the roadway, irregular-shaped stars of safety glass twinkling under the glare of a streetlight in Claire's dark hair. She'd landed on her back and Ingram was atop her yet already moving off and around the car. The Helms truck was backing up and he got a quick glimpse of the man at the wheel wearing a sport coat. He was white and had an abrasion on his chin. Stevens.

The two shared a malevolent look and Ingram ran after the truck as it continued to back up at a high rate of speed, steam hissing from its ruined radiator. Apparently, there were still a few baked goods on the truck. The slide drawers behind the driver had popped open on impact and a few donuts spilled out onto the roadway. The truck's front bumper hung down from one side of the smashed-in front. Neighbors had come out on their porches to see what the commotion was about. As Ingram ran after it, the Helms truck slammed into a car that had just turned the corner on the other end of the block. There was more rending and destruction of manufactured parts. This crash sent the top of Stevens's head into the windshield, cracking it. He was dazed as Ingram got hands on the man and slugged him, once, knocking him to the ground. Stevens hit him back.

"Gonna put you in your place, Ingram." He was back on his feet, punching and taunting. "You and your half-breed gonna get taken down a peg or two. Teach you to try and be a goddamn Brer Rabbit, those people in the bar cheering you." Despite a wounded head, he sent a blow to Ingram's mid-section that had him stumbling backward.

"Fuck you." Claire clubbed Stevens from behind at the base of his neck with a broken-off side-view mirror. Bits of glass showered his shoulders.

"Yellow bitch," he exclaimed, hunched over and turning to grab her.

Ingram leaped on him and drove him back to the ground again. "You ofay motherfuckah . . ." He wailed on Stevens's upper body and face, bloodying him despite his attempts to defend himself. Then he became inert. Ingram continued hitting him.

"Harry, that's enough. Stop." Yanking on his shoulders, Claire wrapped her arms around his upper body. "You'll kill him. You have to stop," she shouted.

"Harry!"

As if a fever had broken, Ingram looked back at her, lost, breathing heavily. She put her hands on his face and her forehead atop his, the sweat of her brow cooled his rage. By the time the police and ambulance arrived, Ingram was standing off to one side. His neighbors, Black and white, were around him should the police try and come at him. His bruised hands were at his side, inert and lifeless.

CHAPTER SEVENTEEN

A day later, when inquiries were made by Crossman for the *Sentinel*, Tackwood for the Freep and Mike Piedmont, the reporter at the *Herald Examiner*, the police would claim that the booking record for the supposed Helms driver had been misplaced.

When Claire brought Ingram back to himself, he had taken a picture of the beaten Stevens. The *Sentinel* and the *Herald Examiner* wouldn't run the shot, given the image was distorted due to him being beaten. The *Free Press* did run the picture with an accompanying piece that asked if this man was an undercover cop. Further inquiries yielded no results as to where the man was or his name. A spokesman for Helms said the truck and uniform had been stolen and an internal investigation was ongoing.

THE DAY after the picture of Stevens came out in the Freep, Ingram got a call at home. "This Harry Ingram?" a voice said on the line. He told the caller he was.

"This is Len Beck. That item you were asking about has come in."

"Great, I'll be right there." Ingram drove to the elder

Beck's secondhand shop. Sure enough, his grandson was there. So was Mose Tolbert.

"We finally meet." He extended his hand. There was gauze wrapped around his bruised knuckles.

Tolbert was Ingram's height with a mane of white-gray hair in need of a trim. He also needed a shave. They shook hands.

Ingram asked, "What convinced you to surface?"

"Your photo."

"Of Faraday?

"The cop that attacked you. Don't seem like you're inclined to let up. Heat on you could be heat on me. Better to have a meet, I realized."

"Sorry, but I'm in it up to my neck. Couldn't walk away if I wanted to."

Mose nodded toward Deebeck. "And they've been bugging me too."

"You couldn't just disappear in a poof for good. You have too many entanglements," Ingram observed.

"There's that," he admitted.

"Was Neal Atkins part of your takedown crew?"

"Get right to it, huh?" The three had moved to the back of the shop, sitting amid items being readied for display.

"You going underground worried Betty about Rickler. But it wasn't about that, was it? You'd found the listening device. The Criminal Conspiracy squad was on to you. Keeping tabs on you, what with you being a fellow traveler and so on. But also got hip to your other activities. Or maybe it was the other way around."

"Not only did that rattle me, but I was trying to figure out if Gavin or Rickler were informing."

"And you came to him with what Neal Atkins found, a burglary he must have pulled off during the riots. Only he stumbled onto something else, something he couldn't have expected."

Tolbert remained mum.

"Files of field reports, photos, and who knows what all else the Criminal Conspiracy Section kept on restless natives and anyone else they targeted. It has to be that, because of what happened to Atkins, and you knew the name of the carpet service they used as a front."

"That's right," the younger Beck affirmed.

Ingram figured Atkins probably sold some of his stolen goods out of this shop with the Becks taking a cut.

Tolbert said, "Because of our friendship, and Donnie knowing my background, he came to me about those damn files."

"After Atkins's supposed suicide?"

"That's right. Up until then, Neal had been trying to angle how to make some money off them."

"Blackmailing the LAPD is not the brightest of ideas."

"Greed gives you goofy ideas," Tobert said straight-faced.

Ingram understood his meaning. To Beck, he said, "You're still looking to cash in on the files some other kind of way, aren't you?"

"Why not? Could you get them published as a special in a magazine with my illustrations, something like that? Get some attention like with your photo."

"Unlikely. Anybody who published them would be sued and harassed out of business." Ingram looked from him to Tolbert, who was blank faced. "Those files are radioactive, man, no doubt naming undercover police infiltrators and who they targeted. Setting up people and who knows what all else."

Tolbert said, "Maybe I should just burn 'em then. Longer I hold on to them, the more heat it's gonna bring. So far the cops ain't been on to me since I split and I intend to keep it that way. Don't want a Helms truck trying to run me over."

"But you haven't," Ingram said. "You know what this could mean if the information were to get out." Tolbert's conscience was at odds with his self-interest as a part-time crook, Ingram concluded. He probably used his end of illicit profits to plow back into the business.

Tolbert said, "If no newspaper or magazine will touch the files, what can be done?"

Ingram massaged his bandaged hand. "There may be a way."

"What way?" Beck asked.

Ingram smiled enigmatically.

INGRAM KNEW one of the print shop teachers at L.A. Trade Technical College, a former employee of the now defunct *Eagle*. Through him, he, Claire and Berkson were able to use one of the mimeograph machines during night-time when no one else was around.

"The Glasshouse Papers," Claire said as she regraded the hand-drawn logo on the front sheet of their effort.

The so-called Papers included a traced line drawing of a Starbrite truck from a photograph and an illustration of a listening device. Both had been done by Deebeck, and for safety reasons, both were not in his usual style and of course, unsigned.

"Let's get these run off and make sure when we're done,

we gather up all the masters, bad copies, everything," Ingram reminded them.

"Right," Berkson said.

They'd brought used shopping bags along to collect all evidence of them being here. The pages of their clandestine publication had been typed and prepared at Ingram and Claire's home. Essentially, mimeograph masters were waxy carbons produced on a typewriter. The ribbon was removed, and the typist typed directly on the receiving sheet. The mirror image was produced on the reverse side—usually in a purple ink because of the color of the stencil.

They got busy duplicating, collating and stapling. When they were done, they got all their trash together, sweeping the floor for any scraps, which also went into a paper bag. They wiped down the machine and surfaces, the light switch and the doorknob. They exited a side door out onto the street.

So as not to tempt fate, particularly given Ingram's notoriety with the police, Berkson had driven here in her car. She being white, the odds were better she wouldn't be stopped by a traffic cop. She drove away with the four hundred copies of the underground expose.

WHILE THE general strike didn't shut the city down, thousands of people did fill the streets around City Hall, police headquarters and the courthouses. Not as many as what converged on the March on Washington in '63, but an impressive turnout nonetheless. Ingram was there taking pictures and notes, as was Claire in her official capacity. Copies of the Glasshouse Papers had been left at various locations of the rally, like on a bus bench weighted down by a rock, to be seen and eventually read by the protesters. A sea of placards called for jobs, fair housing and demands for an end to police brutality—now. Ingram got a particularly telling shot of a ring of such protestors and signs addressing police treatment ringing their headquarters. The chant repeated over and over, and loudly and exuberantly, for Chief Parker to resign. Ingram joined in.

Like the famous gathering in D.C., there was domestic and foreign press covering the event. Calls for police reform were echoed by several speakers throughout the day. A row of balsawood coffins painted black were leaned upright against a wall representing those who died under questionable circumstances at the hands of the LAPD and Sheriff's Department. A blowup of the conclusion from the independent medical examiner showing the path of the bullet that killed Faraday Zinum was on display as well.

At one point, as Ingram worked his way through a knot of people to get a shot of Paul Newman and Harry Belafonte talking, he happened to glance past them and saw a man he recognized. Among the throng was Shoals Pettigrew. Momentarily, their eyes locked. Later, when he told Anita Claire about this, he couldn't tell her what kind of emotion he'd felt, as he didn't know. The grouping Pettigrew was among shifted, blocking him from Ingram's view. When the crowd shifted again, Pettigrew was gone. Ingram went on too.

Later, he talked with Dorrell Zinum who told him about the suspected agent provocateur identified to Anita at the town hall days after the riots. "The dude in the picture calls himself Rivers. He'd been riling up some of the young bucks." Dorrell Zinum found Ingram again as the event wound down. "He was set to meet them this morning supposedly with some rifles in his trunk. He'd talked them into using them to shoot at police cars and so forth today," she'd continued.

"Glad they didn't," he said. "But you know there's more of them been planted."

"Yeah. If we're not careful. We gonna be our own worst enemies in the years to come."

"**THIS UNSUBSTANTIATED** incendiary Glasshouse Papers purports a police intelligence unit has been spying on numerous negro and left-of-center individuals and organizations for several years," Stan Chambers said on air. "Further, this radical handiwork alleges in some cases operatives of the unit fomented discord among these groups or at times sought to entice members of these groups to commit criminal behavior to have them arrested. This was termed acts of agent provocateurs."

Chambers paused to shuffle the pages he held. On the screen came the image of a torched and blackened Starbrite panel van. Over this image, he said, "This company was said to be in the Glasshouse Papers as a cover for the intelligence squad. While this is also considered to be an outlandish assertion, an act of arson was committed on this particular vehicle. The station has been attempting to get in touch with a representative of the company." Spray painted on the van were the words KEEP OUT.

The LAPD was occupied in the ensuing weeks post the distribution of the Glasshouse Papers. Chief Parker's office initially sought to brand the Papers as clearly being of Soviet manufacture. But, as various leads were followed up on, there was too much specificity to merely be a propaganda ploy.

IN A room where smoke from expensive cigars lingered and Macallan single malt was consumed, the captain of the Criminal Conspiracy Section sat with Winston Hoyt in their respective wing-back chairs.

"Well," the man said, gesturing with the long stem of his pipe. "No matter how you cut it, the coloreds have gotten one up on us this time."

"If only momentarily," Hoyt allowed. "Time and resources are on our side. We set the pace of their progress."

"A lot of them go around quoting Che Guevara and Malcolm X."

Hoyt regarded his drink. "The Anglo-Saxon made this country what it is, created the culture and is the backbone of the economy. Our negro operatives understand that."

"Satchmo was no paleface and far as I can tell, it's not your relatives out in the hot sun of Delano picking strawberries. Hell, not even my relatives." He grinned at that.

"Sounds like you've been in the bush too long."

"Figure I'm going native?" The captain grinned.

"You would know better than me." Hoyt drained his glass and held up his tumbler, signaling for more at the waiter passing through.

Elsewhere, in a room with spare furnishings, Ingram, Anita Claire and her parents met to discuss what their next steps should be regarding the Providers' record of bribes, payoffs and other such machinations discovered in the Morning Bandit's final heist. Tea had been brewed and there was a plate of cookies.

"Mimeographing the contents and leaving them laying around isn't gonna do it," the daughter stated.

Steam rose around Dorothy Nielson as she regarded the contents of her cup held aloft. "It's one thing to take a chance, honey, and another thing to willingly walk into the lion's den."

Ingram poured his drink, watching the tea leaves swirl about.

SITTING IN his photo lab in the garage, Ingram hunt and pecked away on his typewriter. It was slow going even though he'd roughed out an outline. While the idea was this would be a photo book filled with his reflections about the shots, he felt it was necessary to begin with how he came to pick up the camera in the war. As he wrestled to get the wording right, he admitted handling the camera became his way of hiding in plain sight. He could intrude on others' lives, yet have this instrument create distance between him and his subjects. But it turned out the more he witnessed through the viewfinder, the less distance there was.

One day as he left the garage to use the bathroom in the house, John Outterbridge called to him from the driveway.

"Harry, look what I found." A big grin on his face, he held up the Speed Graphic. "This has to be yours."

The camera wasn't in good shape and required several weeks' worth of Ingram hunting down the parts he needed to fix it, but he did so. Lovingly, he regarded his handiwork after he got the camera working again. He rubbed one of the bullet grooves for good luck. He damn sure knew he and Anita were going to need it.

ACKNOWLEDGEMENTS

The author wishes to thank for inspiration those behind the 1973 publication *The Glass House Tapes*. As the subtitle stated, it was the story of an agent-provocateur and the new police-intelligence complex by the Citizens Research and Investigation Committee, which included the Bar Sinister Law Collective; editor (and playwright, novelist and screenplay writer) Donald Freed; and the agent provocateur himself, Louis E. Tackwood.